ANNIE BURROWS

A Marquess, a Miss and a Mystery

ISBN-13: 978-1-335-63527-3

9 781335 635273

50650

EAN

"That is, I mean, most men shy away from women like me, don't they? Men don't really like women to be cleverer than they are. Especially not a woman who has a tendency to voice her opinions, whether they run contrary to their own or not."

She would have thought he'd agree with her. Make a joke of it. Break the strange tension she could feel taking over her better senses. Stop her from making a total fool of herself.

Instead, he took her face between his hands. Looked at her mouth. "Most men," he said gruffly, "are idiots, though, aren't they? Cowards."

Her heart was now beating so fast she rather thought it was making her tremble. He was going to kiss her!

Was he going to kiss her?

No, of course he wasn't. Men like him didn't kiss girls like her. Not even when they were taking part in a *pretend* pursuit. Or, perhaps they did. If he thought he needed to convince people he was really smitten, or at least, determined to make her fall for him. But in that case, he wouldn't set about it like this. He'd have made sure there was at least one witness...

Oh, why was she thinking of a thing like that at a time like this? When he was still holding her face in his hands. And looking at her mouth. And...lowering his head!

She gasped.

Author Note

While I was writing *A Duke in Need of a Wife* I became very interested in the duke's dysfunctional family, in particular the half brother who was pushed aside when the duke came back to Theakstone Court as the rightful heir. I mentioned, briefly, that there was a lot of resentment from this side of the family, but didn't need to bring it into Oliver's story.

However, as a writer, I couldn't stop wondering about the little boy who was told he was going to be a duke, and instead got packed off to a small estate in the country with his mother and sisters. Would he ever be able to get over such rejection from his father? Would he ever be able to trust anyone again?

And would he attend his half brother's wedding?

And then, of course, being a writer of romance, I couldn't help wondering what sort of woman would be able to break down all the barriers he would have built around himself after suffering such a betrayal at an early age. And touch his heart. And into my head came Horatia, a woman on a mission...

I hope you enjoy the story of how these two apparently mismatched people find love while they are looking for something entirely different!

ANNIE BURROWS

---

*A Marquess,
a Miss and a Mystery*

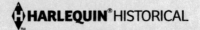

Recycling programs
for this product may
not exist in your area.

ISBN-13: 978-1-335-63527-3

A Marquess, a Miss and a Mystery

Printed in U.S.A.

Annie Burrows has been writing Regency romances for Harlequin since 2007. Her books have charmed readers worldwide, having been translated into nineteen different languages, and some have gone on to win the coveted Reviewers' Choice Award from CataRomance. For more information, or to contact her, please visit annie-burrows.co.uk, or find her on Facebook at Facebook.com/annieburrowsuk.

Visit the Author Profile page
at Harlequin.com for more titles.

To Holly Rose, who was coming into being
along with this book.

Chapter One

There was nothing for it. Horatia Carmichael was going to have to do something drastic.

She peered round at the congregation, who were gathering their prayer books and Bibles together as the Duke of Theakstone's elderly chaplain mumbled the service to a close, and swallowed. The Duke's private chapel was awash with lords and ladies. She didn't think anyone below the rank of viscount had been invited to stay at Theakstone Court for the week preceding his wedding. Apart from her. Which made her feel a bit like Cinderella must have done at that ball to pick a bride for Prince Charming, or whatever his name was. She'd never paid all that much attention to fairy tales. They were always full of pretty people getting unlikely rewards simply for being pretty. Or titled. She'd have been far more impressed if, for once, cleverness had been the virtue that won the prize.

But anyway, even though Cinderella was undoubtedly pretty, she must have felt completely out of her depth walking into a castle packed with titled people. Just as Horatia did, right this minute.

But then desperate times called for desperate measures. Two months it had been since Herbert's murder. Two months during which she'd waited, with mounting impatience, for the Marquess of Devizes to come and offer his condolences, so that she could pass on the information which could prove vital to tracing her brother's killer.

But the…the… She wrestled with a suitable word to describe the character of the man who'd been her brother's best friend and colleague in his clandestine work…and could think of nothing polite enough to voice, not even in her mind, while in a chapel.

But anyway, the point was the…the…she had it! The puffed-up popinjay hadn't come anywhere near her. And, of course, she hadn't been able to simply go to him. A lady could not just walk up to the door of a single man's residence and gain admittance, not without drawing attention to herself. Especially not a single man with the kind of reputation he had. He was the kind of man who could persuade just about any woman into his bed with just one slow smile. And so he did.

Nor would Lord Devizes have welcomed her visit, not even when he heard what she had to tell him. Marching up to his front door in broad daylight, or at any other time, would have drawn the attention of the very people they most needed to outwit. They would have put two and two together and that would have been that.

Which meant she'd had to find some way to approach him that wouldn't arouse suspicion.

The trouble was, since she was in mourning, she couldn't attend any of the balls or parties where she might have simply walked up to him. Especially since they weren't the kinds of events she'd gone to very often, even before Herbert's death. That would have raised as many eyebrows as if she'd gone to one of the gambling hells she knew he attended, or walked into a cock fight, or a coal-heaver's tavern, or any of the other disreputable places he'd gone with Herbert in pursuit of information. Or so Herbert had maintained. Though she hadn't forgotten he'd gone to such places even before he'd started looking for the group of people he'd told her were trying to drum up support for the exiled French emperor, Bonaparte.

It was a good job the Marquess's half-brother, the Duke of Theakstone, had suddenly decided to get married, or heaven knew what stratagems she might have been obliged to adopt. Fortunately, a friend of hers, Lady Elizabeth Grey, had an invitation to the wedding, so all Horatia had had to do was persuade her to bring her along in the guise of a companion. She'd assumed that once here, while everyone was wandering around the grounds, or taking tea, she was bound to find an opportunity for sidling up to Lord Devizes and passing on her translation of the coded letter Herbert had given her, to decipher, the very night he'd been murdered.

But, drat the man, even here she hadn't been able to get near him. There were too many other females fluttering round him, like so many brainless moths dashing themselves against a glittering lantern. Or pigeons, perhaps. Preening themselves and cooing up at him. Well, whatever type of brainless creatures they resembled, at any given time, he always behaved like a…pasha, surrounded by an adoring harem. As though feminine adulation was no more than his due. He lapped it all up, doling out that lopsided smile of his like a kind of reward to any that particularly amused him, though his lazy-lidded eyes made him look as though he was on the verge of laughing *all* the time. As though life was one huge joke.

Which made her want to wring his neck. Or kick him in the shins. Or something equally violent, because while he was lounging about, flirting with every female in the place under fifty, the trail that might have led straight to Herbert's killer was getting colder and colder.

To her left, the friend who'd played fairy godmother to her Cinderella was getting to her feet. Which meant that she would have to do the same. And then follow meekly back to the main part of the house for refreshments. And it was no use telling herself she could approach him over nuncheon, because it was far more likely that she'd feel so out of place that instead of confronting Herbert's friend, she'd retire to a corner where she'd perch like a little black crow and watch the gaudier females flock round Lord Devizes.

It was now or never. Pushing her glasses back up to the bridge of her nose, she got to her feet and shuffled to the end of the pew, then pulled open the strings of her reticule and took out a handkerchief. Behind her, Lady Elizabeth's mother, the Dowager Marchioness of Tewkesbury, breathed in sharply though her nostrils. Something she was wont to do whenever Horatia crossed her line of sight. The Dowager made no secret of the fact that she disapproved of her daughter becoming so friendly with a mere Miss. In fact, if it wasn't for the fact that mother and daughter were barely speaking to each other at the moment, she suspected she would have forbidden Lady Elizabeth from bringing her along.

However, she was here. And Lord Devizes would be sauntering past the end of her pew any second now.

She blew her nose, then thrust her handkerchief back into her reticule, her heart thundering. It was too much to hope he might pause and bid her good morning. He'd had ample opportunity to do so any number of times since his arrival at Theakstone Court. But over and over again, he'd looked right through her. As if she was beneath his notice. As if he didn't recognise her.

Though why should he? Though Herbert had introduced them, during her one and only Season, while he'd still been trying to persuade her that he could make her 'fashionable', Lord Devizes had clearly been highly unimpressed by his friend's dumpy, dowdy little sister. He'd danced with her just the once. And that clearly only as a courtesy to his friend. Lord Devizes had barely spoken to her during that dance. Had never subjected her to an iota of the charm for which he was so famed, let alone actually progressed to flirting with her.

But never mind that now. This wasn't the time to indulge in ancient resentment. Especially since he'd treated her no worse than any other of the so-called gentlemen who'd been persuaded to take pity on such a frumpy little wallflower. He was within three yards. A couple more steps and she'd be able to reach out her hand and tug at his sleeve.

Like a beggar, seeking alms.

So, no, she wouldn't do that. She had to make their contact look accidental, or she'd be drawing attention to her desperate need to speak to him. Which she must not do.

And so, as he drew level with her, she fumbled her

Bible off the pew and tossed it at his feet, hoping it would look as though she'd dropped it.

He stopped. Looked at the Bible lying in his path. Looked at her. Placed one hand on his hip and raised one corner of his mouth into a…a cynical sort of sneer.

Her face flooded with heat. The…the…*bad name*. The *swear word*. He was making it look as though he suspected her of dropping her handkerchief at his feet, in the age-old way women had of attracting the notice of a man they could not get to notice them any other way. Which she was. But not because she was *lovelorn*. Surely he could not be as stupid as he looked? Surely he must realise that it was because she was Herbert's sister that she needed to speak to him? About Herbert? And his work?

Even if he was that stupid, didn't he have even a modicum of good manners? Surely he could go through the motions of polite behaviour and bend down to pick up her book?

Apparently not. He just stood there, that cynical smile on his face, his mocking eyes regarding her steadily as her face heated with all the pent-up frustration this aggravating man had caused her recently.

'I can't believe,' she muttered, stepping forward, then bending down to reach for her Bible, 'that Herbert rated you so highly when you cannot even pick up a *hint*, never mind—'

She'd been going to say *my Bible*, but unfortunately, at the very moment she bent down to snatch up her Bible, he finally leaned down as well.

With the result that her head clashed with his out-stretched arm. And, as she'd been bending down angrily and his arm was the consistency of an iron bar, she bounced off it, then off the end of the pew, and ended up sitting on her bottom on the cold, hard chapel floor.

She heard a lot of muffled sniggering.

'I cannot believe,' said the Dowager Marchioness of Tewkesbury, presumably to Lady Elizabeth, although Horatia could not see either of them from the chapel floor, 'that you could have brought a person like that to a place like this, even if you are—'

'Mother!' Horatia heard Lady Elizabeth's skirts swish as she whirled round in her pew and, to judge from earlier altercations, glared at her mother.

While she glared up at the agent of her misfortune, who was smiling a little wider now as though barely holding back laughter himself.

And extending his arm, as though to offer his help in getting to her feet.

'I don't need your help,' she snarled, ignoring his hand and grabbing hold of one of the finials on the end of the pew she'd just bounced off, which had lots of knobbly bits to give her purchase, instead. 'Not to get to my feet, not to find Herbert's—'

'You are Herbert's sister?' He raised one eyebrow, as though the fact astonished him. 'I never,' he said, running his eyes over her bedraggled frame, 'would have guessed.' Not many people did. Herbert was so handsome and elegant. Even *he* had laughingly said that while she had all the brains in the family, he had all the beauty.

'You...' she stuttered. 'You...' Once again, her vocabulary didn't come up with a word sufficiently insulting to hurl at him that she could possibly use in a chapel.

He lowered his hand. 'Take your time, Miss Carmichael,' he said with infuriating calm. 'I feel certain that you will be able to think of a suitable insult, should you take a deep breath and count to ten.'

The sniggering grew a touch less muffled. Although there was a roaring sound in her ears, now, almost drowning out the sounds of mockery.

She hated him. She really, really hated him. It had been bad enough that he'd neglected to do the decent thing and at least come to visit her, given how closely he and Herbert had been working, to offer his condolences. But to first pretend he did not recognise her, then to make her a laughing stock…

'There isn't one,' she grated. And whirled away before giving him the satisfaction of seeing the tears that were burning her eyes. Tears she absolutely would not shed, not in front of such a…

She strode down the aisle and slammed out of the door of the chapel. And as the heat of the sun struck the crown of her bonnet, she finally let the bad words come. In English, and French and Italian.

And it wasn't just because he'd humiliated her in front of all those titled people. It was because she'd wasted so much time and effort. Instead of thinking of ways to get in touch with the man Herbert had referred to as Janus, she should have gone on the hunt for his killer herself.

Because it was clear he wasn't going to be of any help to her. At all.

She was on her own.

As always.

Chapter Two

As Herbert's sister flounced out of the chapel, Nick bent down to pick up her discarded Bible.

Talk about indiscreet. If he hadn't deliberately goaded her into losing her temper with him, she'd have blurted out her suspicions regarding Herbert's death in the echoing space of a chapel where even whispers carried further than they had any right to go.

No wonder Herbert had been so protective of her. No wonder he'd worked so hard to shield her from the realities of what his recent lifestyle entailed. She had no idea how to conceal what she was thinking. He'd been able to read every single thought that had flitted across her disapproving little features from the first moment she'd walked into Theakstone Court.

She had no control over her mouth, either. If she'd ever suspected the half of what Herbert had recently uncovered, she'd have blurted it out heaven alone knew where, or to whom.

Worse, to judge from the slip of paper he could see tucked in between the pages of her Bible, she'd been attempting to pass him a note. A note! In full view of the entire congregation.

He took a swift glance at it before tucking it neatly back into place as though he had no interest in it. It took every ounce of his self-control to conceal his reaction when he saw what turned out to be a drawing, rather than a written message. For it was a sketch of the two-headed Roman god Janus. Which just happened to be his code name.

'Dear me,' he couldn't help saying. What the devil was she playing at? Revealing the fact that she knew his identity in such a blatant fashion? He masked his shock with a wry smile as he turned the book over in his hands. And swiftly turned it into a jest.

'Whatever will the little black crow do without her Bible to beat us poor miserable sinners over the head with?'

His sisters laughed. As did the pair of rather fast matrons at their side who'd been casting him lures ever since they'd arrived.

Lady Elizabeth Grey, however, whirled away from the heated, whispered altercation she'd been having with her mother, with a frown.

'How can you be so unkind? You, of all people, must know how devastating she found her brother's death. Is it surprising if she acts a little…awkwardly around his former friends?'

'The surprising thing,' he said, slipping the Bible into his pocket while Miss Carmichael's friend was too busy berating him to notice, 'is that she is attending such a *joyous* occasion during what ought to be her period of mourning.' He couldn't resist putting a slightly contemptuous tone into the word *joyous*. Everyone here must surely share his opinion regarding his exalted half-brother's ridiculous, hasty marriage to an unknown. Especially Lady Elizabeth, who'd been one of the leading candidates for the position of Duchess herself.

'It isn't the least bit surprising,' she said heatedly. 'She needed to get out of that gloomy little house she lives in and well away from that gorgon of a guardian who is enough to give anyone the fit of the dismals even if they weren't missing the brother who provided the only bright spots in her existence through his daily visits,' she said without drawing breath.

Daily? He'd gone there as often as that? Hmm...he'd always thought of Herbert as an exceptionally devoted brother, from what he knew of sibling relationships. Nick's own sisters rarely did more than give him a nod of recognition, should their paths happen to cross while they were all in London. And it never occurred to him to visit them in their sumptuous town houses, either. Not without an invitation to some sort of formal event. Let alone every day.

They had, it was true, been making a great deal of fuss over him since they'd come to Theakstone Court. But that had more to do with showing their half-brother, the present Duke, that although they'd accepted his invitation to attend his wedding, they'd done so out of deference to his title, not because they'd forgiven him anything, or now considered him a part of the family. Because in contrast to the way they cooed over Nick, they were always icily formal with the Duke.

Not that Nick could blame them. He couldn't stand the sight of the swarthy, sullen brute himself.

'Without those visits to give her thoughts a positive direction,' Lady Elizabeth was saying, 'she was in danger of going into a decline. I thought a change of scene might lift her spirits. Or at least help her to get over the worst of her unhappiness. Her brother's death devastated her, as you ought to know, being one of his closest cronies.'

Yes, he supposed he should have considered that. But then, his own family were so distant from each other, it was hard to imagine any of them being devastated should anything happen to him. His sisters would express regret and go into black gloves, but a good deal of their regret would be at having to forgo many of their pleasurable pursuits during the period when they were supposed to be mourning him.

Also, whenever he'd thought about her and wondered how she was coping, he'd always come to the conclusion that the best thing he could do for Herbert's sister was to stay well away from her. She'd never seemed to have that shiny, brittle coating which every other woman donned like armour whenever they went out in public. She was open and unaffected in her manner. Which gave him the uncomfortable feeling that he could easily tarnish her.

But…had Herbert perhaps been doing more than merely visiting his sister? Was he, perhaps, supporting her? Financially? Now he came to think of it, Herbert had mentioned something along those lines, just after he'd abandoned the attempt to bring her out into society. Something about their fortunes being linked.

Which made a huge difference.

If any other operative had died during the course of an investigation, he would have gone straight round to their dependents to make sure they were not going to suffer financially. He had access to funds to make sure of it.

'But, as usual, men like you don't see anything past the end of your own nose!'

With her own nose stuck in the air, Lady Elizabeth flounced off. And in this case, he could hardly blame her. He'd assumed that Miss Carmichael must have an income of her own. Assumed, without double-checking.

He'd blundered there. Possibly rather badly.

He should have gone to visit her, to make sure she was provided for, he could see that now. Only...she was of gentle birth. And a man with the reputation he'd cultivated could not simply call upon a single lady of gentle birth, not without raising eyebrows. Not even if her brother had been his closest colleague.

Though what good would it have done, really? He could easily arrange a pension for a widow of a certain sort of man. But he couldn't just offer to support a woman of Miss Carmichael's status. If it ever came out that he was supporting her financially, it would be as good as ruining her.

'You will, I hope, find it in your heart to forgive my daughter's manners,' said the Dowager Marchioness of Tewkesbury, sidestepping along the pew until she reached the aisle. 'This week is terribly hard for her, considering the hopes we had...' She left the rest unsaid. The shake of her head expressed her disappointment that the Duke of Theakstone had passed over her own daughter and chosen instead to make a mere Miss his new Duchess.

'There is nothing to forgive,' he said, giving her the

smile he reserved for women of her age and station. 'It does your daughter credit that she leaps to defend her friend with such…loyalty. And such vehemence.'

The Dowager Marchioness narrowed her eyes to see if she could detect a hint of criticism in his statement. He kept his smile in place, looking directly into her eyes with as much innocence as he could muster. Which wasn't all that hard. Because, actually, he did admire Lady Elizabeth's loyalty. Not many people went against the prevailing current to voice an opinion that ran counter to it. And she had drawn his attention to a facet of the case he'd overlooked. He was grateful to her for jolting him out of his own personal malaise and reminding him that there was at least one other person who missed Herbert just as much as he did. For whatever reason.

'That is so generous of you, Devizes,' trilled his sister Mary. 'To overlook such extraordinary behaviour. And I do not mean,' she said, laying a languid hand on his sleeve, 'that of Lady Elizabeth, of course.' She shot an arch look at the Dowager, for everyone knew about her daughter's shrewish nature. Nick had actually been a little surprised when his half-brother had, apparently, included her on his list of possibilities. And not at all surprised when he'd as quickly crossed her off it.

'I was speaking of that strange little companion of hers,' Mary continued. 'Fancy storming off like that!'

He could understand Miss Carmichael doing so, now, if she was experiencing financial hardship.

Perhaps what she had wanted to say about Herbert related to the way he'd supported her. Perhaps she was finding it hard to make ends meet.

He would ask her, when he returned her Bible to her.

As well as finding out why she had a sketch of Janus in between the pages of her Bible. Had Herbert not been as discreet as he'd claimed? Had he been so close to his sister that he'd let slip some things which should have been kept secret?

Or had she merely stumbled across the picture when she'd been going through his personal effects? He thought he'd cleared Herbert's rooms thoroughly, but perhaps there had been some papers hidden in a place that only she knew about.

Which changed everything. He'd been determined to carry on shielding her from the people who'd killed her brother, by persuading anyone who might care to see that he had no interest in her and, therefore, no connection to her whatsoever, now that Herbert was dead.

But if Herbert had let something slip...

He had to warn her that if anyone suspected she had information, of any sort, relevant to Herbert's work, then she would be in danger. Dammit, somebody had killed her brother rather than let him pass on whatever it was he'd discovered that last night.

And Herbert would never forgive him if Horatia became the next person on that assassin's list.

Dammit, he wouldn't forgive himself.

Chapter Three

Horatia was a few yards beyond the paved area surrounding the chapel, which contained monuments to generations of deceased Norringtons, the family from which the current Duke had sprung, when she became aware of rapid footsteps crunching over the gravel behind her.

She'd been walking so fast, driven by a volatile mixture of anger, humiliation and determination to just *show* them—whoever 'them' might be—that the person she could hear must be determined to catch up with her.

She braced herself to deal with whatever accusations or recriminations she might have to face. And sighed with relief, after glancing over her shoulder, to see that it was Lady Elizabeth who was drawing up behind her.

'Well,' said Lady Elizabeth, slowing down to match her pace to Horatia's, 'you certainly know how to make an exit.'

Since Horatia could hear a distinct thread of amusement in her friend's tone, she knew she hadn't mortally offended her. Still, she owed her friend an apology.

'I'm so sorry for my…outburst,' she said. 'I swore that I would give you what little support I could in the days surrounding the Duke's wedding. Instead, I've just given your mother even more reason to berate you.'

'At least if she is complaining about your behaviour, she isn't complaining about mine,' pointed out Lady Elizabeth with a wry smile.

'As if you *made* the Duke fall for Miss Underwood,' scoffed Horatia. 'It is obvious to anyone who sees them together that they have eyes for nobody else,' she added, jerking her head in the direction of the couple who were strolling along arm in arm along another gravelled path which led in the direction of the house. Making Horatia aware she had not taken the most direct route.

'Ah, but,' said Lady Elizabeth, aping her mother's frosty tones, 'if I had only exerted myself more, I could have eclipsed her.'

Horatia made a very unladylike noise, expressed partially through her nose, to demonstrate what she thought of that particular argument.

'You cannot make a man fall for you, or even notice you, unless he chooses to do so,' said Horatia morosely, coming to a standstill. Could she strike out across the lawn and join the path along which the Duke and his intended were walking? Or would that draw even more attention to herself and the fact that she'd shot out of the chapel in such a state of turmoil that she hadn't even been able to steer her feet in the correct direction?

'I…had wondered about your, um, fascination with Lord Devizes,' said Lady Elizabeth, coming to a halt as well. 'I did not like to say anything, but…'

'You cannot think that I have a *tendre* for him?'

Horatia gaped at her. 'Or that, if I did, I would fling myself at him, like one of the muslin company?'

'No. Neither,' said Lady Elizabeth staunchly. 'Which is what makes your...' She lowered her head and traced a swirl through the gravel with the tip of her parasol. 'No, no, I shall not pry. I have enough of people telling me how to live my life to know how detestable that is. Only...' She paused as if choosing her words with care. 'I am a little worried. You seem...'

Horatia turned her head away from Lady Elizabeth and studied instead the direction of the path they were on. After a bit there was a fork to the left which would lead back to the house, rather than on to the formal gardens. Which solved her most immediate problem. However, she still wasn't sure she could confide in Lady Elizabeth about her motives for coming here. Although they called each other friend, they'd only fallen into each other's company after catching each other rolling their eyes at a particularly fatuous comment made by an extremely pompous Member of Parliament who'd been invited to speak at The Ladies Society for the Advancement of Scientific Knowledge. They'd gravitated to each other over the teacups, then started looking out for each other at various other meetings they both attended. It had only been after Herbert's death that Lady Elizabeth had started visiting her house and offering what comfort she could. But since Aunt Matilda had always refused to let Horatia's visitors *drive her from her own sitting room*, she'd never had an opportunity to tell Lady Elizabeth that she was practically certain that her brother had been deliberately murdered, rather than being the victim of a robbery.

Perhaps it was time she did. She certainly owed her some sort of explanation for the tantrum she'd thrown just now. And since nobody else was taking this path she could speak freely without being overheard.

'Herbert was murdered,' said Horatia, setting off once more along their path.

'Yes, I know,' said Lady Elizabeth, setting out beside her. 'And I know how it shocked you. As indeed it shocked everyone who knew him. It is an awful thing that a man may not walk home from…even from the kind of place to which…that is…'

'He had been to a gaming hell, you mean,' said Horatia. Which was, possibly, true. But he hadn't been killed during the course of a robbery. She just knew it. 'And, yes, he was in one of the poorer parts of London. But it wasn't—' she stopped short of saying that it had been no accident. Herbert had been so insistent that nobody knew about her involvement in his work. That it might put her in danger. So…if she told Lady Elizabeth, might it put *her* in danger, too? 'That doesn't mean he deserved to die,' she finished, lamely, 'does it?'

'Of course not.'

'Well, then,' she continued, focusing on one of her views which was perfectly safe to air, 'don't you think that somebody should be trying to find out who killed him? But nobody is! They came and stood in my aunt's sitting room and droned on about the deplorable dangers of the streets of London at night and said there was nothing anyone could do, that if gentlemen frequented such areas these things happened, that—' She broke off, as the resentment at the way those men had spoken to her, as though she was an idiot, swelled up all over again.

'And you thought that Lord Devizes might be able to…what, exactly? It isn't as if a man like him,' Lady Elizabeth said with a hint of derision, 'would stir himself to go looking for criminals, is it?'

Oh, if only she knew! From what Herbert had told her, Lord Devizes had already unmasked a couple of plots against the government and brought several criminals to justice. Because of his rank, and his well-known propensity for pursuing unsavoury pastimes, he could move with ease anywhere from the highest *ton* parties to the lowest gaming hells without anyone raising an eyebrow. What was more, in society, people regarded him as, well, the way Lady Elizabeth did. As an idle, wealthy, wastrel. They didn't see the more serious side of his nature, because he kept it so well hidden behind a sort of mask. To look at the amused, indolent expression he generally adopted, nobody could possibly guess what he was really thinking. Or even suspect he was thinking very much at all.

Which was the way he wanted it.

She glanced across the triangular section of lawn to the path which all the other members of the congregation were strolling along. Where *he* was strolling, with a lady on each arm. And smiling, as though he had not a care in the world. Even though the traitors he and Herbert had been trying to find, the ones responsible for Herbert's murder, could well be close by.

His assailant definitely came from the *ton*. Or had connections to someone who had access to state secrets, such as the Duke of Theakstone.

So…perhaps that was why he was playing at not having a thought in his head beyond the formation of the next witty remark. He had to make sure nobody suspected him of being capable of doing anything as strenuous as tackling a traitor and murderer.

Which, therefore, meant she must not do anything likely to expose the serious nature of his secret work either. Including confiding in Lady Elizabeth.

'He was Herbert's closest friend,' she said, dragging her gaze away from Lord Devizes and fixing it on her feet. 'I thought he might at least have been prepared to listen.'

'Some people,' said Lady Elizabeth tartly, after they'd walked in sombre silence for a few paces, 'prefer not to hear anything unpleasant, though, don't they? They would rather avoid somebody who is in difficulty altogether than have to talk about things that might make them uncomfortable.'

Horatia flinched at the reminder she was not the only person to have gone through a very difficult time of late and saw that this girl's own troubles were probably what had made her capable of showing such sympathy when Horatia lost her brother. 'Yes, you know how... unkind people can be, don't you? People you thought were your friends?'

'Yes. But you never really know who your true friends are until trouble comes, do you? Before Papa died, I was the toast of the *ton*. I was invited everywhere. And then...poof! They all vanished like...like... well...' she gave a bitter laugh 'like our fortune. Only a very few people treated me no differently after his... disgrace. Which is why I...' She tucked her arm through Horatia's and gave it a brief squeeze. 'Well, I don't suppose I need to remind you that I consider you one of my closest friends. No matter what Mama says.'

'As I consider you to be mine,' said Horatia, swallowing down a lump of guilt. For although she was swearing friendship, she was holding back all sorts of things from her. And not only about the nature of Herbert's work and the circumstances surrounding his death. And it was all very well saying she didn't want to put Lady Elizabeth in danger, but it was more than that. She didn't really know if she could trust her.

'I was so angry with Lord Devizes and with Mama,' Lady Elizabeth said ruefully, 'for the way they talked about you just now that I rather lost my temper with them both after you'd gone.'

'I do wish I was not adding to the bad feeling which already exists between you and your parent,' said Horatia, feeling guiltier than ever. 'Particularly since so much of what she says about me is nothing but the truth. I am not well born. So I am not really a fit person to be your friend, not if you wish to maintain a fashionable appearance.'

'But I don't! Wish to maintain a fashionable appearance, that is. You above all people should know that.'

'Yes, I must admit that is the one aspect of having to go into mourning I can embrace. It is such a relief not to have to try to work out what colours match with which others. Having to have everything black removes most of the difficulty out of choosing what to wear in the mornings. And during the rest of the day, too.'

'No.' Lady Elizabeth clapped one hand to her mouth. 'I didn't mean to imply you are unfashionable, in that sense...'

'Nevertheless, it is true. I have never been able to comprehend how it is that in nature there can be brown trees,' she said, pointing with her free arm in the direction of the woodland on a nearby hill, 'and green grass dotted with lots of different coloured flowers—' she indicated the vibrant blooms tumbling from containers standing on the steps leading up to the terrace spanning the length of the house '—capped by a brilliant blue sky and it all looks charming. But put the same combination of colours and patterns next to my little body and...' She shrugged and grimaced.

'When you are out of mourning, I shall take you shopping. I am sure—'

'No, please do not bother. Herbert did try to supervise my wardrobe when I first made my come-out. For he always looked so elegant, you know, that he was sure he could bring me into style.' That was probably one of the reasons he and the Marquess had hit it off to start with. Both of them were beautiful, fashionable young men with a taste for mischief.

'What happened, then?'

'Well, do you know, he made the offer while we were at the theatre, just after one of his fashionable friends had turned his arrogant nose up at me for...well, I suppose I had been a touch rude, but then he was such an idiot. Anyway, there happened to be one of those acrobats upon the stage who could wrap her legs around the back of her head. And I felt as if he was urging me to become like her. You know, tying myself into a knot in order to fit in with society's expectations.'

'Now that,' said Lady Elizabeth vehemently, 'is something I completely understand. The way people expect you to make yourself something you are not in order to gain acceptance.'

'Particularly men looking out for a bride. None of them wants to know what you are truly like. They just want you to become whatever it is that they want. If you express an opinion that is different to their own, they call you a bluestocking. And if you actually dare to inform a man that his own opinion is based upon a fallacy, then he will say you are a gorgon.'

'Or a shrew,' said Lady Elizabeth, pursing her lips. 'It is only because of my rank that anyone still invites me anywhere.'

'At least I don't have to go anywhere I do not wish to any longer,' Horatia said with satisfaction. 'Not since Aunt Matilda has given up trying to marry me off respectably.' Deciding she wasn't going to tie herself in knots had been the first step along a course that had led, by progressive stages, to her obtaining relative freedom. 'Nowadays I only ever attend events where I am sure of mingling with like-minded people.'

'Apart from this wedding. Which I thought,' said Lady Elizabeth shrewdly, 'you had agreed to attend more as a favour to me, since you knew how difficult I was bound to find it. Instead…'

'Ah. Yes. I have to admit, it was not my only motive…'

They reached the fork that would lead straight back to the house. As they turned on to it, Horatia couldn't help gazing along the immense length of the ornately decorated façade. It made her wonder why the Duke's ancestors hadn't called this place Theakstone Palace, rather than Theakstone Court. Its size alone surely qualified it for the title.

'At least it has meant we can share a suite of rooms, rather than me being left to the mercy of my mother. Last time we were here, as I'm sure you know, we had rooms in the main part of the house,' said Lady Elizabeth, pointing to the central block, which was about the size of an average cathedral, 'rather than one of the guest wings,' she finished with a distinct note of disdain.

Horatia chewed on her lower lip for a moment or two. The suite of rooms she was sharing with Lady Elizabeth seemed very grand compared with what she was used to. But it sounded as if their only virtue in Lady Elizabeth's eyes was the fact they afforded some sanctuary from her mother.

'Are you really upset about that?' Horatia said tentatively.

'The Duke choosing somebody else, you mean?'

She hadn't, not exactly, but rather than explain, Horatia took another tack. 'I know it would have solved a lot of your troubles…'

'What? Marry that man?' Lady Elizabeth tossed her head. 'I would have gone through with it only out of duty to my family. He may be rich, but he is so…' She shuddered. 'One would never believe he is related to the Marquess of Devizes, not unless one knew it for an absolute fact. What with one being so dark and satanic, and the other being so fair and charming…'

'Well, appearing fair and charming can also be an attribute of a satanic creature, according to the Bible,' Horatia couldn't help commenting. 'Such beings are even called angels of light. They set out to deceive people with their charm, don't they? At least you know where you are with the Duke.'

'Yes,' said Lady Elizabeth tartly, as they began to mount the steps to the terrace that ran the length of this side of the house. 'No longer fit to be housed in the main part of his palace.'

'Surely that is a good thing. Since it means you are not sharing rooms with your mother.'

'*Touché,*' cried Lady Elizabeth with appreciation. 'And thank you for reminding me that I ought to be grateful she thinks more of her consequence than she does of keeping a close watch upon me.'

'What? But she…'

'You think pouncing upon me whenever I put one toe out of the door is keeping a close watch upon me? You have no idea. Oh. I am sorry.' Lady Elizabeth looked stricken. 'Of course you have no idea…'

'Lady Elizabeth, I scarcely remember my own mother, so if you are about to apologise for being insensitive about my orphaned state, then please, I beg of you, do not.'

'And I suppose witnessing the relationship I have with my own mother is not likely to make you pine for one of your own, is it? Lord, how I wish that I…' She pulled herself up short. 'It is just,' she said, lowering her voice as they drew closer to the group of people waiting their turn to enter the house through a set of French doors, 'that if I was an orphan, with no title, nobody would mind if I fell in love with a man with nothing to recommend him but his brains. There is nobody to prevent you from following your heart.'

Something inside Horatia twisted at the mention of following her heart. 'You are forgetting,' she said, 'that even men with brains are governed very much by what they see. They don't fall in love with awkward little dabs of women with no fashion sense.' Which meant there was no point, absolutely no point, in hoping such a thing might happen. 'They fall in love with pretty, witty, blondes,' she finished, giving her friend a pointed look.

'It is useless anyway.' Lady Elizabeth sighed, halting a short distance away from the rest of the churchgoers. 'Theakstone arranged for Mr Brown to go to Leipzig. And while it is of great advantage to his career, he might just as well have flown to the moon. We will never see each other again, and...' She stopped on a hiccup that sounded suspiciously like a choked sob. 'Mama will get her way, I dare say. I shall have to marry someone with money and the standing to overcome the disgrace Papa brought to our family.'

'I'm surprised she isn't pushing you at the Marquess, then.'

'Lord, no. He has the money, but apparently even Mama knows it would be a waste of time attempting to snare such a one. Too slippery to be caught in the parson's mousetrap. Too busy enjoying himself with the ladies who flock round him and no pressing need to sire an heir. No, she is hoping to match me up with somebody older. With more substance about him. A widower, perhaps, with only daughters.' She shuddered.

Not for the first time, Horatia thanked her lucky stars she was a mere Miss. Nobody expected her to marry to save the family fortunes. There never had been any fortune to lose in the first place. Herbert had had a small income, which he'd supplemented by doing nominal work at a post gained for him through the influence of a distant uncle.

Until that day he'd come to her with the tale of how he and Lord Devizes had found a brilliant way to earn a little extra. And to serve their country at the same time. Someone, he'd said, tapping his nose to indicate that person's identity must remain secret, was going to pay any expenses incurred while they rooted out traitors to the Crown. To that end, they'd each chosen their own code names, to keep their own identities secret from anyone who didn't need to know they were involved in such work. Lord Devizes was to become Janus, because he would present one face to society, and another to the criminal underworld, while Herbert was to be known as Portunus, after the Roman god of keys and doors. When Horatia had frowned in bewilderment, he'd burst out laughing.

'I've boasted that I can unlock any code or cipher anyone could possibly devise.'

'And can you?'

'No!' He'd grinned, then. 'But you can. You love puzzles and have a knack of solving them. So if we ever come across any coded messages I can bring 'em straight to you. You'll enjoy doing such work, won't you? Give you something to keep your mind off...' He'd grimaced and jerked his head at their aunt, who was jabbing away at her tambour frame at her seat before the fire, embroidering one of her samplers which invariably quoted the sterner verses from the scriptures.

Which reminded her.

'I don't suppose you picked up my Bible, did you?' It wouldn't do to leave it lying around, where anyone could see the sketch she'd drawn of Janus, to indicate she needed to speak with Lord Devizes in his role as a secret investigator.

'No, I'm sorry,' said Lady Elizabeth distractedly as she removed her bonnet, for, by this time, they'd reached the doorway and there were several maids waiting to relieve the Duke's guests of their outer wear, so that they could go straight to a reception room where refreshments were being served. 'I didn't notice it after you'd gone. I thought you must have picked it up yourself.'

No. She'd been too angry to bend back down again. So...where had it gone? If it wasn't on the floor of the chapel when Lady Elizabeth had emerged from her pew, then somebody must have picked it up.

She gripped her reticule tightly, for want of any other way to express her sudden spasm of panic. She'd just have to hope that it had been Lord Devizes. That he'd picked it up while everyone else's attention was on her storming out and Lady Elizabeth and her mother having one of their altercations.

Because if it was anyone else...

No, no, surely she was worrying unnecessarily. Only people who worked for, or with, Lord Devizes knew about his code name. Anyone outside their fraternity would make nothing of a sketch of an ancient Roman deity. Would they?

Although...somebody had discovered that Herbert was on to them. He'd told her, after dropping off yet another of the coded messages, that he was following up a lead that could take him right to the heart of the group of people who were involved in passing information about the state of England's military power to the exiled French emperor. He'd been close, he'd told her with excitement.

Too close, she'd later realised. So close that who-ever it was he'd been tailing had turned round and mur-dered him.

A chill ran down her spine as she stepped out of the sunshine and into the shaded interior of the house. She fumbled at the strings of her bonnet. She had good reason to believe that Herbert's killer was going to at-tend the Duke of Theakstone's wedding. And if she was going to be hunting that person down on her own, she was going to have to be a great deal more cautious.

Chapter Four

Since Horatia and Lady Elizabeth had not taken the direct route back to the house from the chapel, practically everyone who'd attended morning prayers had already reached the yellow salon before them.

Horatia followed in Lady Elizabeth's wake to the tea table, which was manned by a brace of the Duke's liveried footmen. Having procured drinks, they then proceeded to another great long refectory-style table, which was piled with all manner of the kinds of things she would have taken on a picnic. There were huge hams, chicken legs, slices of bread, whole boiled eggs and fruit that was so artfully arranged on a sort of pedestal that it would have felt as if she was desecrating it if she dared remove so much as a single grape.

She picked up a plate and handed it over to one of the footmen, pointing out what she wanted rather than helping herself to any of the tempting delicacies on show. Once it was filled, but not piled high, Horatia looked about for somewhere to sit and eat it. Lady Elizabeth had already dutifully gone to sit beside her mother. But there was no way Horatia was going to try to squeeze on to the sofa beside them. The vinegary expression on Lady Tewkesbury's face was enough to give her indigestion. And there were loads of other chairs dotted about, in little clusters, and sofas set at angles so that the occupants could chat.

Though Horatia had the horrid feeling that what they were chatting about was her. Several times she caught a sly look, or somebody nudging someone else to make them aware she was about to walk by. And, of course, there was Lord Devizes himself, surrounded by a gaggle of giggling females, his eyes following her progress, his mouth slightly tilted in that mocking smile he very rarely went without.

His flirts must all be wondering how she could possibly show her face in public after the scene she'd made in the chapel earlier. If only she had the courage to take her plate and cup up to her own sitting room where she could avoid the stares. Or if only there was a bank of potted plants behind which she could hide.

But there wasn't. For all his vaunted wealth, the Duke had not a single plant, in a pot, anywhere in this room, never mind a whole bank of them. The best she could do would be to find a corner and hope that once she'd sat down in it, and applied herself to her nuncheon, *certain people* would find something else to laugh at. She couldn't help darting the Duke a rather resentful glance before beginning her search. He was standing with a group of men by one of the fireplaces, the over-mantel of which they were using as a shelf for their drinks while they tucked into their food. Which did nothing to improve her mood. It was all very well for men. They could eat standing up and put mantel shelves into use as tables, and all anyone would say was that they were making themselves at home. If she were to do the same…

She resumed her search of the room for a secluded corner and after only a few moments finally spotted a straight-backed chair standing against the wall by a window. It had the advantage of being partially shielded by a heavy velvet curtain. With a sigh of relief, Horatia made straight for it. It was only once she'd sat down that she realised that it was going to be virtually impossible to eat anything while she had her teacup in one hand and her plate in the other. The windowsill was too narrow to be anywhere near as useful as a mantelpiece, as well as being a bit awkward to reach being swathed by such a bulky curtain. Why, oh, why did people not provide their guests with handy little tables? And not just the gregarious ones, who sat upon the sofas in the middle of the room. They were all amply catered for. They had tables to the front of them, tables at their elbows, even tables directly behind the sofa back should they take it into their heads to reach for their teacups over their shoulders.

She was just wondering which of the groups of people who were in possession of tables she could go and join, when the Duke's intended came bustling over, a little white dog bounding along at her skirts.

'Miss Carmichael,' said the dark-eyed, dark-haired, dark-skinned slip of a girl that nobody could believe the Duke would prefer over elegant blonde beauties such as Lady Elizabeth. 'I am so sorry that I have not had a chance to speak with you before now. I am…' She hesitated, a tide of pink rushing up her cheeks. And then she took a deep breath as though deciding she might as well say whatever it was she'd thought twice about. 'As you can probably tell, I am not used to entertaining on such a vast scale. Well, any scale at all, to be honest. But, oh, dear me...' She waved to a footman stationed at the door. 'Peter, can you go and fetch a little table for Miss Carmichael? I am so sorry,' she said the moment he'd strolled away. 'I should have thought to have a table placed here.'

The girl was so uncomfortable, so clearly out of her depth, that even though Horatia had just been mentally berating her for not thinking of providing a table, she started to feel some sympathy for her. Even though that smacked of disloyalty to Lady Elizabeth.

'I don't suppose you expected any of your guests to wish to sit behind a curtain,' she said by way of a compromise.

'Oh. But I should have known, since the first time I set foot in this room I only lasted five minutes before... I mean, well, that is, how are you finding things at Theakstone Court?' Miss Underwood spoke in such a flustered manner that Horatia would have assumed, if she didn't know better, that the girl was even more unused to polite company than she was. 'It must be so awkward for you, being here at such a difficult time,' she then continued. 'Were you very close to your brother? Oh.' She coloured up again. 'That is not the kind of question I should have asked, is it? Oh, where is Peter with that table?' She looked around with an air of desperation.

And Horatia didn't have the heart to maintain any sort of hostility at all any longer. After all, Lady Eliza-

beth herself didn't seem to begrudge Miss Underwood
the Duke. 'I was very, very close to my brother,' she
said, in an attempt to lay to rest one of her hostess's
concerns. 'And, yes, I do feel a bit awkward here, but
then, to be frank, I was not that much less awkward
before. In society, that is. In fact, I rarely went about
much, even though I live in London.'

Now it was her cheeks that heated. But at least Miss
Underwood looked less uncomfortable.

'Then it was very brave of you to attend.'

'Loyal, I should have said,' drawled Lord Devizes,
who had somehow managed to make his way across
the room without either of the ladies noticing. Both
she and Miss Underwood jumped, though she was the
only one to spill tea down the front of her gown. Fortunately, since it was black, the stain would hardly show.
Which was yet another advantage of not having to wear
the fashionably pale colours Aunt Matilda had insisted
she wore in the past.

'You came, primarily,' Lord Devizes was continuing,
'to provide support for your disappointed friend, Lady
Elizabeth Grey, did you not? Against the woman who
stole her intended from beneath her nose.' He turned
to give Miss Underwood a smile that was just about
the most disdainful expression she'd ever seen on anyone's face.

Which made her want to leap to the girl's defence. 'It
was as much to my advantage as Lady Elizabeth's. That
is,' she said, belatedly realising that she'd been on the
verge of giving too much away, 'she thought that getting me out of Town might help to, um, lift my spirits.'

'I can see that she is doing her utmost,' he said, indicating the sofa on which Lady Elizabeth was sitting with her mother, at the far end of the room, 'to do so.'

Sarcastic beast.

'Well, it must be very difficult,' put in Miss Underwood, 'to know what to do for Miss Carmichael. I mean, what with her being in mourning, it isn't as if she can join in all that much with any of the activities we have planned for the entertainment of our guests this week.'

No, but then she hadn't wanted to do any joining in. She'd wanted to contact Lord Devizes and let him know what she knew, so that he could bring Herbert's killers to justice. Once she'd shared all the information she had, she'd planned to stay in her room as much as she could, out of the way of all the festivities, and hand the work over to him.

What a fool she was. She should never have assumed that a man, any man, even a man like Lord Devizes would have been better at tackling the active work. When had any man been any better than her at anything?

Except dressing well and being charming, that was, at which both Lord Devizes and Herbert excelled. Which wasn't surprising, the amount of time they spent gazing at themselves in mirrors. Why, Lord Devizes was doing so now. Though he was standing close enough to hold a conversation with her, he'd also chosen a spot which gave him a clear view to the mirror which hung between her window and the next one along. And was openly checking out the set of his neckcloth.

'*You* were involved in the planning of the entertainment, were you?' Lord Devizes raised one of his eyebrows in mock surprise at Miss Underwood.

'I... Well, no, it was more my aunt, as I expect you know, but...'

'Well, I certainly knew that it could not have been His Grace,' he said, apparently satisfied with his appearance and turning to direct a sardonic smile in Miss Underwood's direction. 'Since he cares nothing for anybody's pleasure but his own.'

Miss Underwood gasped. 'That is not true. He is a truly generous host—'

'I shall have to take your word for it, having never been in receipt of his hospitality.'

'What?' Miss Underwood looked completely taken aback. 'Has he never...? I mean, I know that there is some bad feeling on your side, but...'

Lord Devizes managed to let Miss Underwood know that she'd seriously offended him by letting his smile slip just the tiniest bit and doing something with his eyes that made them look positively freezing. 'Bad feeling?' The tone of his voice matched the iciness of his eyes.

'Oh, um, I see Peter coming over with the table,' said Miss Underwood, wrenching her gaze away from Lord Devizes and turning to the footman as though he was her saviour. After flapping about for a minute or so placing it in a position that meant Horatia had both cup and plate comfortably to hand, Miss Underwood scurried off with her footman at her side.

Leaving Horatia alone with Lord Devizes.

'That was a bit unnecessary,' she said.

'Possibly,' he conceded. 'But I gathered, from your little demonstration in the chapel earlier, that you were desperate to have private speech with me.'

'Well, yes, I am, but...'

'Then why waste the few moments we have in questioning my methods? We probably have two minutes, at most, before somebody comes to break up our tête-à-tête. Here,' he said, holding out the Bible she'd been worrying about. 'My pretext for approaching you.'

Gone was his fatuous smile and the lazy droop to his eyes. Even his voice had changed. Now she could see the man her brother had worked with. The man whom very few people ever saw when they were in the presence of Lord Devizes.

'What is so important that you needed to accost me in that fashion?' he said, in a tone of voice that finally persuaded her that he could really have run the kind of organisation Herbert swore they'd been involved in. 'Money, is it? I know Herbert supported you.'

'He did not!' She was fortunate enough to have a small competence of her own. Along with Aunt Matilda's jointure, the two ladies managed to rub along in their little house very comfortably, in a financial sense, at least. 'And if I was in that sort of difficulty, do you really suppose I would apply to you for help?'

'Then the sketch you tucked in the pages of your Bible really was a message. Herbert *must* have been speaking out of turn,' he said, half to himself. 'What more,' he said, applying himself directly to her again, 'do you know about the business beside my code name?'

'Probably a sight more than you do, since I was the one who unravelled all the ciphers you gave him.'

'You?' He looked at her as though he'd never really seen her before, in a searching, piercing way that made her want to wriggle in her seat.

'Yes, me,' she said, feeling her cheeks flush. Though why they should do so she could not think.

Or perhaps she could. This was the first time he'd really turned his full attention on her. And it was having a most remarkable effect. She could now see why he was so attractive to so many women, even though she'd never cared for his wispy fair looks before. He had a great deal of…presence, that was what it was. She could not call it charm, since he couldn't be less charming, insinuating she couldn't have possibly done so much of Herbert's paperwork for him. Well, whatever it was about him, it was a bit galling to discover that she was not immune to it.

'Surely,' she pointed out, reminding herself that she was a rational, intelligent creature who was in the middle of a very important conversation, and, therefore, had no business melting into the chair, let alone noticing that his eyes were blue, not grey as she'd previously thought, 'you cannot really think he had the time to work out some of the earlier ciphers he brought to me with all the carousing he did with you? Or the brains, come to that. You knew him at Oxford, didn't you?'

'Herbert was clever…'

'In some ways, yes. But he didn't have the patience to sit down and work through the thousands of possible permutations each cipher could represent. Don't you have any idea how many hours such work takes?'

'I truly sympathise,' he said in his more typical lazy drawl, his expression suddenly assuming that mask of fatuous insincerity that he'd briefly dropped. And then turned to face the Duke, who was, Horatia saw, approaching them with a look of dark intent on his face. 'Well,

well, if it isn't my exalted half-brother, His Grace the Duke himself. Deigning to grace us with his presence.'

The Duke came to a halt. His brows lowered still further. 'I have not come to quarrel with you.'

'No? You have not come to inform me that I have insulted your poor deluded little bride? Even though, not two minutes after she reported our conversation to you, you come over here when hitherto you have exchanged barely two words with me.'

Horatia got the peculiar sensation that she'd just become invisible. For all the notice either brother was taking of her, she might as well be.

'I wonder you accepted my invitation to my wedding at all, if that is your belief,' growled the Duke.

'Perhaps it will give me more pleasure to be a thorn in your side in person, than to merely express my dislike of you and all you stand for by staying away,' replied Lord Devizes.

Oh, Lord. Was there anything more uncomfortable than being caught in the middle of what she knew to be a long-standing family feud?

'I suppose that now you are going to accuse me of, what, upsetting Miss Carmichael? Or attempting to compromise her over the teacups?'

The Duke's eyes turned to chips of black ice. 'You had better not attempt anything of the sort,' he said, evidently taking Lord Devizes's throwaway remark as some sort of threat.

'It would be useless to explain, I suppose,' said Lord Devizes, his own eyes gone as cold as his brother's, 'that I was a very close friend of Miss Carmichael's brother. That I was offering my condolences. And that if it appeared as though I had upset her, it was hardly surprising, his demise being so recent, and the manner of his departure from this life so particularly unpleasant.'

The Duke, who looked as though he'd been robbed of the pleasure of taking his younger brother by the neck and heaving him through a window, muttered his own condolences, before nodding his head and walking away.

'I suppose that will grant us another minute or so,' said Horatia, watching the Duke retreat to his fiancée's side. 'Even if it was a pack of lies.'

'It was no such thing.'

'Oh, please,' she snorted. Which she knew was a very unattractive habit of hers when talking to men and no doubt contributed to their universal failure to offer for her hand in marriage, but which she simply could not stop. 'We both know why you have come here. And it has nothing to do with annoying your brother. I apologise for underestimating you.'

'Apology accepted,' he said with a smooth smile.

'Then you *are* on the trail of Herbert's killer? I wasn't sure Herbert had managed to pass on that last note I deciphered for him. I had thought that was why they killed him, to stop you getting it, but since you are here...'

'That's enough,' he said firmly. 'Good God, woman, have you no sense? You don't blurt out words like...in public, when anyone can hear.'

'No, no of course not, I'm sorry, I just...' She swallowed. 'And you are right. One of the people in this very room could be...' She glanced round her nervously. Nobody was standing close enough to overhear their conversation, she was fairly sure. And Lord Devizes had angled his body so that nobody could see all that much of her at all, so they couldn't even guess what she might be saying. Though it had been careless of her to blurt out what she knew. Particularly after vowing she was going to be more cautious. 'I know I am not much good at this side of things.' She was never at ease in groups of people. She was no good at hiding what she felt, or keeping her opinions to herself. Which made her rather unpopular. 'I just got a bit...that is, I'd thought I was going to have to do it alone. But now, knowing that you are secretly on the trail, that you have even followed them here, just as I have...oh, you have no idea how glad I am.' She was no longer alone. She could trust Lord Devizes, just as Herbert had done.

Before she could think better of it, she reached out and clasped his hand. Squeezed it and said, 'Thank you. Thank you. And if there is anything I can do to help you in your search...'

He withdrew his hand abruptly. 'There is not. You are not cut out for this kind of work. I concede that you may have played a part in Herbert's success with...that is, that you were more aware of things than he led me to believe, but he would want you to stay out of it.'

'No, he wouldn't!' He'd brought the ciphers to her in the first place because he'd known how much she would enjoy unravelling them. At doing work that not even most men could take on.

But Lord Devizes had turned on his heel and was striding away.

As though the matter was closed.

Chapter Five

Nick walked across the room as though he had some destination in mind, though in truth his mind was reeling too much for him to pay attention to such mundane matters as where he was going, or who he'd just smiled at as he'd brushed past them.

Because her claim of being his codebreaker rang with so much truth it was like a peal of bells. Hadn't he always marvelled at Herbert's ability to stay up all night drinking, then roll up with a deciphered message the very next day? There had been no denying Herbert's charm, or his ability to cosy up to some low-life and ferret out his deepest secrets. But he'd wondered, more than once, if his friend might be using someone else to do the hard graft behind the scenes.

Someone like a sister who was so awkward in social gatherings that she'd rather sit at home poring over tables of ciphers. And who doted on her brother so much that she gladly let him take all the credit.

He'd wandered over to the buffet table. Deciding he might as well make it look as if he'd gone there on purpose, he picked up a fresh wine glass and held it out for the footman to fill. His hand, he noted with consternation, was trembling slightly.

He took a deep draught of the fortifying drink and then strolled to the nearest mirror, as though to examine his reflection. He looked calm, thank goodness. Slightly amused, if anything. Which was a relief. He did not want anyone to know that, after his encounter with Herbert's sister, his heart was pounding with excitement, his mind racing with possibilities. Because this revelation that his codebreaker, his Portunus, still lived, changed everything. If she really was what she claimed, then he wasn't finished after all.

'I'm not surprised you need a stiff drink after that little scene,' came a bitter voice from just below the level of his left shoulder. The fact that his sister, Lady Twickenham as she now was, had managed to approach him without him noticing warned him that he needed to pull himself together. So what if little Miss Carmichael was his Portunus, had been acting as his codebreaker and opener of the doors to all the secrets England's enemies were trying to pass on to the French? He wasn't going to be able to carry on his work if he could allow himself to become this inattentive to all that was going on around him in a room.

'Yes,' he drawled, turning from the mirror to give his sister back the kind of sarcastic smile she'd expect. 'It did all rather escalate.' Had escalated beyond anything a feather-brained creature like she could imagine. Jane's life revolved around fashion and status and gossip. And she assumed he was as shallow as she.

He'd taken pains to make sure of it. Although recently, he'd been starting to feel the muscles in his face creating smiles that held far more disdain than amusement. And when he checked those smiles in a mirror, more often than not he appeared cynical. Jaded. The way Jane looked all the time.

'I only wonder,' she said, 'that you took notice of such a dowdy in the first place.'

'It had the effect of annoying His Grace,' he pointed out, as though that had been his sole intent on approaching his friend's sister. And Jane, being the kind of person she was, assumed that was what he'd meant.

'You are a wretch,' she said with a maliciously approving smile, rapping him lightly on the wrist for good measure. 'I had wondered why you came, knowing how you must feel about the Cuckoo.' She darted a look of loathing in the direction of their half-brother.

He followed the direction of her gaze. Their half-brother was looking straight back at them, his beetling brows drawn down into a scowl with which Nick was all too familiar. A scowl which sent his mind flying right back to the first time they'd encountered each other, as boys. In their father's study, here at Theakstone Court. And the shock he'd experienced upon hearing that the surly, swarthy oaf who'd looked, dressed, and smelled like a farm labourer was going to inherit the house and the title that Nick had been encouraged to believe was his by right. And what was more, that Nick was no longer even going to live here, but in a smaller, distant estate that he'd never even heard of before.

Nick turned his head away, set his glass down on the mantelpiece and raised both his hands to his cravat. Demonstrating, should anyone else be taking note, that he cared more for his own appearance than he did for his half-brother's opinion. It was an attitude he'd adopted very early on, in order to conceal his devastating pain at being cast off like an old shoe. Oliver might be the first born and the rightful heir, and nowadays also one of the wealthiest men in England, but Nick was never going to let him forget that, once, Nick had seen him standing hat in hand, shuffling his feet in their scuffed boots.

After adjusting the set of his already perfectly arranged neckcloth, Nick returned his gaze to the scowling Duke, raising his quizzing glass as he ran a disparaging eye over the bulky frame in its sombre clothing, before allowing his lips to twist in just the hint of a disdainful grimace, before switching his attention back to his sister.

Who'd so bitterly referred to the Duke as a cuckoo.

But then that was how it had seemed, to start with. As though the moment he'd come to Theakstone Court, Nick and his sisters, along with their mother, had been tossed out of their cosy nest.

The truth was, however, that even though they'd all resented the boy whose appearance had made their father look at them all differently, the analogy fell down under scrutiny. Because no matter where Oliver Norrington had spent the first eleven years of his life, there was no disputing the fact that *he* was the legitimate first born. And that Nick would remain second best for ever. No matter what he did.

'Should I,' said Nick, quirking an eyebrow at his sister's reflection, 'ask why you are here, then?'

She gave a little shrug. 'Anyone who is anyone has been invited. It is the event of the Season. Even the

Wortley-Fortescues are posting back from Paris to attend.'

Yes, so they were. He turned to his sister slowly, giving his mind the leisure to ponder that fact before having to come up with the kind of spiteful witticism she would expect.

The Duke had put it about that he had invited so many of the great and good of the land to Theakstone Court because he wanted to introduce his bride to society from his own home, rather than pitching her into the hothouse that was London. Yet, what better excuse could there be for getting all the members of a network together? They could exchange the latest information they'd gathered over a hand of whist, or while out riding in the park, to whoever intended to take it to their paymasters in France. That must have been what Miss Carmichael had meant by her comment about him having the same reason for coming here as she did. She clearly thought he'd come to Theakstone Court on the trail of those responsible for her brother's death.

And he'd said nothing to disabuse her of that opinion. Because he wanted her to think he was at least as clever as she. Yet only now did he regard the way the room was already thronging with all the noblest and most influential members of society left in England with suspicion. For many of them, as his sister had just pointed out, had already taken advantage of Bonaparte's defeat and crossed the Channel to see Paris. Or Brussels. Or any other of the cities that had been impossible to visit while Europe had been at war. And once the celebrations for the Duke's nuptials were done, many more of them would take to ships and flock to the Continent.

And only a very few people, who knew that information was being passed to the French. would think anything other than that the fashionable were determined to keep up with the latest trend.

'I cannot deny that it has also given me a great deal of pleasure to install my own children in the nursery where we all used to play,' his sister added, with a flash of malice. The sister who'd correctly deduced why he was here.

Because she knew him. She knew that he could, and frequently did, act from petty motives. Over the years, he'd gone from doing his utmost to prove to his father that he was the better son, to creating the biggest scandals he could simply to get the old devil to notice he still existed.

'Mary did the same. We thought we should make a point, you know.'

'And what point would that be,' he said, 'precisely?' That they were still pouting over the fact that their father had been unjust and unkind? 'She was only a babe when we left. She can surely recall nothing of this house, or what it was like to live here.' He'd only been approaching his sixth birthday himself. Though some things were impossible to forget. Like this room. He let his eyes wander over the nymphs frolicking about the frieze below the elaborate plaster adorning the ceiling. All that yellow. Like sunshine, Mother had always said, although today it put him in mind of lemons and the bitter taste they left in the mouth.

'We still have more right to be here than…than anyone else.' She shot a look of sheer loathing at Miss Underwood, who was hanging on to the Duke's arm and gazing up at him with a worshipful expression. He couldn't quite believe that any woman could look at any man with quite so much open adoration, let alone a man like the Duke.

'Especially that by-blow of his.'

'His what?' He whipped round to look at her.

'Oh, didn't you know? Our perfect brother has blotted his copybook. And rather than making any attempt to be discreet, he has brought the fruit of his misdeeds into his house and is forcing that stupid girl to acknowledge it. And she is making a mull of things, from what I hear. The schoolroom is in total chaos, at any rate, since there is no governess in residence.'

She'd said it at the top of her voice. As though hoping anyone within earshot would hear. Because she was furious. And no wonder. It was bad enough to have been thrown out as though they were chaff. But to hear that Oliver was prepared to bring an illegitimate child here really turned the knife in the wound.

He turned to stare at his half-brother with resentment. Was he doing it to make a point? To tell the world that he held even a bastard in higher esteem than his own legitimate siblings?

By God, he hoped that Miss Carmichael was right. That this week-long celebration of the Duke's nuptials to a nobody really was a front to disguise the true purpose of gathering this particular set of people here. That among them all was a small group who were dedicated to betraying their country by passing on highly sensitive information to the French. Specifically, to those segments of the French population who persisted in supporting Napoleon Bonaparte and stirring up as much unrest as they could. Who'd do whatever it took to see him restored to power, even if it meant plunging Europe back into a state of warfare.

When he and Herbert had first been alerted to what was going on, he'd leapt at the chance to find out who the traitors were, believing there could be nothing more satisfying than preventing Europe from descending into warfare again. But if the Duke was mixed up in this particular act of treason…then, oh, yes, that would really be something.

Even if the Duke wasn't mixed up in it, at the very least Nick would stir up a hornet's nest.

He looked round the room at the wedding guests who'd already arrived. Miss Carmichael seemed to believe that her brother's killer was here. Possibly in this very room. Why? What did she know that he didn't?

Hah. Probably a great many things. He'd been so distracted since Herbert's death that he hadn't even heard about the Duke's love child.

He had to pull himself together. The room was teeming with nobles, politicians and high-ranking clergy. Any one of whom could have turned traitor and then had Herbert killed rather than risk exposure. Because Herbert had been getting close. Too close for someone's comfort, clearly. Else why have him killed?

He altered his stance, just a touch, so that he could see the corner of the room in which Herbert's sister was sitting. She was nibbling at a slice of chicken, rather disconsolately. Because he'd told her she was no good at this line of work.

And she wasn't. Yes, she could decipher codes, but she had no talent for the kind of double-dealing that had come to Herbert naturally. She couldn't sit up all night drinking a potential source of information into a stupor, lulling them into a false sense of security by ladling on the charm. She couldn't befriend someone and, under the guise of gossiping, gain their sympathy and get them to reveal far more than they should.

And yet she wanted to track down Herbert's killer. It was why she'd come here. It must be. It certainly couldn't be for the reason most women would attend a wedding. She wasn't one of those who went to any lengths to get invitations to the most fashionable events, to get a rich, titled husband. Since she'd stumbled through her first Season without *taking*, she'd gained a reputation for disliking men. You only had to look at her to see she had no interest in fashion, either.

And from what she said, she had information that, when put together with what he knew, might blow the whole conspiracy wide open.

But how could he involve her in an affair that had become so dangerous that even Herbert, a skilled operative, hadn't survived?

And Herbert had been so determined to keep her out of things that he hadn't let anyone, not even Nick, know she was making any contribution to their work at all.

Not so determined, however, that he'd had any scruples about getting her to decipher the coded messages that had occasionally fallen into their hands.

'Whatever is it about that creature that has you so fascinated?' His sister's strident tones broke into his thoughts, making him aware that for the last few minutes he'd been staring at Herbert's sister, while debating with himself whether he could, in all conscience, bring her on board.

'I am wondering whether it would be profitable to cultivate her acquaintance.'

'What, a drab little thing like that? Not your usual style, Nick.' Though then she grinned. 'What mischief are you plotting? It has to be something exceptionally wicked for you to get that particular look on your face.'

'I shall not tell you,' he said with sincerity. The last person he could tell of his sensitive dealings with government ministers was a gabblemonger like Jane. He might as well take out an advertisement in *The Times*. 'But what I can promise you is that our half-brother is not going to like it.'

'Oh, goody,' she said. 'If there is anything I can do to help, you have only to let me know. I would give almost anything to see that smug expression wiped off his face.'

Yes, even to the point of conniving in an innocent damsel's downfall, by the look she was shooting Miss Carmichael.

Though was he any better? His plans for her were not of the sort Jane assumed. But they would bring her into just as much danger. And not merely of her virtue, but possibly of her very life.

If he was a less selfish man, he wouldn't dream of involving her. But he was selfish. The work he'd begun with Herbert had given him a sense of purpose for the first time in his life. And he was good at it, too. He simply didn't *want* to give it up.

Besides, preventing a war was more important than the welfare of one insignificant female.

Wasn't it?

Chapter Six

The chicken was probably delicious, but to Horatia it might as well have been shoe leather she was chewing. Lord Devizes was just like every other man she'd ever known, apart from Herbert. They thought she could not possibly be of any help with their manly, important work. He'd walked away with a sort of sneer, though how on earth anyone could express disdain by the way they walked she could not say. And then she'd watched him discussing her with his scarily dainty, fashionable sister, to judge from the way they kept glancing at her and laughing nasty little laughs.

The rebuff was doubly hard because at one point he'd more or less acknowledged the contribution she'd made, just before he'd dashed her hopes by pointing out how unfit she was for the kind of work Herbert had undertaken. And then rounded it all off by saying that Herbert would want her to stay out of it.

Which was true, of course. Herbert had been terribly protective of her. He'd stressed how dangerous the people were he hunted down and how important it was that nobody ever find out she was involved in bringing them to justice.

And he'd been right. They were so dangerous that one of them, sensing Herbert was getting close to exposing them, had killed him. But did that mean she was going to just sit back and let them get away with it?

She dragged her eyes away from Lord Devizes, and his titled sister, and gazed round the room, wondering which of these lofty personages could possibly be not only a traitor, but also responsible for the death of her brother. Not that they would have soiled their aristocratic fingers with the dagger themselves. They'd have hired some low, common person to do the dirty work. But somebody here was the one who signed his notes by the code name of The Curé. The presence of Lord Devizes had at least confirmed that much, even if he wasn't going to share any other information with her. His animosity for his half-brother the Duke was so tangible nothing else could possibly have induced him to attend the wedding.

Just as her thoughts turned to him again, he started stalking in her direction, eyeing her the way she'd imagine a lion would look at its next meal.

'The chicken not to your liking?'

'Um,' she said stupidly, her mouth suddenly running dry. What was he playing at? And why was he looking at her like that? As though…as though he'd like to sink his teeth into her.

'Come, come, Miss Carmichael, if you are going to mix with the great and good of the land, you are going to have to come up with a wittier response than *um* when somebody makes a conversational gambit.'

'Oh…er…'

'That is even worse. You are making it obvious to all that my presence overwhelms you. And now you are blushing,' he said mockingly. 'Gauche. That is what you look. Gauche and ill dressed, and totally out of place.'

Well, she might be a bit gauche, but he was being extremely rude. Deliberately. As though he was trying to upset her. 'You are not going to scare me off,' she said fiercely, having suddenly seen what he was about. 'I have come here to find out who is responsible for…' She pulled herself up on the brink of saying the words he'd warned her were not to be uttered, and changed them to, '*You know what*…and insulting me isn't going to make me…cry, or run away, or…or whatever it is you are attempting to do.'

'Well, well,' he drawled. 'Quite the little vixen, when provoked. Perhaps,' he said in a voice suddenly turned all…caressing, 'there is more to you than meets the eye.'

Now what was he doing? She narrowed her eyes. He was looking at her the way he looked at all those silly women who fluttered round him, hoping to become his next bed partner. With smouldering eyes. And a smile that she could somehow only describe as inviting. 'It is of no use ladling on the charm,' she said firmly. 'Not when it is so patently insincere. Besides, I have a mirror. I know perfectly well what I look like.'

'Ah, but I was pointing out that there is more to you than meets the eye. Things that a mirror cannot show.'

'I am not going to fall for that plumper, either,' she said. She would have said a great deal more, only Miss Underwood was coming over.

'I do hope you are, I mean, that everything is…' said

Miss Underwood, looking anxiously between her and the lazily smiling Lord Devizes.

Horatia found that she was clutching her plate in such a tight grip it was a wonder the fragile porcelain had not snapped. Her irritation must be obvious to everyone in the room, while Lord Devizes was lounging against the side jamb of the window, the epitome of cool, calm masculinity. No, no, not cool and calm. Smouldering and confident, that was what his stance portrayed. As if he was sure she was going to be his next conquest.

'What can you possibly be implying?' he said, folding his arms across his chest and raising one eyebrow.

Exactly! He could not possibly be attempting to make a conquest of her, no matter how it might appear.

So what was he about? Did he just delight in making sport of poor little dabs of females? Or was it Miss Underwood and his brother he was trying to provoke?

'Oh, well,' said Miss Underwood, 'I am sure it must be very hard for Miss Carmichael to cope with…um, having been so recently bereaved, I mean she must be… and really, we ought to be trying to be more…'

He straightened up. 'Are you trying to teach me my manners?' His smile had gone. 'Miss Underwood?'

'Of course she isn't,' said Lady Elizabeth, who must have also approached while she'd been talking to Lord Devizes. Or at least, fencing with him verbally. 'Horatia, I can see you have finished with your food. Shall we retire to our rooms now?'

Lord Devizes was smiling again down his perfectly formed nose at her. And no wonder. Not just her hostess, but also her friend, had noticed her mounting annoyance and come dashing to her rescue before she disgraced herself by doing something like flinging her plate to the ground so that she could stand up and launch into a proper duel with him.

'I suppose,' she said in a voice that was as humble as she could make it sound, 'that would be best.' She got to her feet and set her plate on the side table the footman had brought her, before she could change her mind about turning it into any kind of missile.

'Best for whom?'

To her surprise, it was Lord Devizes who'd spoken.

'You may be pretending to be concerned for her welfare,' he continued, eyeing Miss Underwood in a very disdainful manner, 'but isn't it the truth that you want to shuffle her out of the way? So that she cannot bring a shadow to your glittering show?'

Miss Underwood and Lady Elizabeth both gave gasps of outrage.

'Indeed it is not,' said Miss Underwood. 'I could see that *you* were making her uncomfortable and...'

'Was I making you uncomfortable?' He turned to her and gave her one of those knee-melting smiles. And in spite of knowing he was up to something, a part of her, a very small, yet wholly feminine part of her, wanted to sigh and smile back, and say *Of course you were not making me uncomfortable*. So, of course, she clenched her knees and flung up her chin.

'I think you were deliberately baiting me,' she replied.

'Ah, yes, but after only a very little of that you ceased drooping over your plate, looking as though you wished to shrink behind the curtains, didn't you?'

Miss Underwood and Lady Elizabeth both looked at her. And then at him.

'It occurs to me that you are both being overprotective,' he said. 'What Miss Carmichael needs is not cosseting and being hidden away, but something to do. Something useful. Something that will occupy her mind. Is that not so, Miss Carmichael?'

The ladies looked at her again. She could see them both reaching the same conclusion. Though they both disliked Lord Devizes, and the way he went about things, on this occasion, he just happened to be correct.

'I did bring you here hoping that a change of scene would distract you,' said Lady Elizabeth thoughtfully.

Horatia rapidly reviewed the last words Lord Devizes had spoken. About wanting something useful to do. And about how she didn't need cosseting and protecting. Did that mean he had changed his mind about keeping her out of his investigative work, while she was here at Theakstone Court? Her heart gave a funny little kick in her chest. She studied his face carefully.

He gave her a surreptitious wink.

If she was going to prove that she could work with him in an active role, then she was going to have to pick up little hints like that and run with them. Although she had no idea what his plan was, he looked as though he definitely had one.

And if she didn't want to end up trying to track down Herbert's killer on her own, then she supposed she would have to follow his lead.

'I do think it might help if I could be useful to you, Miss Underwood,' she therefore said, 'in some way. I know I must be a most difficult guest to have at such an event and the last thing I want is to cast any shadow over your enjoyment.'

'And I just happen to know that Miss Underwood is in dire need of help,' said Lord Devizes, with a knowing smile.

'Oh?'

All three ladies turned to him. And as they did so it occurred to Horatia that they must look exactly the way all the other ladies looked when they gathered round him. As if they were hanging on his every word. Though at least none of them had silly looks of admiration on their faces while they were doing it.

'Yes, I have just learned that the nursery is in a state of chaos.'

The nursery? What did she know of nurseries? Or children of any sort, come to that?

'Lady Twickenham informs me that there is no resident governess to preside. I imagine that the children must be behaving like little savages while the visiting governesses are battling it out for supremacy.'

Miss Underwood clasped her hands at her breast. 'I deny...that is, I cannot be everywhere at once...'

'On second thoughts,' said Lord Devizes, giving her a considering look, 'perhaps Miss Carmichael is not the best person to put in charge of such a task. After all, what can a spinster know of children? Or what might keep them out of mischief?'

This calculatedly disparaging remark immediately caused both Miss Underwood and Lady Elizabeth to leap to her defence.

'I am sure Horatia is perfectly capable of restoring

order over some squabbling servants,' said Lady Elizabeth loyally.

'Most governesses are unmarried ladies, you know, of good birth and...' said Miss Underwood at the same time.

Lord Devizes raised his hands, as though in surrender. And then sauntered away, a satisfied smile curving his lips in a way that made Horatia simultaneously want to slap him and applaud him for the masterful way he'd just manipulated them into installing her into the very arena he wished her, for some reason, to investigate.

Chapter Seven

'Lord Devizes is quite correct,' said Miss Underwood despondently. 'I really do need to do something about a new governess. Although, I do not regret dismissing the last one,' she said, raising her chin and shooting his retreating back a defiant look. 'She was totally unsuitable.'

'He was also correct in pointing out that I have no experience with children,' said Horatia.

'Never mind standing about talking about how clever Lord Devizes is to point out everyone else's faults,' snapped Lady Elizabeth. 'Let's go up to the nursery and put our minds to solving your immediate problem, Miss Underwood.'

Miss Underwood shot her a grateful smile and led them to the door.

Oh, Lord, how Horatia hoped she wouldn't discover that either Miss Underwood or her husband had anything to do with Herbert's death. She seemed like such a nice girl, if a bit out of her depth, attempting to manage a ducal household.

However, Lord Devizes clearly wanted her to investigate something, or someone, connected with the nursery. She must not waste this chance to prove she could be a valuable agent in his organisation. So she had to think of some questions to ask. The kind of clever questions that would sound perfectly natural for someone in her position to ask, yet could also lead to the unmasking of a traitor.

That was all.

'Um,' she said, as they began to climb a flight of stairs, 'pardon me asking, but why would you need a governess at all? I mean, you have no children yet. Obviously, since you are not even married.'

'Oh, Oliver has a little girl already,' said Miss Underwood, before glancing over her shoulder at Lady Elizabeth with a worried expression. 'I dare say there has been a great deal of gossip about her.'

Lady Elizabeth nodded.

'I have not heard any,' said Horatia. 'I don't mix much in the kind of circles where such gossip flows, you know, besides being out of circulation altogether since Herbert—'

'Well, the truth,' Miss Underwood cut in, before Horatia could mention a word that was surely taboo at wedding festivities, 'is that he had no idea he even had a daughter until Livvy's mother died. And because of... some things that happened to him in his own childhood, he could not bear to foster her out to some family who would only look after her for financial gain. He hired a governess and a nurse for her, and brought her here, to Theakstone Court, in an attempt to...to learn how to be a real father to her.'

That sounded commendable in some respects, if

rather eccentric. However, it did rather suggest that the Duke didn't care what anyone else thought of him, since most illegitimate children were hidden away and raised by foster parents. Was this disdain for prevailing opinion the kind of attitude that could lead him to pass government secrets to a foreign country, though? Even if he was well placed to obtain such secrets and also had the contacts to pass them on?

'So why,' Horatia plucked up the courage to ask, since Miss Underwood seemed not to mind talking about what was surely rather a sensitive subject, 'did you dismiss the governess the Duke hired?' And when Lady Elizabeth jabbed her in the side with her elbow, added, 'If you do not think my question impertinent?'

'You may as well hear it from me,' said Miss Underwood with resignation, 'as anywhere. That woman was most unkind to Livvy. She went around referring to her as The Duke's Disgrace. And worse, addressed Livvy to her face as such when she could be bothered to spend any time in the schoolroom, which wasn't all that often.'

'How horrid of her,' said Horatia.

'I wonder the Duke hired her without finding out about her attitude towards children born on the wrong side of the blanket,' muttered Lady Elizabeth in her ear.

Miss Underwood, who clearly had very good hearing, said, 'Well, she came highly recommended, apparently.'

'Oh?' Horatia wondered, if the woman was so unsuitable, if someone might have introduced her into the household to help further their nefarious plans. Because if she was hardly ever where she was supposed to be, then it might be because she had other fish to fry.

Or was she clutching at straws?

Well, nothing ventured, nothing gained.

'Who was it who recommended her?'

'Perceval,' replied Miss Underwood, with a wry twist to her lips. 'Oliver's secretary. Have you met him? Perhaps not. He has been terribly busy with various things lately and isn't one for socialising all that much. But he is generally so efficient in business matters that Oliver trusts him completely.'

Aha. A shadowy figure, who had access to all the Duke's papers and was trusted implicitly. If he wasn't a likely candidate then she didn't know who was.

'Only he is a bachelor,' Miss Underwood continued, 'with no experience of working in a household with children. Oh,' she said suddenly, looking contrite, 'please don't think that it will matter that you don't have any such experience, either...'

Horatia was pretty sure it did matter, but that wasn't what she'd been thinking about. Or not exactly. No, what she'd been wondering was how he came to pluck this *'highly recommended governess'* out of thin air, if he had no previous experience in hiring them.

'Because I don't think you will need to do much more than let all the visiting governesses know that I have placed you in charge,' said Miss Underwood, darting her a glance which made Horatia suspect she didn't really believe what she was saying. 'The governesses who have come know their work, I expect. You will just need to act as a kind of...umpire? Is that the word? Oh, dear,' she said, looking harried. 'I never imagined so many of our guests would bring their children with them. Usually, so Oliver says, people leave their offspring at home on their country estates the year round, no matter where they go.' She puffed as they began climbing a third flight of stairs. 'My Aunt Agnes has organised a very full programme of activities for the ladies. And Uncle Ned for the gentlemen,' she said over her shoulder, as she led them along a very plain corridor, right up in the eaves. 'But nobody spared a thought for the children,' she said, reaching a door through which there emanated rather a lot of shouting. 'Well, as I said, we didn't expect any to come,' she said, putting her hand to the door latch and opening the door rather gingerly.

For a few moments, none of the occupants noticed their arrival. Two plainly dressed women were engaged in a heated argument before the fireplace, while what looked like about ten children, of varying sizes, were doing exactly as they pleased all over the room. Two boys were happily dismembering a doll in spite of the efforts of a little girl, who was screaming at the top of her lungs, to stop them. A tiny, red-cheeked infant was wailing on the lap of a rather distressed-looking nurse while on the floor, before a bookcase, another girl was busily cutting pictures out of what looked like copies of a fashion magazine, and, to judge from the pot of glue at her side, using them to illustrate a pile of textbooks.

Horatia swallowed and reached out to grasp the nearest solid support, which turned out to be Lady Elizabeth's arm. Lady Elizabeth patted her hand.

'It isn't as bad as it looks,' she said bracingly. 'Why, nobody is…bleeding, or anything, are they? They are all just playing…'

At that moment, just as Miss Underwood appeared

to be about to say something along the same lines, an older girl, with long, dark curls, came rushing over to the door and flung her arms round Miss Underwood's waist. Miss Underwood returned the embrace without the slightest hesitation.

'Sofia,' said the little dark-haired girl, who Horatia assumed must be the Duke's illegitimate daughter, to be on such familiar terms with his affianced bride. 'How long do we have to have all these people here? You will be sending them away once you have married Papa, won't you?'

Miss Underwood bit her lower lip. 'I do hope so,' she finally said. And darted Horatia a look of appeal.

'I am Miss Carmichael,' said Horatia. 'Your st—I mean, Sofia,' she said, darting Miss Underwood a glance, hoping that using the child's name for her had not caused offence. 'Sofia hoped that I might be able to help…arrange some…er…activities to keep you all amused.'

It wasn't exactly what Miss Underwood had asked of her, but the moment she'd seen how unruly the children all were one of her Aunt Matilda's sayings, *'The devil makes work for idle hands'*, had sprung to mind.

'Oh, goody,' said the little girl. 'I keep asking if we can go outside to play, but those two,' she said, pulling a rather rude face in the direction of the quarrelling governesses, 'keep saying we are supposed to stay out of sight and out of mind. Which doesn't seem at all fair. All the grown-ups are doing all sorts of fun things from what Uncle Ned says, so why shouldn't we?'

'Oh, dear,' said Miss Underwood. 'Well, the thing is, Livvy, that while we have so many people staying, it might not be quite safe for these children to wander about the place. I know that you would be sensible, but I would never forgive myself if one of the others fell out of a tree, or into the lake, or ran across in front of one of the gentlemen when they are out riding and got trampled.'

Livvy looked at the two little boys intent on torturing the little girl and her doll, and pulled a face as if to say she wouldn't mind very much if some of them did get trampled.

Horatia swallowed again. She had no idea how to restore order to the children running about in the nursery. And the prospect of taking them outside and seeing them scattered to the four winds, some to drown in the lake while others ended up ground to paste beneath the horses of the visiting gentlemen, made her feel a touch queasy.

Why on earth had she told Lord Devizes that she could work with him to unmask the traitor at Theakstone Court? Why had she not simply stuck to what she knew, sitting at a desk, poring over tables of ciphers? And how on earth could any woman do anything with this…this mob, when even trained, experienced governesses could not?

Which made her wonder if Lord Devizes had set her this task to test her mettle. It was just the sort of sneaky, underhanded thing he might do, in order to teach her how unsuitable she was to become one of his team. There was probably nothing worth finding out regarding Herbert, or the nest of spies that seemed to centre on Theakstone Court, at all. In fact, she wouldn't be a bit surprised if he'd sent her up here to keep her out of his way while he got on with his own line of enquiry.

Right. She would just have to show him, then, wouldn't she? That not only could she meet this challenge, but also use it to further her own pursuit of the truth. She'd already unearthed some information about the former governess and the Duke's secretary that he might not know and might be pertinent. And since servants always knew all sorts of things that went on in the houses where they worked, no matter how hard their employers tried to keep them secret, she would just have to see what more she could learn from these two governesses. And the nurse.

She eyed the children again. As Lady Elizabeth had just said, they were only displaying signs of being bored. So she'd have to start devising some sort of activity that could keep them all entertained, within doors.

She might not know much about children, but she was by no means stupid. And she had spent most of her childhood within doors. In fact, her own governess had to practically drag her outside for a daily walk, so keen had she been to sit at her little desk devising or solving acrostics. She could soon prepare some simple ones for the older children.

While she was still turning over various possibilities and discarding them as unworkable, the two battling governesses stopped arguing, and turned to face the doorway in which Horatia was standing. And dropped deeply respectful curtsies. It would have been wonderful to think they had finally noticed her and Lady Elizabeth, and Miss Underwood. But the truth was that somebody else had joined them.

Lord Devizes.

'Good afternoon,' he said affably to the servants.

At the sound of his voice, the children, as one, paused in their various acts of destruction and looked up at him.

'Uncle Nick, Uncle Nick,' yelled the two boys, surging to their feet and dashing across the room to his side.

'No, no, don't paw at my coat, you young rascals,' he said, pushing them aside. They didn't seem to take this as an insult, however, but only grinned and launched themselves at him again, so that he'd repeat the rebuff.

Boys. She'd never understand them. Why did they take so much pleasure in fighting and destroying things?

'Look what they've done to Minny,' wailed the little girl, toddling over with what was left of her doll and holding it up for his inspection.

'I shall buy you another,' he said offhandedly and then turned to Horatia. 'It struck me, after you had all left the yellow salon, that in relegating you to this bear garden, I was doing practically the same thing as Lady Elizabeth had attempted, only with rather more aggravations attached.'

Good gracious. Was he attempting to apologise?

Surely not. In her experience, men *never* felt the need to apologise for *any*thing. So this must all be part of his plan.

'In fact, upon several occasions I have not acted well in my dealings with you. So I have come to make amends.'

Lady Elizabeth's eyes narrowed. 'You? Make amends?' Clearly she'd had similar experiences with the males in her life.

'Why not?' He returned her suspicious stare with a cold one. 'Miss Carmichael's brother was one of my oldest friends. No matter what I, personally, think of *her*, I owe it to him to do the right thing.'

'Why, you…'

'No, no, Lady Elizabeth,' said Horatia, giving her arm a gentle squeeze. 'Let the insult go. He cannot help it, I don't suppose.'

'Precisely,' said Lord Devizes. 'And I can think of no better way of making atonement for my many grievous affronts than standing at her side as she tackles the task of entertaining these…' he waved a languid arm round the occupants of the room '…brats.'

Miss Underwood's jaw dropped. Lady Elizabeth made a rather rude sound, part way between a laugh and a snort.

'I should have thought you, of all people,' he said to Lady Elizabeth, 'would approve. You made your feelings about my treatment of your friend perfectly clear after chapel this morning.'

'Don't quarrel,' said Horatia. 'Please.'

'*Pas devant les enfants,*' said Lord Devizes, in the kind of superior tone which was starting to make her want to slap him. Even though he was backing her up.

'Well, if you really…that is,' said Miss Underwood, gazing round the stilled room in a mixture of awe and appreciation. 'I do think we can leave Miss Carmichael and Lord Devizes to, um, sort things out, however they wish. Yes, thank you. Thank you both,' she said, hastily tugging Lady Elizabeth from the room before she could say anything else to antagonise anyone.

'Not up to snuff,' Lord Devizes observed, as the door shut upon a flurry of skirts. Livvy gave him a resentful glare before going over to a window seat and curling up on it, her back to the room as she gazed out over what was probably a splendid view of the estate.

And then, before Horatia could say anything in her hostess's defence, he added, 'Not used to living in such a grand house, or organising so many guests, from what I hear. Not brought up to it.'

'Well, nor am I, come to that,' said Horatia hotly in Miss Underwood's defence.

'Ah, but you have not set your sights on becoming a duchess, have you? You are far too sensible a person to attempt a task for which you are not qualified.'

She gaped at him. Although she'd heard no hint of sarcasm in his voice, he couldn't really have meant that he thought she was sensible, could he?

'I can think,' she therefore retorted, 'of no two people less qualified to entertain children than you and I, Lord Devizes.'

'Stuff,' he said. 'You have a keen mind and I have a way with children, as you have seen,' he said, sweeping an arm in the direction of his two little nephews, who had now taken the glue pot from the little girl by the bookcase and were using it to try to mend the doll they'd previously torn to bits. With the result that now it was a different girl who was crying.

He gave one of the governesses a look. She dropped a curtsy, went to the crying girl and set about drying her tears.

Golly. Miss Underwood had been correct. All the battling governesses needed was an umpire. So long as that umpire had an air of command, Horatia reflected. She didn't suppose she would have been able to achieve the same result with just one look.

'So,' she said, deciding she might as well take the bull by the horns, 'why have you really come up here?'

He grinned at her. 'That's one of the things I like about you. The agility of your mind.'

'Um. Thank you?'

'You should thank me. Because, after giving the matter careful consideration, I have decided that you could be of some assistance in my pursuit of Herbert's nemesis.' He leaned closer. 'For one thing, you are the only person as keen to discover who that may be as I am. I will never have to question either your loyalty or your commitment.'

'No. Well, precisely,' she said, pressing her hand to her heart, which was beating rather erratically all of a sudden because he'd finally agreed to let her work with him. Even if it was only on this one occasion. It had nothing to do with the fact that he was so close she could feel his breath fanning her cheek and smell the scent of clean linen and shaving soap.

'Now, to business,' he said, in a firmer voice, straightening up and glancing round the room. 'I am going to suggest, to both of them at once,' he said, indicating the governesses, who were both now doing their utmost to prove their superiority over each other by tidying up the wreckage and indiscriminately clipping their charges round the ears, 'that we—you and I—take the entire nursery party out into the grounds to play.'

'Outside?'

'Yes.'

'No. I mean, just a minute ago, Miss Underwood was pointing out all the reasons why the children ought *not* to go outside.'

'Which were?' He folded his arms across his chest and raised one eyebrow, as if preparing to demolish whatever argument she might put forward.

'Well, firstly, the dangers of letting them run around—'

'We shall not be letting them run around. We shall be taking them, at a sedate pace, down to the Crinchley Beck.'

'The what?'

'It's a stream that flows into the boating lake.'

'We cannot possibly take them anywhere near the lake. Miss Underwood said she'd never forgive herself if any of those children drowned.'

'Not even my nephews? Never mind. Let me assure you we shall not be taking any of them anywhere near the lake. We shall be going to a spot on the stream which flows through the woods, where they can splash about in a stretch of water no more than a couple of inches deep.'

'I...I don't think the governesses will permit it,' she said dubiously.

'Miss Underwood did say we could sort this out however we wished,' he reminded her. 'Besides, we are not going to give the governesses the chance to object. We shall just inform the children we are going to take them outside, then open the door. The governesses will not be able to stop a single one of them from making a dash for freedom.'

'Oh, dear,' she said, chewing her lower lip. 'You're about to incite a rebellion. I don't think this is quite what Miss Underwood envisaged when she left us in charge...'

He grinned at her. 'It is all in a good cause, though, isn't it?'

'Is it?'

'You know it is,' he said. 'For once we have success-fully arranged one such event, we will have the perfect excuse for spending more time together, ostensibly coming up with more activities to amuse the infantry.'

'Whereas, we will actually be…'

'Comparing notes,' he said with a decisive nod. 'Because each of us will no doubt have information the other does not.'

Goodness. She blinked up at him owlishly through her spectacles. Not only was he nowhere near as stupid as he looked, to have come up with a plan in the short time between stalking away from her in the yellow salon and arriving in the nursery, but he was also acting as if he trusted her. Something lightened inside. She blinked again, though this time it was to dispel the tears that were welling in her eyes.

'What is the matter? What have I said to upset you?' He frowned down at her. 'I thought this was what you wanted?'

'It is! I am just…' She reached out and squeezed his hand. 'Thank you,' she breathed. 'From the bottom of my heart.'

He snatched his hand away. Took a step back.

Gratitude was clearly the last thing he wanted from her. No, he wanted a cool, clear-headed woman who could be sensible. She ducked her head and delved into her reticule for a handkerchief. If it was what he wanted, if that was what it took to be a part of his plan to discover the traitor and Herbert's killer, then she could be sensible, she vowed, blowing her nose. In a sensible manner.

Chapter Eight

Just as he'd predicted, the moment he announced an outing to a stream and opened the schoolroom door, there was nothing that could have stopped the children stampeding from the room. Even the poor little nurse leaped to her feet, her infant tucked under her arm, and made a bid for freedom.

He could see Horatia biting back some pithy retort about him being a bad influence as she stepped out on to the landing. She was too grateful that he was going to give her what she wanted to voice any objections.

Which meant now was probably the best time to tell her just what working with him was going to entail.

He tucked her arm in the crook of his as they began to descend the staircase in the wake of the nursery party.

'There's just one thing—no, actually two, which I should mention before we go any further,' he said.

'Yes?'

'And one of them is crucial to the success of our operation,' he added, causing her to look at him sharply. 'This,' he said, waving his free arm at the backs of the escaping children, 'is out of character for me. People are bound to remark upon it. So I need to provide them with a convincing motive for taking an interest in children for the first time in my life.'

'Of course you do,' she said, with a sincerity that made him suspect she'd now consider coming up with one herself. She was clever enough to do so. Clever enough, probably, to come up with a better one than the one he'd already thought of. So he had to tell her what he'd decided before she had time to put her mind to the problem.

'And believe it or not,' he said, pausing on a half-landing to tidy his hair by his reflection in the window, 'it was the Duke who gave me the idea.' He tugged at his neckcloth. 'You may not like it, but I know that you will be sensible about it.' He adjusted the set of his cuffs. 'Because you are committed to finding Herbert's killer.'

'Go on,' she said, with a touch of wariness.

'I am going to attempt to seduce you.'

To his surprise, the wariness vanished, to be replaced by a look of sheer disbelief.

'Nobody in their right mind is going to believe you would do that, any more than that you'd suddenly become interested in children.'

'Oh, yes, they would,' he retorted. 'Haven't I said? The Duke already suspects me of being capable of toying with you for my amusement. He said so, at nuncheon, don't you remember?'

The frown returned. 'No, he…'

'Very well, if you must be pedantic about it, he warned me that I had better not attempt to compromise you. But if he sees me doing just that, then he'll assume I have taken it into my head to defy him and ruin his wedding party at the same time by creating a scandal. That is a motive that everyone will believe.'

'You really think they will believe you capable of such dishonourable behaviour?'

She looked utterly taken aback. As though the thought of him misbehaving had never crossed her mind. It made him want to kiss her. Right there on the staircase.

No, not kiss her. Hug her. The way he'd sometimes hugged her brother. Like a friend.

She had many of the same qualities he'd valued in Herbert, he suddenly saw. She was fiercely loyal, would stop at nothing to avenge the death of her brother, not even the prospect of agreeing to a fake seduction. Which reminded him.

'The other thing I need to say, before we go any further, is thank you.'

'For what?'

'For persisting. For not giving up until you'd made me take action. Herbert was the best of fellows. I owe it to him to find out who killed him and make them pay.'

Before she could demand to know why he hadn't done so before, he let go of her arm.

'Excuse me, but I have just noticed that the entire nursery party has reached the lower floor and are heading in the direction of the corridor that leads to the back of the house and the door to the outside world. Stop right there,' he shouted, running down the rest of the stairs two at a time. 'From here,' he informed the children in his sternest voice, planting his fists on his hips for good measure, 'you will all walk behind me and Miss Carmichael.' He held out his arm to her as she reached the ground floor. 'And anyone who steps out of line before we get there will be sent straight back to the house. One of the governesses will be only too happy to escort you,' he added, crooking one eyebrow at the two disgruntled women who had finally reached the top of the last flight of stairs, having paused to collect an assortment of rugs, parasols and other paraphernalia, as well as strapping severe bonnets to their heads. They both nodded. But then, as he'd already deduced, neither of them really wanted to venture outside in the first place. And the children, sensing the very real danger that their outing might be cancelled before it had even started, settled down. A bit.

'And if any of you misbehave while we are out there...' he pointed to the corridor to freedom '...I shall change my mind about concocting a treasure hunt for you next.'

'A treasure hunt?' One of his nieces, the one whose doll the boys had been tearing limb from limb, gazed up at him in awe.

'With real treasure?' The nephew who'd been the instigator of the dismembering, if he knew anything about it, was looking up at him with a touch of the cynicism that so often marred his mother's pretty face. The cynicism that was so conspicuously lacking from Miss Carmichael's expression. She might look fierce, or angry, or determined, but never, not once in all the years since he'd first met her, had he ever caught her looking petulant, or spiteful, or jaded.

'Plenty of treasure,' he assured the boy. Who, while still not looking totally convinced by anything an adult promised him, still appeared to be considering whether it was worth reining in the worst of his impulses, just in case.

'For worthy children only,' Nick added. 'We don't want anyone taking part who cannot be trusted with the Duke's breakables.'

'We can be good, Uncle Nick,' said the larger, yet strangely more docile of his nephews.

'Well, we shall discover whether that is true this afternoon, won't we,' he said, darting a wink at the governesses.

Having done what he could to ensure their compliance, he took Miss Carmichael's hand, tucked it back into the crook of his arm, and set off along the corridor.

'A treasure hunt?' She darted him a look that held almost as much suspicion as that of his nephew.

'Yes. You do know what a treasure hunt is, don't you?'

'Of course I do,' she retorted.

'Only, the way you repeated the phrase sounded to me as though you'd never heard of one before.'

'Nothing of the sort! You just took me by surprise, that is all. I never thought...'

'That arranging a treasure hunt could be a way of convincing everyone I am doing my utmost to seduce you?'

'No.' She blushed. 'That is, I was just amazed that you came up with the notion so quickly. Not that I don't think you are intelligent,' she added, going even pinker in the face.

'I know, I look far too elegant to be capable of having a single thought in my head, don't I?'

'I never said that.'

She'd thought it, though. A lot of people did. And

that assumption served him well. He smiled his most affable, not to say vacuous, smile at her as he led her through the door which led to the kitchens.

'Oh,' she said, glancing along the long stone-flagged passage that led past the kitchens, butler's pantry, housekeeper's sitting room and staff dining room. 'You, um, seem to know your way around this house very well.'

'I do. I spent the first few years of my life here. Until the true heir returned, that is. Nevertheless,' he added, before she could ask him exactly why he'd had to leave the minute his older brother had come back, 'telling everyone I am planning a treasure hunt will give us carte blanche to wander all over the house. No matter where anyone may catch us, we can tell them we are trying to ascertain whether it will be a suitable place to hide some treasure.'

'Brilliant.'

He eyed her warily. 'Exactly what do you mean by that?'

'Exactly what I said,' she said. 'You have come up with a brilliant plan that will enable us to work together. To hunt all over the house for the…' She pulled her lips together as though with an effort to bite back the words he'd warned her she must never utter aloud. 'I suspected you would do something of the sort when you first suggested I go to the nursery. I was sure there must be some good reason behind it and I am most impressed with what you have thought up in such a short span of time.'

He paused, since they'd reached the end of the corridor, and leaned forward to open the door that led into the kitchen courtyard. 'No caveat? No adding, *Impressed, considering*? Or *Brilliant for the likes of you*?'

'Goodness,' she replied. 'That sounds almost as if you are not used to receiving compliments.'

'Well, I'm not. Not from you, at least.'

'For which I apologise,' she said stiffly. 'Herbert always did insist you had a brilliant mind. I just never truly believed it, until now. I...' She flushed. 'I suppose I have been guilty of only looking upon the image you have deliberately created. The...' She waved her hand about his midsection, which made him pull in his stomach muscles, just as if she'd stroked him there. 'The perfectly cut coat, the quality of the satin from which your waistcoat is made. All that shiny gloss you apply to dazzle the beholder.'

'And do I dazzle you?' he leaned down to murmur into her ear as the children went streaming past, apparently forgetting their promise to follow behind in the excitement of seeing the light of day.

Her blush turned a deeper shade of pink. She lifted her chin. 'Absolutely not. Not now that I know it is a deliberate attempt to make people believe you are nothing more than a fribble. Not that it ever did,' she added hastily.

'A...*fribble*?' he muttered, after allowing the door to close after the exit of the last governess. 'I will have you know, Miss Carmichael, that I have never attempted to make anyone think of me as anything less than a dangerous rake.'

'Surely most rakes do not spend quite so much time preening themselves? You did not even get halfway down one flight of stairs just now before checking your appearance by the reflection you could see in the window.'

'It is of paramount importance to preen on a regular

basis. How can any rake worth his salt be assured of cutting a swathe through the female half of the population if he cannot be absolutely sure he has not dripped gravy down his cravat?'

'I...' She pressed her lips together once again, though this time it looked as though it was a giggle she was attempting to suppress, rather than a pithy retort. The triumph was a small one, but a triumph none the less. She needed to smile more often, did Miss Carmichael. All that frowning and scowling made her look far less appealing than she did right at this moment.

'But what am I thinking,' he said, 'to drag you outside on this expedition without even giving you time to run and fetch a bonnet to protect your complexion?'

'Don't worry about that,' she said, linking her arm through his so that they could set out, side by side, across the courtyard, the governesses having rounded up the children and formed them into a line behind them. 'I don't care all that much about my complexion.'

'Well, you should.' Her skin was pale as milk, tinged with rose-petal pink along her cheekbones. 'You have the kind of complexion most females spend a fortune on cosmetics to achieve.'

She gave an inelegant snort. And then peered up at him with a wry smile. 'Ah, I see. This is an example of the way you speak to ladies you are attempting to seduce, isn't it? Well, there is really no need to bother with all that flummery. I know what I look like, thank you very much.'

'You look...' He paused as she stiffened, as though hearing any sort of compliment would make her uncomfortable. And he did not want to make her uncomfortable. He wanted her to be able to keep talking to him in her open, frank manner. If he stopped her from feeling she could do that, he saw, he would be losing something rather precious.

'Very well, no flummery,' he conceded. 'We shall just discuss sensible things. Like the weather.'

'Now you are being absurd. We need to discuss what we are going to do about...*you know what*.'

'Yes. But not until we reach the stream and all those little ones are so busy playing there is no risk of any of them hearing anything unpleasant.'

'Absolutely,' she said, glancing over her shoulder at the procession of little people who were struggling not to overtake them. Even though they had little idea of where he meant to take them.

'Ah, just one moment,' he said, relinquishing her arm. 'I see you had the foresight to equip yourself with several parasols,' he said to one of the governesses bringing up the rear of the procession. 'Would you be so good...?' He smiled and held out his hand. As soon as the governess handed one over, he unfurled it, and held it over Miss Carmichael's head.

'There,' he said. 'Now I look the very picture of an adoring swain, shielding my fair damsel from the elements.'

'Oh, stuff,' she said gruffly. 'Though I suppose you must keep up the act. To convince everyone you are in earnest about pursuing me for nefarious reasons.'

'Exactly,' he said. Although, it hadn't been an act. He really did want to protect Miss Carmichael, since there was nobody left now to do so but him.

Chapter Nine

The time it took to walk through the Duke's formal gardens to the rising ground topped by woods, in which was the stream Lord Devizes was leading them to, felt interminable to Horatia because, since various other guests were wandering about, taking the air, he wouldn't discuss anything but trifling things, like the weather, or the flowers in the borders, or even, at one point, the waistcoat he planned to wear at the Duke's wedding.

She knew it was all in keeping with the persona he wanted everyone to believe was the real him, but now she'd caught a glimpse of another version of him, it was irksome having to pretend the fribble was all there was.

At last they left the main path, which wound its way through the woods and which was clearly used by horse riders on a regular basis, and plunged into what looked like a tangle of undergrowth but which turned out to be fairly easy to push through. It didn't take long to reach a small clearing through which a stream chuckled its way over a bed of sand and gravel. The grass on its banks had been nibbled short by rabbits all the way back to the trees, making a natural lawn upon which the governesses, and any children who didn't wish to paddle in the stream, could sit.

'What a lovely spot,' said Horatia, gazing round admiringly.

'I remember it being bigger. The banks steeper,' said Lord Devizes with a slight frown. 'I suppose it is because I haven't actually been here since I was about the size of those two,' he mused, pointing to a pair of little boys who were tugging off their boots and slithering down the banks, shrieking as their toes plunged into the cold water.

'But I thought…oh, yes, that's right, you mentioned having to leave when your brother returned. And now I come to think of it, Herbert told me there was some rift in your family, which meant you and your mother got sent to live on one of the lesser Theakstone estates while your half-brother grew up here.'

He stilled. 'Herbert talked about me a lot?'

'I wouldn't say a *lot*. Although…'

'Yes,' he said grimly. 'He told me a deal more about you than I suspect you would like, too.'

While she was pondering what that might mean, she noticed the governesses making a great play of laying out blankets under the trees while turning their backs to the boys, indicating that since Lord Devizes had brought them down here, it was up to him to supervise.

'Um, you did promise you wouldn't let any of them drown,' Horatia pointed out, as one of the bigger boys pushed one of the smaller ones so hard he sat down in the stream bed with a splash and a wail.

'Yes, I'd better give them something to do, since they seem not to have the brains to think of anything beyond fighting,' he said disparagingly, then began stripping off his coat. 'Here,' he said, spreading it on the grass. 'You may as well make use of it while I'm teaching the next generation of Norringtons how to dam a stream.'

Horatia gasped. 'But…rabbits!' Not only had they nibbled the grass short, they'd also left plenty of other evidence of their presence. 'Your coat will be ruined.'

He shrugged and sat down on the jacket himself. 'I have plenty of others. In fact,' he added airily, as he removed his shoes, 'I was never truly happy with the buttonholes on this one.'

In that moment, she knew that in spite of all the money he appeared to spend on them, he didn't really care tuppence for any of his clothes. He couldn't be rolling down his stockings with such…nonchalance, if he was truly a dandy. And those legs… She cocked her head to one side as he exposed them to her view. His feet might be slender and elegant, with long toes that matched the fingers of his hands, but his shins and calves were so hairy! For some reason, the very hairiness of them convinced her that the glimpses she'd seen of a different man proved there was more to him, much more than the elegant façade he created with all his fashionable clothes and cutting wit.

'I shall return in a few moments,' he said, getting to his feet. 'As soon as I have given them a direction for their energies.'

'Yes,' she said. Although, from the way his face started to alter, she suspected he was anticipating splashing about in the stream for his own sake, too. A suspicion which proved correct, when he proceeded to organise all the children who cared to get in the water, tasking them with fetching rocks and piling them up, so that they'd create a pool and a miniature waterfall.

She tucked her knees to one side as she sat down to watch him. Twirled the parasol he'd handed her, deciding that he was not pretending anything at the moment. He was simply enjoying himself. He laughed whenever the children splashed sandy deposits on to his waistcoat. Delved about for rocks with such enthusiasm that his shirtsleeves became so wet they started sticking to his upper arms—revealing a set of sharply delineated muscles.

By the time he'd returned, she couldn't imagine why she'd ever believed he was nothing but a fribble. He smiled at her in a friendly, almost boyish way when he sat down beside her on his jacket, leaned back on his elbows and stretched out his legs in the sun to dry.

'So,' he murmured, half-turning to her and gracing her with a more sensual sort of smile, which she could tell now was completely fake. 'Now that the children are all occupied and the governesses are far enough away that they cannot hear a word we say, let us discuss our strategy.'

She glanced round the clearing. Some of the girls had joined the boys in the stream now and the nursery maid was busy making a daisy chain for her little charge, who was lying on her back with her thumb in her mouth, apparently fascinated by the way the sun shone through the leaves of the tree above her head.

'I am going to tell everyone,' he murmured in what could only be described as a caressing tone of voice, 'that we will need to spend all day tomorrow going all over the house finding good places to hide treasure, along a route that is suitable for even the tiniest ones, as well as thinking up clues that they can solve without too much difficulty.'

'We should probably only have five or six stages,' she said.

'Yes, I've already decided on five of them. The music room, library, hallway, portrait gallery and that vile yellow salon,' he said, making her wonder, if he'd already made up his mind about them, why he was bothering to discuss it with her at all. 'They all contain, believe me, items that stick in the minds of children, so at least one of them will be bound to have noticed them.'

'And prizes?' She rather thought Miss Underwood would be able to get her cook to bake some small biscuits or something children would like. She was just about to say so, but he got in first.

'We shall send footmen into the village to buy sweets and toys, of course,' he said, tucking his hands behind his head and half-closing his eyes against the glare of the sun. And before she could voice any objection, added, 'It will mean even fewer servants about watching what we will be getting up to.'

Drat the man, he'd thought of everything. Or had he?

'Do you really think the Duke is going to permit us to commandeer his staff? For a children's game?'

'Oh, yes,' he replied with a cynical smile. 'Rumour has it that the Duke will do just about anything for that girl of his, even marrying a woman with no dowry, as long as she appears capable of accepting his by-blow.'

'I think it is a bit more than that,' Horatia said, sitting up a bit straighter. 'Have you not seen the way they look at each other?'

He waved his hand as though her argument was irrelevant. 'The point is, everyone believes that he dotes on the child to the extent he will look favourably upon anyone who acknowledges her. Why else do you suppose so many people have brought their children to what is, really, an adult house party?'

'Well, I...' She looked around the clearing and the band of children who were splashing about in the water with the Duke's illegitimate daughter.

'You cannot suppose that so many people have suddenly developed such fondness for their offspring that they cannot bear to part with them, even for a week? It's ambition, Miss Carmichael, and their children are merely pawns in the game they are playing with the Duke.'

'That's a really cynical thing to say.'

'Nevertheless, it is true. You, and Herbert, had the advantage of being orphaned before your parents could use you in this way. I was not so fortunate.'

He rolled on to his side, lifted his quizzing glass and examined her through it, his expression challenging.

'Nothing to say?'

Not about something as personal as his horrid childhood. Or hers. But there was something she rather ought to mention.

'Yes. I do wish you will be careful with that thing.'

'What thing?'

'Your quizzing glass. I was thinking about ways to amuse boy children earlier, before you came up to the schoolroom, and I remembered how much Herbert had enjoyed holding a magnifying glass to a sheet of paper to see if he could set it on fire. And I have a horrid suspicion those boys would enjoy doing the same. And if one of them should discover they could do so with your quizzing glass, or anyone else's, and chanced to set the house on fire, I would feel it was my fault.'

For a moment he just stared at her. Then he threw back his head and laughed.

'Miss Carmichael, you are a treasure,' he said, tucking his quizzing glass into a pocket of his waistcoat. 'No wonder Herbert was so fond of you.'

Her cheeks heated. 'I thought I made it plain that I do not want you to talk flummery to me.'

'It is not flummery. You are...' A frown flitted across his face. 'You are very easy to converse with. In that, you remind me of Herbert. I could say anything to him and admit to anything and never feel...oh, I don't suppose you would understand.'

'I think I could,' she said sadly. 'Because that was exactly how I felt about him. He was the most easygoing, understanding person I've ever met. No matter how badly I behaved at one of those stupid society things he kept dragging me to, he never...gave up on me. Oh, he gave up trying to make me fit in with his sort of people. But he never liked me any less because I couldn't be like everyone else.'

'That's it in a nutshell,' said Lord Devizes. 'He was the one person who accepted me exactly as I am. And remained loyal. And made me laugh at myself.' He reached out and took her hand. 'And we are not going to give up on him. Whatever it takes...'

'Whatever it takes,' she vowed, squeezing his hand in agreement.

But before either of them could say anything else to the purpose, one of the governesses got to her feet and clapped her hands.

'Time to return to the house, children.' She gave Horatia and Lord Devizes a steady look. 'Routine is important. Their tea will be served in the schoolroom very shortly.'

'Ah, yes,' said Lord Devizes, reaching for his stockings and shoes. And then, in a lower voice meant only for her ears, 'And your virtue has been saved, to boot.'

'What? What do you mean?'

'I think that woman suspected I was about to kiss you. Kiss your hand, that is,' he said.

Which was what he'd intended the woman to think.

Horatia got to her feet with a feeling that a shadow had passed across the sun, rendering the little glade gloomy and dank. Because even though he'd been saying such lovely things, he'd still had an eye out for the impression he was making upon everyone else.

Whereas she had forgotten everything but the pressure of his hand and the determined look in his eyes.

Chapter Ten

Getting back to the house took far longer than the walk to the stream, because the children, this time, were dawdling. Yet Horatia felt as if the afternoon had flown by. She certainly found it hard to believe that the clock hanging on the wall in the servants' corridor could be telling the correct time.

My word, if she didn't hurry up, she was going to be late for dinner. She flew along the corridor and up the stairs, and flung open the door to the rooms she was sharing with Lady Elizabeth, reaching for the fastenings at the back of her gown. Connie, Lady Elizabeth's maid, came bustling over.

'You let me help you with that,' she said firmly, taking her by the shoulders with her big, work-worn hands, and turning her round. 'I've laid out your second-best dinner dress on your bed,' she said as she efficiently undid the hooks, 'and there's hot water in the ewer, or at least it was. It should probably still be fairly warm.'

Horatia really did need to get a move on. If Connie was actually helping her to change, then she must already have finished with Lady Elizabeth. Sure enough, just as she was stepping out of her grass-stained, rabbit-soiled gown, Lady Elizabeth emerged from her bedroom in a stunningly expensive-looking creation in blue.

'My goodness, you must have been having an exciting time of it in the schoolroom,' said Lady Elizabeth. 'Though,' she added when Horatia started stuttering a series of explanations without actually managing to form a single comprehensible word, 'Lord Devizes would have the same effect upon any single woman, I dare say.' She pretended to fan herself. 'You simply must tell me everything.'

Everything? Out of the question. But Lady Elizabeth was following her into her room and, as Horatia poured water into her basin to take the wash she felt so sorely in need of, her friend sat on the bed, an expectant expression on her face.

'So, did he flirt with you? Or was it simply being with him all this time that has resulted in that flushed face and shining eyes?'

Were her eyes really shining? She peered into the mirror on the dressing table next to the washstand. And noted mainly that her hair was escaping its pins, which made her look a bit of a mess.

'Jan...' She pulled herself up short. She must not refer to Lord Devizes by his code name. In fact, she'd better stop thinking of him by it, too, or heaven knew who she would blurt it out in front of. 'That is, Lord Devizes led the entire nursery party out to the woods. And if my face is flushed, it is because we lost track of the time while building a dam in a stream and I ran all the way up the stairs so I wouldn't be late, or make you late, for dinner,' she said, removing her glasses, tossing them on to the dresser top, then splashing her face with water that was nowhere near cool enough to have any effect on her heated cheeks.

'Well, that accounts for the flushed face, yes. But what about the sparkle in your eyes?'

Horatia buried her face in a towel for a moment or two while thinking what sort of an explanation she could give. It was probably down to the fact that Lord Devizes was going to help her find Herbert's killer after all. Or, to be more accurate, he was going to let her help him. Not that she could tell Lady Elizabeth that.

'I can see there is something,' Lady Elizabeth persisted. And Horatia reminded herself that Lord Devizes wanted everyone to think he was intent on seducing her, so that nobody would suspect he could have any other motive for wanting to spend so much time with her.

Although, it would be very hard to tell Lady Elizabeth an outright lie.

To stall for time while she considered what she could say that would satisfy both Lord Devizes and Lady Elizabeth, as well as her conscience, she picked up her comb.

'How…how has your mother been this afternoon?'

Lady Elizabeth let out a crow of laughter. 'I do believe you are trying to change the subject. Oh, how glad I am that I persuaded you to come here with me,' she continued as Horatia turned to reach for her fresh gown. 'I feared I was going to find it excruciatingly uncomfortable, what with Mama being so disappointed with me over failing to catch Theakstone in the matrimonial net. But I never dreamed you would entertain me so much, let alone make me laugh out loud. We haven't,' she said, sobering considerably, 'had much to even *smile* about of late.'

'No,' said Horatia thoughtfully, stepping into her second-best evening gown. Sometimes it was hard to remember that the Dowager Lady Tewkesbury's bad temper could well stem from the trials she was having to endure, rather than from innate nastiness. Both she and Lady Elizabeth dressed so well, and moved with such assurance in society, that it was easy to overlook the fact that they'd been living in very reduced circumstances since the death of Lord Tewkesbury. She really ought to be more understanding when Lady Elizabeth's mother was snappish with her, more forgiving when she was irritable for no apparent reason.

'But to answer *your* question,' said Lady Elizabeth pointedly, 'Mama has been lying down in her room all afternoon, on the advice of Theakstone's own physician, apparently. According to that aunt of Miss Underwood's, she was starting to look pulled and he said she should go and rest to prevent her from developing one of her megrims. She'd already gone when I returned to that ghastly yellow room, so I have had rather a pleasant time chatting with, of all people, Miss Underwood. She seems to have forgotten we were rivals for Theakstone's favours and is treating me like a bosom bow.'

'Well, I expect she feels in need of a friendly face,' said Horatia, through a mouth full of hairpins, as she twisted the bulk of her hair into a neat bun at the nape of her neck.

'What do you mean?'

'Well, according to Lord Devizes,' she said, stabbing pins ruthlessly into her hair to keep it in place, 'who heard it from his sisters—' stab '—or their governesses—' stab, stab '—I'm not completely sure, it sounds as if a lot of people are trying to, um, get close to the Duke by currying favour with, well...' To be truthful, he'd said that the favour-currying was going on via the children in the nursery. But if people would go to those lengths, then there were probably other ways they would try to use those nearest the Duke. Especially his bride-to-be.

'Yes, she told me much the same,' said Lady Elizabeth, promptly confirming Horatia's conjecture. 'Who would want to marry a duke, eh?'

'There,' said Horatia, turning her head from side to side to make sure all was as neat as she could make it. 'I'm ready.'

'Amazing.' said Lady Elizabeth. 'It always takes me a good half an hour and the assistance of Connie to achieve anything.'

'Well,' said Horatia, glancing between their two outfits, 'you are attempting to create a wholly different impression from me, are you not? You look absolutely stunning, whereas all I am attempting is to look clean and neat.'

'Pfft,' said Lady Elizabeth with a dismissive wave of her hand. 'If you spent as long as I do primping and preening, you would be far prettier than I.'

'What?' Horatia shot her a suspicious glance. 'Don't be absurd.'

'It's true,' said Lady Elizabeth, sliding off the bed

and coming to stand beside her in front of the dressing table mirror. 'You have such thick, lustrous hair, in comparison with mine which is all…wispy, bland and dull.'

'It's blonde,' Horatia protested.

'But I have to wield the curling tongs twice a day to get curls like these,' she said enviously, tweaking at a couple of wisps that had escaped the pins already and were curling about Horatia's ears. 'And if you didn't hide your eyes behind glasses, single men with poetical aspirations would write odes to them.'

'Nonsense!'

'No such thing. They have a…well, I don't know how to describe it, not being of a poetical turn of mind, but the colour is unusual, neither brown nor grey, and they are a lovely shape, and you have eyelashes that would be the envy of most women, if you only fluttered them about a bit more.'

On the contrary, if she were ever foolish enough to attempt to flutter her eyelashes, people would just think she had got something in her eye.

Besides, she'd already decided she was not going to go about looking as though she was desperate to gain some man's attention. She'd had enough of that during her Season. Because what invariably happened when she had drawn some man to her side, by *making the most of herself*, as Aunt Matilda had put it, was that they recoiled from the person they pretty soon discovered she really was. It was less painful, she'd discovered, to deliberately repel them with outer trappings such as drab clothes and severe hairstyles and the ugliest glasses she could find in the first place.

'I am not cut out to be fluttery,' she said stoically,

picking up her spectacles and hooking them over her ears. Which also anchored those few stray curls out of sight.

'But then what did put the sparkle in your eyes?'

Horatia sighed. Lady Elizabeth was not going to give up. But by now, Horatia had formed an answer that would satisfy everyone concerned.

'Believe it or not, I think it must have been spending so much time talking about my brother. It was a real comfort, sharing memories with someone who also knew him very well.' And who was, now she'd given him a nudge, as determined to avenge his death as she was.

'Hmmm.' Lady Elizabeth pursed her lips. 'If that is all you are willing to tell me...'

'It is. For now,' she added, because her friend was bright enough to perceive that Horatia was holding something back.

'Then I shall let the matter drop. For now. Since if we do not leave this room straight away, we really will be late down for dinner.'

There were about thirty people already standing in the Rubens room, where everyone gathered before dinner, by the time she and Lady Elizabeth arrived. If it had been left to her, Horatia would have sidled in and found a chair in a corner out of the way. But Lady Elizabeth had other ideas. Her father might have squandered the family fortune, but he had been a marquess and she was not about to let anyone forget it. Head up, Horatia's arm firmly under her own, Lady Elizabeth swept into the very centre of the room and gazed about her as though defying anyone to question her right to be exactly where she was.

It wasn't long before Miss Underwood herself came over, a welcoming smile on her face.

'Good evening. How are you both? I am glad to see your mother seems to be somewhat better after Dr Cochrane took her in hand earlier on. And, um…' she turned to Horatia '…I am so grateful to you for taking the children outside in spite of…that is, Livvy said her Uncle Nick found a lovely spot for them to play in safely and that the promise of a treasure hunt, in due course, has given them something to look forward to.'

'Uncle Nick?' Horatia wondered how Lord Devizes would feel about Livvy calling him that.

At this point, the Duke appeared at her side. Although, from what she'd observed so far, he never let Miss Underwood get very far away.

'Uncle Nick,' Lady Elizabeth echoed, her eyebrows shooting up.

The Duke's drew down.

'Well, apparently, so many of the other children in the nursery called him that,' said Miss Underwood, 'that she asked if he was her uncle, too, and, of course, he *is*, so…' At this point, the look on the Duke's face caused even Miss Underwood to quail. Even though he was glaring over her shoulder at somebody who was approaching. Someone who Horatia could tell, without even looking, must be Lord Devizes. For the Duke never glared at anyone else in quite the same way.

'I am sure His Grace suspects me of having some nefarious reason for encouraging his child to look upon me as her favourite uncle,' came the voice of Lord Devizes, at her elbow.

'Nothing of the sort,' put in Miss Underwood hastily. 'It was very good of you to give up your afternoon to entertain the children so marvellously. And to be willing to organise a treasure hunt as well. You must let me know,' she continued, in a rather desperate manner as the two brothers stood there eyeing each other like combatants in a prize ring, 'if there is anything you need.'

'Prizes,' said Horatia, wishing Lord Devizes wouldn't be quite so antagonistic. 'We thought that we could have small prizes for solving each clue, probably about five or six of them, and then a grand prize at the end. We had hoped that we could borrow a couple of footmen and send them to the nearest village in the morning to raid the sweet shops. Oh, that is, if you have one? A sweet shop, that is, not a footman. I know you have dozens of those.' She felt her cheeks heat as she blurted out the last, stupid statement which must have made her sound like a real...*idiot*.

'We do,' said Miss Underwood kindly. 'What a good idea.'

The Duke took a breath as though about to make an objection. But at a look from Miss Underwood, he kept whatever he'd been about to say to himself.

'And then, of course,' Lord Devizes slipped in smoothly, 'on the day of the treasure hunt, we will need a footman at each stage to give out those prizes and present the teams with the next clue.'

The Duke looked as if the last thing he wished was to allow his half-brother to monopolise five or six of his footmen.

So it was into an atmosphere of tense silence that one of Lord Devizes's sisters came over, her husband, Lord Twickenham, on her arm.

'Well, well,' she said with an acid smile. 'Quite the family gathering.'

'Yes,' said Miss Underwood. 'Lord Devizes is organising a treasure hunt for his nephews and nieces. And the other visiting children, of course.'

'And His Grace's little…'

There was a pause, during which Horatia held her breath as Lady Twickenham appeared to consider how to refer to the Duke's illegitimate child.

'Daughter,' she finally said, to Horatia's relief. 'Though I must say I find it rather odd behaviour for you, Nick,' she said, swatting Lord Devizes on his arm with her fan, 'to get involved in this sort of caper. Not your style, I wouldn't have thought.'

'I have my reasons,' he said with an enigmatic smile.

The Duke, Miss Underwood and Lady Elizabeth all looked from Lord Devizes to Horatia and back again in the manner of persons putting two and two together.

'Do tell,' said Lady Twickenham coquettishly, missing the knowing looks flitting between the others, since she was looking only at her brother.

'The reasons are mine,' he reminded her. 'And if I told you, they would become common property.'

'Oh, but you are accusing me of being a gossip, you naughty boy,' she cried, rapping him again. Horatia was beginning to wonder how any man could put up with a woman who behaved as though she was a cross between a little girl and a pugilist. But most men, from what she'd observed in her short foray into society, appeared to find such behaviour fascinating.

Her fingers curled round her own fan. What would happen if she started swatting men with it and calling them naughty boys? She'd probably either get prosecuted for common assault, or carted off to one of those asylums for the feeble-minded. Which was what such behaviour warranted.

'But, anyway,' Lady Twickenham said, 'it will prove a most onerous task to lay a trail about the house, since you can hardly remember much about the place, I shouldn't have thought. Why, you were a very small boy when the rightful heir—' she shot a malicious look at the Duke from under her artificially blackened eyelashes '—returned and had us all evicted.'

It felt as if a frosty wind had just swirled round the little group.

'He did nothing of the sort,' said Miss Underwood indignantly, stepping closer to the Duke's side and taking his arm. 'He was just a boy. He—'

'I have no need for you to fight my battles for me, my love,' said the Duke, patting her hand. 'Lord Devizes,' he said, turning to his half-brother, 'whatever your motives, I am grateful to you for lending what aid you can to this week's activities. And, Lady Twickenham,' he said in a rather cooler tone, 'it is pointless to bear a grudge against me for what our father did. We all, as children, suffered from his eccentric behaviour. And it is high time we put it behind us. Now that we are adults.'

With a curt nod, he turned and walked away, towing Miss Underwood along with him.

'Well!' Lady Twickenham stared at his back, an indignant expression on her face. She would have said more had not the butler chosen that moment to fling open the double doors at the end of the room and announce that dinner was served.

'Blast it,' whispered Lady Elizabeth into Horatia's ear. 'That was just getting interesting.'

Chapter Eleven

Nick relaxed his jaw so that nobody would see how close he was to gritting his teeth. The patronising b— well, no, his half-brother wasn't illegitimate, that was the trouble. But if he could prove the man was a traitor, and unfit to be a duke, well, that was another matter.

Which would require the help of Herbert's sister, who was inching away from him. That wouldn't do.

'Since we are already standing together,' he said, linking his arm through hers while she was still within reach, 'we may as well stroll in together, and sit next to one another.'

Any other woman would have either taken offence at his casual attitude, or simpered and giggled and tried to make out he'd paid them a huge compliment. Horatia, of course, did neither. She just gave him a direct, rather considering look, before nodding and uttering a gruff, *'Very well.'* He had a feeling she would have behaved exactly the same even if she didn't know he was trying to make everyone believe he was pursuing her.

The current Duke and his intended bride led the way

into the dining room and took their seats at the head of the table together, apparently so absorbed in each other that they failed to notice how their guests were behaving. Nick, however, had no intention of taking place in the melee that had broken out in their wake, as the more socially ambitious fought for the prime places, elbowing the weaker, less thrusting guests aside. His own sister, Lady Twickenham, even stuck out her little foot just as Mrs Turnbull, one of Miss Underwood's married cousins, was about to take the seat she'd clearly set her sights on.

'I wasn't sure I believed what you said earlier about people being so ambitious they would even use their children,' she said, 'but this…' Her eyes rounded in appalled fascination as Mrs Turnbull stumbled into the arms of her bucolic husband.

'It will only get worse as the week progresses,' he murmured into Horatia's ear.

'Why do they not put out place names at the table, or organise things more efficiently?' said Horatia, gazing about her with disapproval as they approached the table in a more leisurely fashion. 'Surely it would stop all this…' She waved her free hand at the spectacle of lords and ladies fighting to establish their precedence and succeeding only in losing their dignity.

'The wealthier, more ambitious ones would only bribe the servants to change them round if they didn't like the places they'd been assigned,' he said. 'But don't let all this distract you from our aim tonight.'

'Which is?' She perked up immediately, like a terrier catching sight of a rat.

'To find out as much as we can about the Duke's

household. To find out who is up to their neck in treason,' he reminded her grimly. 'Now look,' he continued, as she nodded and stiffened her spine. 'Now that
the more sought-after places at each end of the table
have gone, nobody will raise an eyebrow at our taking our own seats next to a man such as Perceval, the
Duke's secretary. If any man knows what is going on
under this roof, then it is him. So I am going to sit you
next to him, so that you can pump him for information.'

Her face fell. 'I…I don't know how to do that. I…
Herbert must have told you I am useless in social situations, never mind actually attempting to wheedle secrets out of anyone, I…'

'Calm down,' he said, patting her hand where her
fingers were clutching at his sleeve. 'The first thing
you need to know about men is that they love to talk
about themselves.'

She nodded, her face clearing somewhat, as if this
was something she already knew.

'Flatter him on getting this important job with such
a high-ranking man. Say how wonderful he must be
to be so much in the Duke's trust, that sort of thing. It
will be easy.'

'No, it won't,' she said, looking anxious again. 'He
will smell a rat. Everyone knows I don't flatter men. I
mostly tell them they are idiots.'

'Well, then, he will be even more flattered if you tell
him that you find him to be the exception to the race of
men you so despise.'

'It will be a lie! I cannot lie to save my life!'

'I think you could do just about anything you set
your mind to, for Herbert.'

She frowned. 'Do you really believe that or are you just saying it to give me some confidence?'

He frowned back at her, although he felt like chuckling. 'It makes no difference,' he said sternly. 'You must do it. But, if it helps, let me remind you that you won't be telling a complete lie. You *are* interested in Perceval, to the extent of wanting to find out what he knows about what may be going on in this household.'

She nodded. 'Good point. I can remind myself of that. After all, it is but a short step from being interested in what he *does* from what he *is*, but…'

Before she could think of any more reasons why she couldn't do what he'd asked, he thrust her at the chair by Perceval's side. 'Good evening, Perceval,' he said affably.

'Devizes,' said the man, giving him a stiff nod. 'Miss Carmichael.'

She shifted from one foot to the other. Bit her lower lip. Looked at her shoes.

'Gauche,' he mouthed at Perceval over the top of her downbent head. Then he helped her into her seat and, before taking his own, leaned over and murmured, 'You will help to put her at her ease, won't you, old chap?'

The secretary sighed, nodded, then took his own seat with an air of resignation. Though Nick turned to his dining companion on his other side, another of Miss Underwood's many cousins, he did not give her anything like his full attention. He was far more interested in listening to what Perceval might reveal to Horatia.

Before long it was all he could do to keep a straight face. Just as he'd predicted, Perceval thoroughly enjoyed talking about himself and how necessary he was to the Duke. And the more he puffed himself up, the more irritated Horatia became, valiantly though she tried to conceal it.

When it was time for him to turn and make conversation with her, he slid his arm along the back of her chair and leaned in close, in order to be able to find out what she'd managed to learn from Perceval.

'Is that absolutely necessary?' she asked, stiffening in her seat.

'Absolutely,' he assured her. 'The level of noise round this table has reached such a pitch it is impossible to converse with you without raising my voice. Or leaning in close,' he murmured, right into her ear.

She sat bolt upright and held out her glass to a nearby footman for a refill. Which obliged him to remove his arm from the back of her chair. A slick manoeuvre if ever he saw one.

But then he saw a thought flit across her face. Swiftly followed by an expression of remorse.

'I do beg your pardon,' she said. 'We are supposed to be making everyone think we are, um…and I really don't know how to flirt,' she finished, going pink with chagrin.

What other woman would admit to such a lack of wiles? And yet, in Horatia, he couldn't consider this a flaw. It was, on the contrary, rather endearing. She was so utterly free from artifice, not only to him, but to everyone. And he didn't want her to try to become as shallow and insincere as everyone else.

'Then don't,' he said. 'Receive all my advances exactly the way you did just now. With disapproval and cool disdain. Give no sign that you are succumbing to my legendary charm,' he said with heavy sarcasm. 'That will not put me off. It will, instead, cause me to redouble my attentions. Because everyone knows I cannot resist a challenge. That will ensure we throw dust in everyone's eyes, while continuing to pursue the real quarry.'

'And you think that will work? No, never mind, you are the expert in these matters. I must,' she said, as though facing swallowing a dose of unpleasant medicine, 'trust your judgement.'

'Thank you,' he said, since he could see that had been a considerable concession on her part. 'But now we've done discussing my legendary prowess as a lover,' he growled in his most seductive voice, which had the effect of making her grip her napkin and twist it slightly, as though she was hanging on to her temper for all she was worth, 'you should really return your attention to the secretary. See if you can find out anything useful.'

She pulled her lips together as though biting back a pithy retort. Gave a little sniff and turned her head from him with all the dignity of an affronted duchess. He smiled, a genuine smile, at the back of her head. Oh, how she hated having to follow his lead. Only her zeal to find the person responsible for her brother's death could have made her do so. And her genuine belief that he, as the more experienced in these matters, knew what he was about.

If only that were true. He had only stumbled on to the trail *she'd* discovered through her own intelligence. Perhaps it was time he swallowed his pride and admitted the truth. Asked her exactly what she knew about the man Herbert had been following the night he'd died. Except…

Except, right at this moment, someone was watching him. With hostile intent. He could feel it. Lazily withdrawing his gaze from the tendrils of hair curling about the nape of Horatia's neck, he caught his brother, the Duke, giving him the same sort of look that Nick so frequently turned upon him. As though he was some kind of pond creature.

Because he suspected him of flirting with Horatia? That was what any onlooker would assume, who hadn't been able to hear their words, but only follow their actions. But what if it was for some darker reason? What if, through his contacts in high places, the Duke had got wind of the fact that he was actively engaged in hunting down traitors? Well, whichever it was, the result was the same. Nick was thoroughly annoying him. Which made him smile.

Which made the Duke look angrier than ever.

Horatia would have thought, with so many other people sitting down to dine, that she would have been able to simply enjoy the sumptuous meal, the way she'd done the night before.

Trust Lord Devizes to ruin it for her.

Though, no, he wasn't ruining things. He was helping her to find out, or, to be more accurate, she was helping him find out who had killed Herbert. Which meant he had to push her to do things she would not normally do. Such as talking to what must be one of the most pompous, boring men she'd ever had the misfortune to meet. Not that she ought to hold that against him. She hadn't been listening to him for long before deciding that, above all else, he was both conscientious and hard-working. Or at least, that was the image he wanted everyone to see.

Oh, dear. Was working with Lord Devizes going to make her suspicious of everyone? For ever? Couldn't people just be what they appeared to be? Did they have to be hiding secrets?

It felt like an age before Miss Underwood rose from her chair to signify that all the ladies should withdraw. Horatia tossed her mangled napkin on to the table with relief, allowed Lord Devizes to help her out of her seat without looking directly at him and made for the exit as swiftly as she could. Even so, Lady Elizabeth soon joined her.

'You simply have to tell,' she said in a low voice.

'Tell you what?'

'What on earth Lord Devizes said to you to put you to the blush? Though everyone must have seen him put his arm along the back of your chair. Has he been flirting with you like that all day?'

'Flirting? He wasn't flirting,' she said bitterly. He was informing her that it didn't matter that she didn't know how to flirt since he was experienced enough to convince everyone to believe whatever he wanted about them. And, lo and behold, here was Lady Elizabeth confirming what he'd said.

'Oh, come. What else can you call it?'

'Well, I…' While Horatia was still fumbling for a reply, Miss Underwood herself approached.

'I do hope you are not too…that is, I noticed that you did not look very happy, whenever I…and Perceval can be very trying…'

'No, no, I do believe he was doing his best to, um, entertain me.'

'He isn't used to trying to amuse young ladies,' said Miss Underwood with a sigh. 'I recall, my very first night here, I had to sit next to him. Although he was a fount of information about all the other people staying there that night.'

A fount of information. Lord Devizes had been correct. If anything underhand was going on at Theakstone Court, he would know. With a sinking heart, she realised she was going to have to cultivate his acquaintance.

'Oh, we are nearly here,' said Miss Underwood as they approached a set of double doors, attended on either side by yet another brace of liveried footmen. The Duke must employ hundreds of them. 'And I shall have to…but I did just want to thank you for all you are doing to help. There is so much to think of and this is my first real…'

'Well, the meals are certainly first rate,' said Horatia. 'And not just to taste, but to look at, too. That dinner just now looked as if it had been created by an artist, not merely a cook.'

'That is down to Oliver's staff,' said Miss Underwood morosely. 'Nothing to do with me at all. And now, oh, dear,' she said, hesitating on the threshold of the withdrawing room, which was already filling up with ladies who all considered themselves to be leaders in society, to judge from the lifted chins and frigid expressions.

'Never you mind them,' said Lady Elizabeth, taking her by her arm. 'They are all jealous of you, that is what it is. Now, if I were you,' she said, leaning in and murmuring into her ear.

As the pair of them were so intent on working out a strategy to ensure Miss Underwood's success, Horatia was able to hang back, unnoticed. And while others jostled for possession of sofas in what they clearly considered the prime locations, she looked about for a chair in a corner somewhere.

Although, that wasn't what Lord Devizes would want, was it? He'd want her to strike up a conversation with someone, to see what she could learn. She gazed round at the occupants of the room, wondering which of the ladies present might be worth interrogating. Who would know enough about everyone attending to be able to guess that they had been involved in passing information to France? She started chewing her thumbnail as she considered, and discarded, one after another. Miss Underwood's cousins lived in the country and didn't have the connections. It would be one of the higher-ranking ladies she should target. Only…would any of them deign to speak to her? They all had their little coteries, to none of which she had ever wished to belong. She'd always been happier sitting at home, working on the puzzles Herbert brought. Knowing she was doing something worthwhile. Something that not many people had the patience, or the ability, to do.

But now, oh, now, she felt like a fish out of water.

And then Miss Underwood's aunt, Lady Norborough, came over.

'I know you are in mourning, but some of us will be playing at cards later on and I wondered if you would consider it appropriate to join in?'

Put like that, Horatia felt she had no choice but to refuse. 'I am sorry, but as you say…' She indicated her black gown.

'Oh. Well…' Lady Norborough made as if to move away.

'But…' Horatia put out a hand to stay her. This lady, Miss Underwood's aunt, was so involved in organising the wedding, she must at least have a working knowledge of the guest list and probably knew many of the people by reputation, if not well enough to suspect them of treason. 'I would… I mean, thank you for trying to…' She took a breath. This was an opportunity she must not waste. 'That is, I should very much like some introductions to…erm…well, anyone really. If it would not be too much trouble?'

Lady Norborough's face broke into a smile. 'Of course not, my dear.' She held out her arm. 'Come along. No time like the present.'

Horatia took it. And prepared to take note of every single word every person to whom she was introduced might say. And to watch for other tell-tale signs that they were not what they were pretending to be. She could do it. For this was not an attempt to make friends, or fit in.

This was setting her mind to solving a puzzle. A different sort of puzzle from the ones she was used to, but a puzzle none the less.

Chapter Twelve

By the time Nick got to the withdrawing room, his younger sister, Lady Anmering, was at the piano, playing one of the dreary dirges she favoured. Trust her to put a damper on the evening.

He spotted Horatia almost immediately. She really stood out amid the other females present. And it wasn't only because she was dressed head to toe in black, either. There was an intensity about her that the other, more fluttery creatures lacked. Although, he probably noticed it more because he knew she was on the hunt for a killer. But, no, on second thoughts, she was definitely not preening and posing, trying to attract the attention of males, or to outshine the other ladies. She never had done. Not even during those few weeks when her duenna had attempted to launch her into society. At the time, seeing how fresh and open she was in her manner, he'd decided that the best thing he could do for Herbert's sister was to stay well away from her. Someone so bright and clever was not for the likes of him. Besides which, she'd have seen through him in next to no time and withdrawn, disappointed to find there was nothing but an echoing empty shell beneath the surface charm.

But now, for perhaps the first time in a room full of society's most shallow, frivolous specimens, she didn't look as though she'd rather be somewhere more interesting. He smiled to himself. She'd really got the bit between her teeth, by the looks of it.

He strolled over to where she was standing, with none other than the aunt of the bride, Lady Norborough, apparently being introduced to one of her daughters. Not the one his sister had outmanoeuvred at dinner, however. It was the other one. The taller, freckled one.

'Good evening, ladies,' he said, making his bow.

Horatia whirled round with an air of suppressed excitement. She'd clearly discovered something she was dying to tell him. It could be their undoing, that open expression of hers. Unless the other ladies mistook it for signs of infatuation. Thank heavens he'd set that little line of subterfuge in motion already.

'Miss Carmichael,' he said, giving her one of his most seductive smiles. Which acted on the other ladies present the way it did on ladies from London to York. They both simultaneously lit up and melted.

Horatia merely said, in a rather impatient tone of voice, 'Yes?'

It made his smile turn from a practised one to something far more genuine.

'If it would not spoil your enjoyment of this evening, I really do think we should discuss the treasure hunt we have agreed to organise for the children.'

'No, of course it wouldn't. Spoil my enjoyment, I mean. Of course we need to get on with, er, the clues and such,' she said, half to him and half to Lady Norborough and her daughter.

'If you will excuse us?'

'Of course,' said Lady Norborough, eyeing the way Horatia had just linked her arm with his, as though they were old friends. 'I have to oversee the setting up of card tables, anyway.'

Horatia gave her one of her brisk nods. 'Thank you for introducing me to so many of the ladies. It was good of you to take me under your wing.'

'Not at all, Miss Carmichael,' said Lady Norborough. 'It was my pleasure...'

But Horatia had turned her back and was tugging him away from them before she'd even finished.

'So keen to get me to yourself,' he teased her.

'Yes. Because we need to get on. It is only a few days to the wedding and every day more guests will be arriving. And I want to know how you plan to flush out the...the one we are looking for,' she said, leading him to a table set between two tall windows. Which was as far from all the other sofas and chairs dotted about the room as possible.

She'd clearly been thinking ahead.

As had he. From an inside pocket of his jacket he produced a sheaf of papers, which he tossed on to the table top.

'Do you happen to have a pencil about you?' he said as he helped Horatia into one of the two chairs set on either side of the table.

'Yes, of course,' she said, delving into her reticule.

'It never ceases to amaze me,' he said, picking up the chair that had been placed on the opposite side of the table and setting it right next to hers, 'how much ladies manage to pack into such tiny, frivolous-looking items.'

'Well, I was surprised at how you managed to have all this paper tucked in your pocket without it spoiling the fit of your coat.'

'My tailor is an expert, now, at fitting concealed pockets into all my clothes. It is often necessary to carry all sorts of things I do not wish anyone else to suspect I have about my person.'

She eyed his coat intently. 'He must be an expert. I would never have guessed that it was not moulded to your...erm—' She broke off and flushed.

'My manly frame?'

'That's enough of that,' she said in the tone he was coming to think of as very nannyish. 'We should get down to business. What is this?' she asked, pulling one of the papers out from the others. 'A map of the house?'

'Yes,' he said, simultaneously glad she was being so businesslike, while mourning his decision to tell her she didn't need to try to flirt with him. He had a feeling that after only a little tuition, she'd become very skilled at it. As skilled as she would become at anything she set her mind to learn.

Though, no, he ought not let his mind stray on to all the things Miss Carmichael could become an expert at with a little tuition. She was Herbert's sister. An innocent.

He cleared his throat. 'I mentioned earlier that I've already started thinking about the route the treasure hunt should follow. I've chosen rooms that give easy access to places we need to search. From the portrait gallery, for example,' he said, pointing to the long gallery that ran along one whole side of the house on the second floor, 'there is a door that leads to the corridor where most of the female guests have been put.'

'Yes, I see,' she said, scanning the simple plan he'd sketched of Theakstone Court, which was roughly a U shape.

'I have already come up with a few clues, in verse, for the first few locations I think would meet our requirements.'

'Already?'

He tried not to preen at her expression of blatant admiration. 'Yes. Only pretty poor sort of doggerel, but the children aren't going to be harsh critics, are they? They will just want to have something that will lead them straight to the clue, which *sounds* as if it is harder to work out than it is. For example, *Underneath the golden dancers, Is a single patch of blue, Here you'll find your second clue.*'

'That is…the blue sofa in the yellow salon!'

'Yes.' He cleared his throat again, determined not to let two such looks, in such rapid succession, go to his head. 'Overnight I'll write the others. And then in the morning it will simply be a case of going round looking as though we are racking our brains to get everything finished in time, while in reality, going through the guests' rooms.'

'Wait a minute,' she said with a frown. 'How are we going to get into everyone's rooms without being noticed?'

'Well, to start with, my esteemed brother is apparently such a creature of habit that you could set your watch by him. He always spends at least an hour on estate matters, his correspondence and so forth, in his study, which is on the ground floor of the south wing.' He tapped at the location on his sketch map. 'Which will give us a clear run at his room.' He pointed to the central block, the base of the U. 'And later, most of the men, whose rooms are all in the south wing…' he pointed to one of the uprights of the U '…will be out taking part in a fishing competition Lord Norborough is running.'

'But, surely, they won't *all* be taking part? They can't all like fishing, can they?'

'Oh, Horatia, Horatia,' he said, shaking his head in mock pity. 'You have not been to many house parties, have you? The event is not about fishing. It is about the wagering. Those not taking part will want to go to make sure nobody cheats.'

Her frown deepened. 'How can you cheat at fishing? Surely you either catch the most fish, or you don't?'

'Wherever there is a wager, there will be ways to cheat. The point is, I can guarantee a clear run at both the Duke's bedroom and the single men's corridor during the morning. And I'm pretty sure we will have a similar opportunity to go through the ladies' rooms after lunch. Lady Norborough has arranged a game of pell-mell on the south lawn,' he said, tapping an area a few inches distant from the main house, 'to which, once again, they will all go, for fear of missing something. And before you say they will not all take part in the match, no, they won't, but they will want to partake of the refreshments being offered.'

'It sounds risky to me,' she said gruffly. 'And you are making an awful lot of assumptions.'

'I shall ignore that remark,' he said. 'And urge you

to study this plan, so that you can become familiar with the layout of the place. This,' he said, tapping the base of the U with his pencil, 'represents the main part of the Court, where we are now. This wing,' he said, tapping one upright of the U, 'is primarily for male staff and guests. The guests have the first floor, directly above the billiard room, gun room, the Duke's study and so forth. The north wing…' he tapped it '…houses female guests and married couples on the first floor. The nursery, schoolroom and accommodation for female staff are on the upper floor.'

'Yes, where we went earlier,' she said, leaning closer to pore over the plan.

'I will search the Duke's rooms, and those of the male guests tomorrow morning, while you stand guard,' he said.

She nodded. A little warily.

'And then during the afternoon, while the ladies are all outside, you will do the searching and I will do the looking out.'

'What?' Her smile vanished. 'Me? Search rooms?'

'Well, I can hardly go rooting through a lady's underwear drawers, can I? Come, come, Horatia,' he said, delighted to have an opportunity to tease her a little, 'have some backbone. You want to catch the…culprit, don't you?'

'Of course I do. But I don't see how we are going to accomplish that by rifling through other people's belongings.'

'I should have thought that was obvious. We need to find…'

But before he could finish, a shimmering reflection

in the window beside which they were sitting alerted him to the approach of a female.

'And the children will, hopefully—' He broke off, looking over his shoulder, as though just becoming aware someone was coming to join them. 'Ah. Mary,' he said as he saw it was his younger sister, Lady Anmering. He should have noticed that the piano music playing now was far livelier.

'Still carrying on with this stupid plan to curry favour with our brother,' she said, eyeing the plans on the table.

'They are your children, Mary,' he pointed out. 'And don't you think,' he said, leaning back and crossing his legs at the ankle, 'they deserve to have some fun while they are serving as pawns in your own game?'

She glared at him.

'Besides,' he continued, 'I am of the opinion they have the right to explore our ancestral home. And if not while engaged in an activity such as this...' he waved his hands at the papers scattered across the table '...then when? It's not as if we are likely to visit very often, is it?'

'Oh, I see,' she said with a shrug. 'I suppose that makes more sense than...' She shot Horatia a disdainful look. She leaned forward to look at the plans and the outlines of clues he'd drawn up.

'Among the Dukes there is a king, and at his feet there is a thing...' she read. 'The portrait gallery. I see. You can show them all our grandcestors,' she said, while Horatia spluttered.

'At his feet there is a thing? A *thing*? Could you not come up with a better rhyme than that?'

'Well, there is a little table standing beneath the

painting of King Charles, in the portrait gallery. And if you think you can come up with a rhyme for table, which will lead children of eight years or less to that spot, then have at it,' he said, tossing her the pencil.

She took it, probably because it was her own pencil, rather than to take him up on his challenge, to judge from the militant gleam in her eye.

But at least Mary looked happier. Or at least, considering her temperament, less dissatisfied than usual.

'You have,' he said to Horatia, getting to his feet and holding out his arm to his sister, who was clearly delighted to have broken up the tête-à-tête, 'until tomorrow morning.'

Chapter Thirteen

Horatia flopped into bed, her whole body aching and weary. This had to have been the longest day of her life. Longer even than the day she'd heard of Herbert's death, because it had been more eventful. And yet she couldn't fall asleep straight away. Her mind was still whirling. Reeling from all the changes of mood she'd been through. She'd started off indignant with Lord Devizes over the way he'd treated her in the chapel, then mustered up the determination to track down Herbert's killer alone. She'd then been surprised and elated when she'd changed his mind and he'd started taking her seriously, before startling her with his plan to try to make people think he was trying to make a conquest of her. She'd veered from despairing at having to investigate alone when she felt so completely out of her depth, to celebrating the minor successes she'd achieved. And while all those waves of emotion had been flinging her up and down, there had also been a constant under-current of frustration, because although Lord Devizes was starting to listen to her, he wasn't treating her as an equal, not by any means.

He'd said they should put their heads together, but he hadn't given her a single chance to tell him anything of import. Not what she'd learned from deciphering those messages Herbert had brought her, nor what she'd discovered since arriving at Theakstone Court.

It felt almost as if she'd been swimming against the tide all day, through a stormy sea.

She sighed and rolled over, burying her face in her pillow. She was going to have to go through more of the same tomorrow. She could only hope that he wouldn't keep leaning in and murmuring in her ear. Though, of course, he had to. It was all part of the plan. And, to be fair, she could see at least one good reason why he should do so. They couldn't risk anyone overhearing what he said. But, oh, how his voice melted her spine. And made her go all…*mushy*. And she couldn't afford to go mushy at a time like this. She needed to be sharp as a tack.

Besides which, she knew that no matter how mushy he might make her go, she didn't have the ability to make him feel anything much at all. Not when she was so plain and dull and inexperienced. Not when he could remain calm and mockingly detached under the assault of the prettiest, wittiest females in society. And especially not when it was all make-believe anyway.

Stop this at once, she chided herself. Instead of fretting over what she hadn't got, she would do better to… to… Well, she could, she supposed, make a list of all the things she had achieved today. Then, once she was in a more positive frame of mind, she might be able to calm down enough to get off to sleep.

First, she had, against all the odds, achieved her main objective in coming here. She had joined forces with Lord Devizes and they were now on the hunt for Herbert's killer together. The fact that she'd discovered she was not immune to his considerable charm, even when she knew he was only play-acting, was a minor issue.

Second, she had learned how to talk to people in a social setting. Lord Devizes had been correct. You only had to pretend to be interested in a person and they would quite happily talk about themselves indefinitely. She'd put his advice to good use not only during dinner, on Mr Perceval, but also after that, in the drawing room with the ladies.

Hah—that was one in the eye for Aunt Matilda. She'd always insisted that to succeed in society, a girl had to be capable of being entertaining. To contribute to conversation by bringing something of interest to everyone else. Which had always been Horatia's stumbling block. By the time she'd thought up something witty to say, the conversation had flowed on to a point where it would no longer have been relevant.

Perhaps she was having more success because, strictly speaking, she wasn't trying to fit in with the people here, or impress them. She was simply trying to gather as much information about them as she could.

Still, she rather thought that if ever she did want to move in polite society, at any time, the tactics she'd employed tonight would work on anyone.

She would rather like to impress Lord Devizes, though, she sighed. If only she could come up with a brilliant rhyme for table…or perhaps king. Anything rather than have a clue end in such a vague way. *Thing* indeed! There must be dozens of better words to rhyme with king. There was spring, for example. Or cling. Or ring.

No, no, those words were all wrong. *Cling* made her think of the way his slightly damp shirtsleeves had clung to his arms when he'd returned from playing in the stream. Which led her mind straight back to the intriguing view she'd had of his bare legs and beautiful toes. With a huff of impatience, she yanked her thoughts away from recalling any part of Lord Devizes unclothed and back to the challenge he'd set her.

Ring. Oh, wouldn't you know it? That word conjured up an image of him sliding one on to her finger, which was never going to happen. She must not allow her thoughts to stray into avenues of romantic fantasy. She'd heard enough fairy stories to know that plain girls never got the prince. Not that Lord Devizes was a prince…

Botheration! Letting her mind stray from princes to puzzles was getting her all…*agitated*. She needed to think of something calming. Something that would take her mind away from all that she'd been through today.

It mightn't be a bad idea to follow the age-old advice for those who had trouble sleeping and start counting sheep. A whole flock of them, jumping over a gate to get back to their field.

She wiggled into a more comfortable position, took a deep breath in and one out, and started counting. One. Two. Three… Just a minute, had that third sheep sneered at her as it jumped over the gate? How dare it? Four…oh, and that one was sneering, too. Which was intolerable, given that she'd invented it in the first place. But then, because it was a product of her mind, it knew that she hadn't been able to come up with a clue simple enough for a child to follow. Able? She was perfectly able to do…hang on a minute. Able. Sable. Table. Surely a portrait of a king would contain some kind of fur? She could change his rhyme to… *Among the Dukes is a king in sable, and under his feet you'll find a table.*

Thank you, sheep! Wouldn't Lord Devizes be impressed when she told him about her improvements to the clue, at breakfast next morning.

Baa…sneered yet another of her jumping sheep, just as she remembered that kings wore ermine, not sable. And as she finally drifted off, the last image in her mind was not of sheep, but of Lord Devizes, leaning on the wall beside the gate and smiling at her in that patronising way of his, as she burbled out a childish rhyme about rings and kings, wearing sable on a table. And the sleep that followed was populated with shadowy figures leaping out of alleyways brandishing knives and Lord Devizes leaping in front of her just in time to save her. And just as he'd put his arms round her and was looking deep into her eyes and saying, *Horatia, I thought I'd lost you*, she would always wake up with her heart pounding and her whole body yearning for what would have come next.

Which meant that by the time she awoke on Monday morning, she was in a thoroughly bad mood. She couldn't tell him about the rhyme she'd come up with. Or that the sheep had come up with, to be completely truthful. He would only shake his head and tell her they had far more important things to think about. Which they did.

'Good morning,' he drawled in his lazy voice as she and Lady Elizabeth entered the breakfast room.

They both dropped the necessary curtsies, before going to the buffet and selecting a plate of hot food each.

'Not many people about this morning, are there?' he remarked as they took seats at the almost empty table. 'I wonder where everyone can be.'

'Well, Mama is taking her own breakfast in her room,' said Lady Elizabeth. 'She rarely rises before eleven. Though I did notice a lot of activity in the courtyard under our window earlier on. It looks as though a lot of the gentlemen are going out shooting, or fishing, or possibly both since they are all carrying either guns or fishing tackle.'

'Really?' Lord Devizes raised a really annoying eyebrow in her direction, as if to say *what did I tell you?* 'Is it possible to shoot fish with guns? I had no idea.'

Lady Elizabeth picked up her knife and fork and attacked her eggs rather than bother to answer that sally.

'Yes, and, of course, Lord Devizes and I,' said Horatia, 'are going to be busy exploring the house to look for places to set clues for the children's treasure hunt.'

Lady Elizabeth pulled a face, signifying the message, *rather you than me.* But then she sighed. Put on a martyred air. 'Do you need any help? I was planning to get outside for a brisk walk, while Mama is still abed. But if you really need me…'

'I think we can manage to arrange something to satisfy the schoolroom party without need of assistance,' said Lord Devizes, in his patronising manner, with the exact smile Horatia had dreaded him turning upon her if she'd told him what the sheep had come up with. 'You go and enjoy your walk.'

Lady Elizabeth shot him a darkling look, then gave Horatia one of sympathy. 'Underneath all that superficial charm beats the heart of a really, really annoying man. He would try the patience of a saint.'

'And I am no saint,' Horatia agreed.

'I shall leave you two to get on with it, then,' she said later, once she'd finished her plate of eggs.

Lord Devizes leaned back in his chair, watching her until she'd left the room, before getting up and coming round the table to take the seat she'd just vacated while pulling out his set of clues and plans.

'As I told you,' he murmured into her ear, 'we will start with the Duke's private apartment, since he is the most likely one to be at the heart of this nest of traitors.'

She wasn't at all sure she agreed. From the grim cast to his features, it looked as if he just *wanted* the Duke to be the one he was looking for, because he disliked him so much. She took a breath to point this out, then paused. If she openly disagreed with him so soon, he might decide not to include her in any further investigations. Besides, the sooner he discovered his half-brother was not the one they were looking for—and she could not believe he was, for how could a lovely person like Miss Underwood have fallen in love with a traitor and murderer?—the sooner they could get down to looking for the real villain.

'And, thanks to the treasure hunt, he has sent the footmen who usually guard that corridor into the village to search for prizes.'

She knew he had to lean close. Even though there were few other guests at the table, a couple of footmen were hovering nearby, ready to whisk away used plates and forks, and they couldn't risk anyone overhearing their plans. But it made his voice run down her spine like warm honey, so that all she wanted to do was sigh and agree with whatever nonsense he cared to utter.

'By all means, let us commence there,' she said, since she was certainly in no fit state to start arguing the case for the Duke. And getting up and setting off did at least mean that he had to move a little further from her, which enabled her to gather her wits about her again.

'Do you have a full set of clues, now?' she said, once they'd passed through the door and were out of earshot of footmen. Which was at least a sensible thing to say, since he'd told her last night that was how he'd intended to spend his evening.

'Yes. I wandered about a bit last night, through the rooms I'd already thought would make good places for a treasure hunt, just to make sure I hadn't misremembered anything.'

'Ah. Your sister was right then. About you being too young when you left to…that is, I beg your pardon. I don't mean to imply that…'

He gave her a cool look. 'There is never any harm in double-checking a plan,' he retorted, leading her up a flight of stairs. 'After the stream, I did wonder if, for example, during the years since I rode my hobby horse along the corridors, artefacts that fascinated me might have been moved.'

'Yes, that's what I meant to say,' she said, as they reached the first landing, cursing herself for her ability to put her foot in it no matter the occasion and the fact that, now she'd irritated him, he was not going to be at all receptive to her ideas about the King Charles clue.

He paused. Turned to her. Seemed to register her chagrin. 'Look,' he said, 'the truth is, what Jane said did make me think. I was very young when I left. And memory has a tendency to…well, let me put it this way. I remember that stream as a marvellous place with great steep banks where rabbits hopped about.'

'All true.'

'Yes, but…it is a question of perspective, I suppose. I had embellished it, in my mind, with a kind of glow of nostalgia until it resembled something not far short of the Garden of Eden. Which led me to wonder, did that suit of armour I admired so much as a boy really have scrollwork like birds in flight up the arms? Or had I embellished that, too, during my years of exile?'

Golly. Had he actually confided in her? Admitted to having doubts about his own brilliance? She had better take great care what she said next, because he had just opened up to her in a way she suspected he very rarely did. Which was a huge compliment. She wouldn't want him to think he'd been mistaken in thinking he could trust her.

So naturally, her mind went blank.

After breathing in and out, and pushing her spectacles up her nose, she remembered the tactic that had worked so well the night before. She didn't need to come up with anything brilliant. She could just ask him about himself.

'And had your mind embellished the suit of armour?

And the rest of the house? With things that had never actually been there?'

A frown flickered across his normally smooth brow. 'Ah. Well, that is a three-point question. To the first part, no, my memories of the suit of armour that stands guard over the foot of the stairs in the entrance hall is entirely accurate. Although as an adult, I wonder at the mental state of whoever ran amok with an engraving tool over what was surely intended for riding into battle.'

'Good. Well, that must have been...um...well, I mean it is a good thing that you have discovered your memory is not at fault.'

'In a way, yes, but...' He took her arm and urged her to a walk. 'We can as easily discuss the efficiency of my memory while making our way to the Duke's rooms.'

'Yes,' she said, resting her hand on his sleeve. For one thing it meant she didn't have to watch his face and wonder if the apparently open expression he'd just shown her was just another mask. For another, she liked the feel of his sleeve beneath her hand. And the presence of his body at her side. Far more than on that one occasion when he'd danced with her, because then he'd looked bored and she'd known he was only dancing with her out of duty. Today...well, never mind the fact that she'd had to ambush him in the chapel yesterday and force him to take notice of her. Today he was treating her as if, *almost* as if, they were friends.

They came to another set of stairs, began to climb them. When they reached the top, he turned and grinned at her.

'Just as I'd hoped. No footmen. The Duke will clearly do anything if he thinks it will benefit his daughter.'

'I don't think it is just that.'

'What else could it be?'

'Well, from what Miss Underwood says, I think he would like to mend fences with your side of the family.'

He gave an insouciant shrug. 'If so, it works in our favour. Come on,' he said, taking her by the arm again and drawing her along the landing.

She'd already been a bit breathless, because they'd been walking so fast. But now her heart did a funny little skip and her stomach went all warm, as though she'd just had a glass of mulled wine.

'The Duke's rooms are just along here,' he said, indicating a cross between a broad alcove and a short corridor branching off the main landing. It was formed mainly by two massive sets of double doors on each side.

'How do you know?' she'd whispered. Why on earth she'd whispered, she couldn't think.

'It was my father's room. And he told me it had always been the master suite,' he said, all trace of humour leaving his voice. 'I can't see a man like my half-brother breaking generations of protocol to move somewhere else. Can you?'

The question was clearly rhetorical, since he carried on without appearing to draw breath.

'The Duchess will occupy the rooms beyond these doors,' he said, waving his hands to the doors on the right-hand side. 'My mother...' A strange expression flitted across his face, then vanished, to be replaced by the smile she was beginning to see he donned whenever he wished to mask whatever he truly thought.

'There, you see,' he said, indicating the deserted corridor. 'No footmen on duty. Nevertheless, I shall need you to stand guard and alert me should anyone come. It is one thing to be caught in a corridor where we shouldn't, strictly speaking, be loitering, but it will take a deal of explaining if anyone knows I was actually inside the holy of holies.'

He looked over each of his shoulders in turn, put his hand to the set of double doors facing the ones he'd said had once been where his own mother had lived and knocked gently.

'Just as I'd hoped,' he said, setting his hand to the door knob. 'Nobody there.'

And then he darted inside, leaving her standing in the deserted corridor, her heart knocking against her ribs.

Chapter Fourteen

Horatia stood perfectly still for a couple of minutes, staring at the closed door. What was she supposed to do now?

Lord, but it was quiet up here in the Duke's domain. Eerily so. It was as if the house, as well as she, was holding its breath.

She let one out. Then sucked one in. Tiptoed a bit closer to the Duke's rooms and pressed her ear to the door.

Nothing. Not a peep. If she hadn't seen Lord Devizes walk through that door a moment ago, she would never have guessed he was in there, turning out drawers and peeking under the bed, or whatever he was doing.

Until he suddenly opened the door and she nearly fell into the room.

'What are you doing with your ear to the door?'

'How could you tell?'

'Never mind that. You must not, ever, loiter right outside the door to any room I may be searching. Especially not with your ear to the door, or your eye to the keyhole.'

'My eye was not to the keyhole.'

'It would have been, in a moment or two, if I hadn't come out and told you not to put it there.'

She opened her mouth to protest. Then shut it, realising that it probably would have been the next thing she would have done.

'Go and stand in a less suspicious place.' He pointed to where the stub of the corridor leading to the Duke and Duchess's apartments branched off from the main landing. 'Keep an eye out to see if anyone comes up the stairs, from either end, so you can give me ample warning.'

'Oh, yes. Yes, of course,' she said, as he shut the door softly, yet firmly, in her heated face.

She went to the end of the short passageway, stepped on to the main corridor and paused. She must not look as if she was loitering in a suspicious manner, yet she had to keep an eye out for anyone approaching. How on earth could you keep an eye out while not looking suspicious? Her hand crept to her mouth and she began chewing on a nail. It was all very well for Lord Devizes; he was experienced at sneaking about. But she'd never sneaked anywhere in her life.

She whipped her hand from her mouth and firmed her lips. She must not start complaining. Or even thinking along the lines of raising a complaint. Hadn't she done all she could to persuade Lord Devizes to allow her to join him in such activities? Yes, she had. So she had better start behaving like a…sneaky person.

Placing her arms straight down at her sides, she began strolling in what she hoped was a nonchalant manner in the direction of the nearest staircase. Only her attempt at nonchalance probably bore more resemblance to a guard patrolling outside a sentry box. Oh, dear, she hoped nobody came. She couldn't look more suspicious if she was holding a crowbar in one hand and a sack full of stolen goods in the other.

And then what she most dreaded came to pass. The sound of a heavy, measured tread upon the staircase. She froze, her heart hammering. Which wouldn't do. She had to warn Lord Devizes that someone was coming.

Although, unless it was the Duke himself, or his valet, or some other servant with the right to enter the master suite, Lord Devizes would probably be safe.

And if it was anybody with a perfectly good reason for going into the room he was searching? She would just have to…oh, no! Lord Devizes hadn't told her how she was to warn him. Unless it was by dashing up to the door and hammering on it, and it was too late for that, because she could now see the top of a white head through the banister, which meant whoever it was coming up the stairs would soon notice her. Particularly if she darted from her place like a startled deer and went bounding along the corridor to the Duke's rooms.

Her stomach turned over. Fine lookout she was, standing here in a panic instead of doing something to the purpose. Like making a loud noise of some sort, something that would warn Lord Devizes of approaching danger, without alerting anyone to exactly where he was. Something like…like…

And then her gaze snagged on a fragile-looking vase of virginal white roses standing on one of those little half-moon tables that were of no use for anything much.

She sidled up to the table, keeping one eye on the man mounting the stairs, and before he could notice her she picked up the vase. And swallowed. She had never deliberately broken anything in her life. And the vase might be worth hundreds of pounds. But, well, if the Duke valued it all that much then he jolly well shouldn't have left it out in a corridor where anyone could chance by and hurl it to the floor. And anyway, desperate times called for desperate measures. Taking a step out into the very middle of the corridor, she raised the vase over her head and then hurled it to the floor with all her might.

It made a satisfyingly loud crash as it shattered, although rather a lot of water seemed to bounce back in her direction, soaking the bottom half of her gown.

'What? What, what?' The man who had been coming so slowly and deliberately up the stairs paused, peering up over the landing like a bewildered owl. Horatia recognised him at once. It was the elderly chaplain, who had presided over Sunday prayers in the chapel the day before.

'Oh, dear me,' she cried, dropping to her knees, right in the middle of the worst of the mess, which would coincidentally block his way if he'd been intending to turn right at the top of the stairs. 'So clumsy of me. Look what a mess I've made.' Then, as though she was the kind of hen-witted female who would try to pick up shards of broken pottery rather than ringing for a maid to fetch a dustpan and brush, and a mop and bucket while she was at it, she began to gather up as much as she could. He'd have to step right over her to get past. Surely that would give Lord Devizes time to…to…well, if he'd heard her, that was, and correctly interpreted her signal.

'Guilt,' said the chaplain sourly, prowling in her direction. 'I have caught you where you should not be. Guilt is writ all over your face.'

A horrid feeling squirmed in her stomach at his condemnation. For she had felt guilty from the moment Lord Devizes had put her on guard outside his half-brother's door.

'Thou wanton,' the chaplain continued, drawing near.

Why was he calling her a wanton? Unless he'd been listening to gossip about her and Lord Devizes and believed it. Well, whatever his reason for looking at her that way, he was certainly succeeding in making her feel extremely guilty.

'At least you have the grace to fall to your knees,' he added, coming to a halt so close to her that she had to lean back a touch to avoid bashing her forehead on his thighs.

'Really, Dr Grimes,' came a soft, disdainful voice from over her shoulder.

Lord Devizes! Oh, thank goodness. Though how on earth he'd managed to leave the Duke's room and appear just there, she could not imagine.

'Did you not receive,' said Lord Devizes, sauntering over as though he had not a care in the world, 'the same warnings I did, upon arrival, about this being a *respectable* house party?'

'I have no need of warnings,' retorted the elderly cleric.

'That is not,' said Lord Devizes with what looked like amusement, 'what it looks like from where I'm standing. If I were not a man with similar tastes, I would be very shocked to see you attempting to coerce an innocent female into such an act, in a public corridor, too.'

For some reason that Horatia could not fathom, that cryptic remark had the cleric taking a hasty step back.

'She...she...' he blustered, pointing a gnarled finger at her. 'She was on her knees when I got here.'

'A likely story,' said Lord Devizes affably. 'You should really come up with something more plausible.'

'I have no need to come up with anything, you infernal scoundrel. The woman is at fault.'

'Ah, the eternal Eve,' said Lord Devizes, nodding. 'The woman is always the temptress, the man but the poor weak dupe...'

The conversation was becoming more and more bewildering, but at least somehow Lord Devizes was getting the cleric so flustered that he was not asking them what they were doing there.

'Miss Carmichael,' said Lord Devizes, finally turning to her. 'You seem to be in a spot of bother. May I be of assistance?'

'Oh, um...' she said, racking her brains for a suitable response. 'That is, I was...'

'Looking for a place to hide a clue, I would guess,' he supplied helpfully.

'Yes. That is it,' she agreed with relief.

'A clue?' Doctor Grimes glanced suspiciously from one to the other of them.

'Yes. Miss Underwood has tasked us, Miss Carmichael and I,' Lord Devizes said, placing one hand on his breast, 'to arrange a treasure hunt for the children who seem unaccountably to have turned up along with the guests invited to my brother's wedding.'

'And she wanted to hide a clue in a vase of flowers?'

'Hen-witted, I grant you,' said Lord Devizes. 'The paper would have gone soggy and the clue become illegible, no doubt. Really, Miss Carmichael,' he said, bending to offer her a hand so she could get to her feet, 'I had expected better of you.'

Oh, had he? Well, for her part she'd thought she'd come up with a brilliant way of distracting the chaplain so that he hadn't noticed that Lord Devizes had been in the Duke's rooms. She shook off his hand as she got to her feet. If it hadn't been for her quick thinking, the chaplain might have wandered into the Duke's rooms and caught Lord Devizes red-handed.

'This part of the house is not at all suitable for a treasure hunt,' said Dr Grimes peevishly. 'Especially not for a bunch of unruly children. Why, look at the damage you have caused already!' He pointed at the mess of broken pottery, petals and stalks seeping into the carpet.

'Come along, Miss Carmichael,' said Lord Devizes, taking her by the arm and steering her past the quivering cleric. 'Let us see if we can find somewhere more *suitable* for our endeavours.'

She was rigid with annoyance. And trying to tug her arm from his grip, so that he was obliged to hold on to her a bit harder than he would have liked.

'I hope you are not one of those people who bruise easily,' he said, when he was pretty sure that he was out of earshot of the snooping old chaplain.

'You wouldn't need to consider it if you weren't so

determined to drag me away like a...criminal being taken to prison,' she hissed at him, still trying to free herself.

There was an alcove ahead. In only a couple more paces, he swung her into it and leaned in after, pressing her back against the wall. 'Spit it out,' he advised her.

'Spit? I don't spit. What do you mean?'

'Then tell me, in plain words, what has set up your bristles.'

She glared at him. 'I should have thought it was obvious. You made me look like a complete fool.'

'That chaplain was already halfway to thinking that. I only needed to give him the slightest push—'

'You did not need to push him anywhere!'

'Oh, but I did. If I had not kept him in a state of irritation, or condemnation, he would have started to wonder what we were really doing up here. And you lent yourself to the part of scapegoat so splendidly, smashing the Duke's priceless Ming vase in that reckless way.'

Her hand flew to her throat. 'Was it really? Priceless, I mean? I would have thought he would have locked it up in a cabinet if it was worth very much...'

'I have no idea. But it was such an ugly thing it ought to have been smashed. And it could not have been broken in a better cause.'

'You heard it, then? When I saw him coming up the stairs, I could not think how to alert you, apart from making a big noise, and screaming would have made him suspicious, and you told me not to act suspiciousiy—'

'Yes, you did very well, considering.'

'Considering?' She gave him that look again. The

one that reminded him of his nanny just before she told him that she didn't believe a word he'd said and that he would have to take his punishment.

'Considering you have never done anything like this before.'

Her face lit up.

'Although…'

Her face fell. She really did have a remarkably expressive face. And didn't seem to be trying to disguise what she felt in the least, unlike most women he knew.

'I didn't have time to do a thorough search. And the chaplain probably wouldn't have entered the Duke's apartments anyway, you know,' he pointed out, as gently as he could.

'You mean, I should have just let him go past? And not smashed the vase? But then,' she pointed out, 'it might have been too late. I thought it would be better to alert you, to give you time to escape, rather than wait to see where he was going.'

'And that was probably for the best. It just means that we will have to come and search another time. The hour is almost up and…hell!' Now he could hear someone else coming up the stairs. He pushed her deeper into the alcove, so that her raised hands became folded against his chest. She glanced up at him in alarm. Curled her fingers into his waistcoat.

And it occurred to him that if anyone did pass this way, they'd assume the worst.

'Hell,' he muttered, stepping back smartly.

'Devizes?' The man who had just reached the landing just had to be his half-brother, didn't it? It was that kind of a day. And, of course, Horatia simply had to stumble out of the alcove, and, with a flushed face, start smoothing down her clothing.

'What,' said the Duke, stalking in their direction, 'are you doing?' Though the expression on his face made it pretty clear what he thought they'd been doing.

'Looking for places to hide clues for a treasure hunt,' he said blandly.

The Duke gave him a look. Turned his head, ever so slightly, to observe Horatia's somewhat dishevelled state.

'Under her skirts, was it?' said the Duke.

'What? Absolutely not!' Horatia took a step forward and clasped her hands at her waist. 'Please don't think badly of Lord Devizes. He…' Her voice petered out as she strove, and failed, to find a plausible excuse for their presence there. In an alcove.

'How can you suggest such a thing?' said Nick, smoothly.

'Because I know you.'

'However, you do not know Miss Carmichael. Or how clumsy she can be.'

'Clumsy?'

'Yes, I…' Horatia looked the picture of guilt. 'I broke a vase, just now.' When she pointed to where its remains lay, the Duke turned to look over his shoulder.

'Miss Carmichael, suddenly overwhelmed by guilt and fear of what you might say or do to her for breaking an object she thought might well be priceless, darted into the alcove to hide. And when I tried to remonstrate with her, she, ah, grabbed me and pulled me into the alcove, as well.'

He gestured to the front of his waistcoat, where he

was pretty sure the Duke would spy a set of damp little handprints.

Though, had she really grabbed him in the way he'd
described, she would have gone for his lapels.

Fortunately, the Duke clearly hadn't ever been pulled
into any sort of alcove by a desperate woman, or he
would have known about their methods, for his expression changed.

'I shall ring for somebody to clean up the mess,' he
said.

'I am so sorry, Your Grace,' said Horatia, her face
pink with mortification. 'I hope it was not valuable.
Lord Devizes said…'

'I joked with her about it being a priceless Ming vase.
I am afraid I rather alarmed her.'

'I see,' said the Duke, as though somehow he might
have known it had to be Nick's fault. And, after standing looking at them for a moment or two, as though
considering saying something pithy, apparently thought
better of it. For he sighed and walked off in the direction of his apartment.

Horatia sort of folded into his side, taking his arm.
She was shaking.

'Well done,' he murmured.

'But I didn't do anything!'

'You followed my lead,' he said. 'Rather than complaining about me putting the blame on you.'

'But I was to blame for it. Although, I have to admit
I was a bit surprised you elected to tell him the truth.'

'Yes, it was not very gallant of me,' he said, feeling
a bit guilty himself, now, for describing her as clumsy.

'No, it wasn't that. It was just I thought we were *sup-*

posed to be making everyone think you and I…' She faltered. And blushed.

'We did. Because he thought I was making up excuses. But he couldn't accuse me of lying, not once you'd backed me up. Or he would have been accusing you of lying, too.'

She wrinkled up her nose as she thought this over. 'I see,' she finally said. 'Very clever. Very effective.'

That praise, given in that matter-of-fact way, made him, for some reason, want to slip his arm round her shoulder and drop a grateful kiss on the crown of her head. She had the most sweet-smelling, lustrous hair. Would it feel as soft against his lips as it looked? She wasn't the kind of woman who would use lotions or oils to style it. Natural, that was Horatia. And clever. Clever, yes…it would be much better if he concentrated on her mental abilities than her physical potential. 'Your quick thinking certainly got us out of hot water that time. For it turns out it was just as well you got me out of his rooms before I was ready to leave, or he would have caught me.'

'Thank you,' she said simply. And then pulled herself upright, her face determined, as though she was giving herself a talking to. 'So, where next?'

'Next?' Given the choice, he'd push her back into that alcove, pull all the pins out of her hair and…

But this was Herbert's sister. An innocent. He had no business thinking such thoughts.

'I think we should adjourn for now. Go to our rooms and tidy ourselves up. Your skirts are soaked,' he said, bending down to pluck a petal from her gown. 'And probably your shoes as well. And look,' he said, tucking the petal into a waistcoat pocket. 'I have grubby little handprints all over me.'

'And then what?'

'We shall meet again at nuncheon.'

'Nuncheon? Why, that won't be for…ages! And we have so little time as it is…'

'Very well, we will meet in half an hour. In the portrait gallery. We may just be able to search a few of the men's rooms before they return.'

She beamed at him. And marched off, leaving a trail of little wet footprints behind her.

Chapter Fifteen

Horatia was rather surprised, when she got back to her room, to see Lady Elizabeth there, pacing up and down before the sitting-room window.

'Is something wrong?'

'I was just about to ask the same thing. What has happened to your gown?'

'I broke a vase,' Horatia said, making for her bedroom.

'I will ring for Connie,' said Lady Elizabeth.

'No need. I can soon dry my feet and change my stockings.'

'It must have been a big vase, to have soaked you so thoroughly,' said Lady Elizabeth with a puzzled frown.

'And that wasn't the worst of it,' said Horatia, reaching for a towel. 'I am now in bad odour with both the Duke and his chaplain.'

'How come?'

'Well,' said Horatia, sitting on the edge of her bed to toe off her damp shoes and unroll her stockings, 'I'm not sure about the chaplain. But when the Duke strolled along, I felt so guilty about smashing the horrid vase that I tried to hide. And made Lord Devizes try to hide, as well. And the Duke thought we were…'

Lady Elizabeth chuckled. 'Oh, my word. I can just imagine what Theakstone thought. It is what anyone would think if they saw Lord Devizes and a woman trying to hide. Um…where, precisely were you trying to hide?'

'In an alcove about three inches deep,' she admitted, shaking her head. 'I think the Duke believed my version of events in the end. Because there was the vase and the roses all over the carpet. And my dress and shoes were wet.'

'And what of the chaplain?' Lady Elizabeth went to sit on the window seat. 'What did he think?'

'Well, it was all rather puzzling. First of all he started calling me wanton. But I wasn't in the alcove with Lord Devizes then, I was kneeling on the carpet trying to pick up the bits of smashed pottery. It was when Lord Devizes said something about having similar tastes that Dr Grimes went very red in the face and sort of…gobbled like a turkey.'

'What else?'

'Oh, something about a cleric coercing an innocent female into some act that was out of place at a respectable house party…'

Lady Elizabeth burst out laughing.

'What? What is so funny?'

'Um… Well, single ladies—respectable ones, anyway—are not supposed to know about such things. But some men enjoy…' She lowered her voice and looked from left to right as though checking nobody could overhear, although only the two of them were in the room. 'Having a female…um…put her mouth, that is, putting their…er…private parts into a female mouth.'

Horatia thought about where she'd been kneeling. And how close the chaplain had been standing over her, so that she'd almost bumped her forehead against his thighs.

'Oh,' she said, placing her hand on her stomach, which had sort of clenched up. 'That is positively disgusting. And the chaplain…he…' she said. 'He is supposed to be a man of God. And he's so…*old*.'

Lady Elizabeth was giggling so much now that she was beyond saying anything to the point for a few moments. Which gave Horatia time to put on fresh shoes and stockings, and get a clean gown from her wardrobe.

'You do me the world of good,' said Lady Elizabeth, wiping her streaming eyes. 'I was so blue-devilled before you came in.'

'Oh, yes, I could see that something was troubling you.'

'It's Mama. The doctor is with her again. And she looks so ill that I'm starting to wonder if…'

'Oh, dear. How will you manage if… I mean, of course, you could come and live with me, if you think you could stand Aunt Matilda, if you don't have anywhere else to go.'

'That is very kind of you. But if Mama should die, then there will be nothing to stop me from going to Leipzig and marrying Mr Brown.'

'Of course. I mean…oh, I must dash. I am supposed to be meeting Lord Devizes in the portrait gallery. The treasure hunt, you understand.'

'Yes. I do. No need to apologise. Just promise to let me know if you have any more encounters like the one with the chaplain!'

The portrait gallery was deserted when Horatia got there. She might have known Lord Devizes would take longer to get changed than she. She ambled along portraits of medieval persons she guessed must be Nick's ancestors, coming to a halt beneath the painting of King Charles. Ermine. Those robes were definitely edged in ermine. Not sable.

She chewed on her lower lip. Even though there was not a scrap of sable in sight, could she really let such a pathetic verse as the one Lord Devizes had scribbled pass unchecked? Should she tell him about the sable and table clue she'd come up with last night? Or would it make him think she was getting distracted from their goal? Or worse, would he be offended at her finding fault with his composition? Even though he'd described it as mere doggerel, one could never tell. Men could be such sensitive creatures.

She turned at the sound of his slow, measured steps approaching. And blinked. Not only because he'd changed his soiled waistcoat for one of black, embroidered all over in an intricate pattern in silver thread, making her wonder if he was deliberately attempting to make them look like a matched pair. But also because she'd *known* it was him without having to turn round.

'I remember him being far more magnificent than that,' said Nick, eyeing King Charles with disfavour. 'And bigger.'

'Oh, just like the stream.'

'Yes. Do you know, it was just as well we took what I thought was going to be a detour yesterday. Or I might not have…' He stopped, frowning slightly, as though wondering why he'd been about to say whatever it was. But it was too late. She'd already worked out what he'd meant.

'Your sister was correct, wasn't she? About you being too young when you left to remember much.'

He gave her a cool look. 'It is not so much not remembering things, as remembering them in an exaggerated form.'

'Like the stream.'

'Precisely. And as for the rest of the house…' He gave a slightly bitter-sounding laugh. 'It has been strange, walking into rooms that are just as I remember them, yet not the same at all. Like the suit of armour. As a boy I found it fantastical. Remembered it as fantastical. But as a man…' he shook his head '…I find it fanciful. Decorative, but ultimately useless. No knight would ride to war wearing such impractical armour.'

'Perhaps it was never intended for use,' she said, as soon as the thought popped into her head. 'Perhaps it was meant to show the skill of the person who made it.'

'Like most of this house,' he agreed. 'Meant for show. Not to actually live in. Except for perhaps a few rooms. But then…' He shook his head. 'Perhaps I can explain it better if I show you something.'

He took her arm and led her further along the gallery, until they came to a portrait of a fair-haired woman with three children at her knee. 'Me, as a boy,' he said, waving an arm at it. 'With my mother and sisters.'

She could see a sort of foreshadowing of the adults

she'd met, in the faces of the children. Mary already had a petulant pout, Jane was looking as though she could swat someone with her fan, if only she'd had one, and he…

Well, she certainly recognised that smile. And the gleam in his eyes as though he was plotting what mischief he was about to get into next.

'Can you see,' he said, his chest rising and falling rapidly, as though under the influence of some great emotion, 'what is missing from this picture?'

'Um.' She looked at it again.

'Or perhaps I should say, *who*?' As he forced that last word through gritted teeth she saw what he meant.

'Your brother and your father.'

As he stared up at the picture, she stared at his profile. His jaw was bunching, as though he was grinding his teeth. 'And yet by their very absence, they send a message, don't they? That we are not a part of all…' he waved his arm to indicate the corridor in which they stood '…this. I was allowed a taste of what could have been mine, only to be banished from it the moment the true heir returned. Like a sinner cast out from the Garden of Eden.'

Horatia's heart went out to him, because he was reaching out to her in his own way. At least, he was attempting to explain why he was the way he was, owning up to suffering years and years of hurt, rather than hiding everything the way he did with everyone else.

But Horatia had no idea what she could say that might be of any consolation. So, instead, she decided to ask him a question that might encourage him to unburden himself further, if he was still in the mood to do so.

'Why were you banished?'

He shrugged. 'My father apparently only had room in his life for one family at a time. My mother always knew, apparently, that he was a widower with a son when she married him, but learned never to provoke his wrath by asking about them. However, the rightful heir came as a great shock to us…' he indicated the three children in the painting '…when he suddenly turned up, large as life and twice as ugly.'

'I wish I could think of something to say that would be of some help,' she admitted.

'There isn't anything anyone can say.' He ran his fingers through his hair in an impatient gesture, then strode away to gaze out of a window, down on to the courtyard. 'It was coming back here as a man which made me see that this…' he waved one arm in a gesture encompassing the entire house '…was never any sort of Garden of Eden. My mother was certainly far happier once we'd moved away from here, even though it was to a small estate with far fewer servants. And a far smaller allowance, I learned later on, when she was attempting to launch my sisters into society. But I… I…'

She went to stand beside him. Stretched out her hand, tentatively, wanting to offer him comfort. Noted the way he'd clenched his hands into fists as he stood gazing out, not at what was there today, but something that had probably happened long ago. Pulled her own back to her side.

'You felt only the pain of losing what you thought you had. Familiar surroundings. Luxuries you took for granted. Like, the sense of belonging to somewhere and someone. It was the same for me. Sort of. I mean…'

He turned to frown at her.

'Herbert must have told you about our own child-hood? How, when our parents died, we had to go and live with Aunt Matilda? How she wasted no time in sending us both off to school, because if there was one thing she didn't want, it was children under her feet.' She smiled ruefully at the memory of her first sight of her eccentric, irritable, spinster Aunt Matilda. 'She really, really doesn't like the fact that I'm still living with her, either. She had such high hopes of washing her hands of me by marrying me off to some...some-body. Anybody. She was bitterly disappointed that I didn't take. And to start with at least you still had your mother and sisters. I had to deal with...' she shuddered '...school.'

'School isn't that bad,' he said. 'At least, I rather en-joyed my time at school. It gave me so many opportu-nities to get into mischief. Because I'd decided, by that time, that it might be the only way to get my father's attention. Although, it turned out to be a waste of my time and effort. It was a measure of his indifference that no matter how badly I behaved, or, as I grew older, how much scandal I left in my wake, he never stirred a finger upon my behalf. All his attention was upon his firstborn.' His mouth twisted in distaste.

No wonder he behaved the way he did. And no won-der he was so determined to find his half-brother guilty. He'd felt abandoned and betrayed by his father. And now he wanted revenge upon what he clearly saw as the cuckoo that had thrust him out of his cosy nest.

'That's all very well,' she said, 'but... I had not a father or mother's attention to gain. So I just sort of…hid inside my books rather than deal with the other girls.'

He flung up his hands as though acknowledging a hit. 'That's true. I have always had my mother's unconditional love. The trouble is,' he said with a wry smile, 'that she also loves my unlovely sisters with the same fervour, which just goes to prove she is no judge of character. Besides which, she behaves as scandalously as I ever did in my wildest days. Not that she's a bad person,' he said, rounding on Horatia. 'I won't have you thinking that.'

'Er…no…'

'It's just that once my father died, she was like a great…puppy, suddenly let off the leash. And, not having any experience of society without him breathing down her neck the whole time, when he did let her out, which wasn't all that often, she naturally tumbled from one scrape into another.'

'I…I see. She certainly looked as though…that is, I saw her once, at one of the very few balls Aunt Matilda managed to get me an invitation for. She stood out from the other ladies of her age, who all looked disdainful, or bored. She looked so…jolly. As if she was determined to wring as much fun out of life as she possibly could.'

'That is her in a nutshell. There is no real vice in her, but she's so determined to make up for all the years of being married to a tyrant that money flows through her fingers like water…but anyway, that's enough of my family,' he said, giving the portrait one last look before leaning back against the stone window frame and adopting a casual pose. 'This place clearly has a detrimental effect upon me,' he said, rearranging his features into the mask she was more used to seeing him wear. As though he'd realised he'd shared far too much and had decided it was high time he closed himself off. 'Instead of wasting time delving into our tragic pasts,' he said in a sarcastic drawl, 'we should be making the most of our chance to search through the rooms of the visiting gentlemen while they are still out shooting the Duke's fish.'

'Yes,' she said, noticing that he was attempting to use humour to brush through a situation that had drawn dangerously close to becoming a bit emotional. 'And I will stand guard,' she added, feeling a bit more confident about the role since she'd managed to brush through her first attempt earlier without exposing Lord Devizes to discovery. Even if the Duke now did suspect her of dragging his brother into alcoves upon the slightest pretext, while the chaplain would probably always start thinking of a certain revolting-sounding practice every time he clapped eyes on her.

'And then this afternoon, while the ladies are outside playing pell-mell, we can search the ladies' rooms.'

Well, that would be a new experience. Essential attributes for anyone wanting to hunt down criminals, that was how she would have to look upon standing guard, or ransacking underwear drawers.

'Any questions,' he said, with a hint of impatience, 'before we proceed?'

'Um…just one.'

'Yes?'

'What, precisely, are we looking for that is so small it can be concealed in a lady's underwear drawer?'

Chapter Sixteen

Nick bit back his initial response, which would have been cutting. The girl was doing her best and so far she'd exceeded his expectations. Not that they'd been all that high. He'd never yet met a female upon whom he could rely. He'd learned very early on, from his own sisters, that they were frail, wayward creatures who could drift from mood to mood depending on the time of day, the weather, or a dozen other factors that bore no relevance to anything that really mattered. And as for his mother...

'The code book, of course,' he said, noting that in spite of attempting to be gentle with her, he had not been able to conceal his impatience altogether.

'A code book?' She looked at him as though he'd just told her they were hunting for a unicorn.

'Yes, of course a code book. What did you think we would be searching for?'

'Something suspicious. Something that shouldn't be there. I don't know, *any*thing but a code book.'

He found himself folding his arms across his chest

as he strove to control his increasing irritation. 'If we are going to find out who was writing the letters Herbert was so excited about those last few days,' he said, 'then the most obvious thing to do is to discover who is in possession of the code book that—'

She gave a little scream. Raised her fists. Brought them swiftly down to her side. 'We have wasted a *whole day*,' she said, quivering with what looked like rage. 'Because you...' she advanced, uncurled her fists and jabbed him in the chest with one finger '...would not *listen*—' jab '—to me. You—'

As she went to jab him for the third time, he grabbed her hand, and then, since she raised it as though to attack him, the other one. 'Calm down,' he said.

'Calm down! Calm down? You expect me to be calm when all this time we have been running all over this, this, *warren*, on a wild goose chase?'

'I thought,' he could not resist saying, although it was becoming clear that she was privy to some information she had not yet shared with him, 'that we had been organising a treasure hunt for the children, not...'

'The treasure hunt was a front,' she cried. 'As you very well know, you...you...'

'Yes, but if you have information that is so crucial to the case that my ignorance of it has reduced you to this state, then you really must calm down, so that you can impart it to me.'

'You...' she breathed. Shook her hands free of his. Took a step back. 'You have lied to me.' She turned and wrapped her arms round her middle.

'I have not...'

'Well, you let me think you had come here because

you knew what was in that last letter Herbert brought me, which you cannot possibly do, or you would not be searching for a non-existent code book.'

'I spoke the truth that night. If you chose to believe something else...'

She made a gesture with her hand that expressed her utter contempt of his prevarication. And he felt a dart of something that felt suspiciously like guilt. He *had* let her think he'd come here in pursuit of Herbert's killer, once she'd hinted that was why she was here.

'You heard me tell the Duke that it was going to give me more pleasure to be a thorn in his side, in person, than merely to express my dislike of him by staying away,' he pointed out in self-defence. 'You chose to interpret that as an excuse, and assumed I knew far more than I did. I never actually said...'

'You let me believe you knew everything! When really you are a great, fat fraud!'

'Not fat,' he said, running his hand down the taut length of his stomach. 'Acquit me of that, if nothing else.'

'You...you...can you not take anything seriously? I *trusted* you! When you started telling me about your childhood and listened to my account of mine, I thought we were being open with each other. But all the time you were still hiding the truth from me.'

She turned great wounded eyes to his. Eyes that were starting to fill with tears.

Usually, the sight of feminine tears made him wish to run a mile. So he couldn't understand why, today, he wanted instead to put his arms round her and tell her that she *could* trust him. Which wasn't true. He wasn't trustworthy, not when it came to women. Nor would it be true if he said he was going to make it all better. So why was he even thinking of saying it? Where had his sense gone? Apart from anything else, if he attempted even just to put his arms round her, in a brotherly fashion, the mood she was in, she'd probably slap him.

'Look,' he said, wishing he had pockets deep enough to shove his hands into. 'I admit, at the time, I did want to…perhaps I did let you believe I knew more than I did…'

'Perhaps?'

'Very well, I did let you assume I knew at least as much as you.'

'Oh, I see,' she said. 'Because you cannot bear to think a woman can possibly have half a brain, you tried to fool me into thinking you knew twice as much.'

'That is unfair. I only said at least as much, not twice as much.'

'Stop splitting hairs! We don't have the time…' She whirled away from him. Raised a hand to her brow. 'When I think of all the people already here and the dozens more expected over the next couple of days, and we've wasted one whole day.' She turned and held up her palm to silence him before he could say anything. 'And don't quibble about what we have accomplished as regards clues for kings and stupid sheep wrapped in sable…' She frowned. Made a slashing motion with her hand. 'Forget about the sable and the sheep. They have nothing to do with…and this is not funny,' she cried, when he couldn't help smiling at her non-sequitur about sheep and sable.

'Are you laughing at me?' She seemed to shrink

about an inch in stature. 'How can you? When we are letting the chance to catch Herbert's murderer slip through our fingers?'

'I am all kinds of a villain,' he calmly agreed.

'Don't try to get round me by agreeing with me,' she snapped. 'Do you take me for an idiot?'

'No. An idiot is the last thing you are. However,' he said, stepping across the corridor to stand toe to toe with her, 'you are speaking far too loudly. I know, I know,' he said, taking her hands when she would have struck him again. 'I am being annoying, and villainous, and untruthful and anything else you like. But just remember that in spite of all my faults, I am your only ally.'

She breathed in deeply a few times, as though struggling to hold back a few more pithy remarks.

'That's right,' he crooned. 'Now you can tell me what you should have told me from the beginning. Which I was too puffed up with my own masculine self-importance to hear from a lowly female.'

'You…you…you have taken the words from my mouth,' she said bitterly.

'Well, I thought it would save time.'

'I…I…I need to scream again. Or break something.'

He looked swiftly along the gallery. And then back at her. 'I don't think you really wish to gain a reputation for smashing ducal porcelain, do you? Besides, there is none to hand. You will just have to scream again. Or…' A wild notion came into his head. 'You could channel all your anger for me into a kiss.'

'What?'

Well, that had the desired effect. She looked about

as shocked as though he had just dashed a jug of cold water in her face.

She pulled away.

'No kissing necessary. I can be calm.' She tucked a stray curl behind her ear. Adjusted the position of her glasses. Lifted her chin. 'I can speak to you in a rational manner, about...' She looked from right to left, as though suspecting the portraits of his ancestors of eavesdropping.

'Well done,' he said. Trying and mostly succeeding in stifling the insulting implication that she regarded a kiss from him in the light of a threat. Then, catching sight of a movement out of the corner of his eye, he lay one finger lightly across her lips.

Her eyes widened, but she did not smack his finger away. Which made him wonder if it had been hearing something, just now, that had made her look about so guiltily.

He turned from her, as casually as he could, and, just where he'd seen the flicker of movement, he saw the sturdy figure of the Duke's personal physician materialise.

'I thought I heard a scream,' said Dr Cochrane, ambling nearer. 'Has there been some sort of...incident?' The doctor looked from Nick to Horatia in the judgemental sort of way that people always looked at him when he was caught, alone, with a young lady.

'I did upset Miss Carmichael,' Nick said, with the smile he always used in such situations. The one that hinted he'd been wicked. And the doctor, like so many before him, chose to believe the worst.

'Miss Carmichael,' the doctor said, stepping closer

and extending his arm. 'I think you had better come with me.'

'What?' The dear girl looked the picture of confusion. 'Why? Really,' she said with a touch of impatience. 'I have far too much to accomplish today to take a walk with you. If that is what you were wanting? Unless... Has Lady Tewkesbury taken a turn for the worse? And you cannot find Lady Elizabeth... That is, I mean her daughter.' She stepped forward, her face creased with concern.

'No, no, nothing of that nature. I just thought you might prefer not to have to stay here with this...young man,' he said down his nose.

'Why?'

'I believe,' said Nick, 'he thinks I have been importuning you. And that you screamed for help.'

'Surely not,' she said with a funny little tilt to her head. 'He must be intelligent, or he could not have become a doctor. Unless he thinks I am such a ninny that I would stand still and allow you to importune me without kicking you in the shins and marching away?' She turned to look at Dr Cochrane, with that nanny-ish expression.

'But, then, why the scream?'

'Oh, that,' she said, making a dismissive motion with her hand. 'Lord Devizes has already told you that he upset me. It was a scream of vexation that you heard. Over a...well, we were arguing about...if you can believe it,' she said, a blush stealing to her cheeks, 'the clues for the treasure hunt. I have been up half the night thinking up rhymes and he has been extremely rude about them.'

If he thought Dr Cochrane had been looking down his nose before, it was as nothing to the way he was looking at Nick now. As though he was a worm.

'A gentleman...' he said.

'Oh, pray do not read him a lecture. He was a friend of my brother's, you see, and tends to treat me the way Herbert did. In a teasing fashion, that...well, sometimes drives me to distraction.'

'Herbert? Your brother, yes... That is, I noticed your state of mourning, of course, but thought you intended to spend your time here quietly away from the vicinity where you could not help being reminded daily of your loss, not dashing about the corridors in a most unseemly fashion with a person whose reputation can only put yours in peril. And as for you...' He turned to glare at Nick again. 'Really, to tease a young lady who is clearly in mourning is not the act of a gentleman. To encourage her in pursuits which can only draw down censure upon her head, which may even put her in moral danger...'

'I have never claimed to be much of a gentleman,' said Nick, leaning back against the window embrasure and folding his arms across his chest.

'No, but he has been trying, in his own fashion, to distract me, you know, Dr Cochrane,' said Horatia. 'And if you two wouldn't mind, I think we really should be getting on with laying the trail of clues for the children. The library, I think you said was next, Nick?'

Never slow to take a hint, Nick extended his arm to Horatia.

'Yes, the library is one of the places I think would

be a perfect place to plant a clue,' he said as she took his arm.

'You intend to persist with this…treasure hunt,' said Dr Cochrane. 'Miss Carmichael? In spite of my warnings?'

'I cannot see what harm I can come to with Nick as my escort. You may not think he is much of a gentleman, but he was my brother's closest friend.' Her eyes looked suspiciously damp, behind those spectacles. 'I trust him.'

She trusted him. In spite of all the ways he'd already let her down.

It made it hard for him to say anything, somehow, as they walked arm in arm to the staircase at the far end of the gallery from where Dr Cochrane still stood, glaring after them. Even if he hadn't wanted to be sure the old quack couldn't overhear, he had to marshal his thoughts. Quench the feelings that had gone tumbling through his mind when she'd spoken in his defence. Because it was true, what he'd told her. Nobody had ever trusted him, or defended him, apart from his flighty, feather-brained mother. And Horatia was neither flighty nor feather-brained. Quite the contrary.

'From what I have been able to learn in the few days since I've been here,' he eventually managed to say, 'hardly anybody ever goes in the library. And we need to find somewhere we can talk without being disturbed.'

'And this time,' she said, very strictly, 'you are going to listen to me.'

Yes, Nanny, he wanted to say. But settled for walking sedately down the stairs and along the short passage that led to the library. Opening the door for her and bowing her into the room which was, as he'd predicted, distinctly free of people.

Apart from the two of them. If he'd been arranging an assignation, he could not have thought of a better place. Apart from the walls lined with shelves, stuffed full of books to deaden the sound, there was a very comfortable-looking leather sofa upon which he could have stretched out full length. He tore his eyes from it to find Miss Carmichael going to a table upon which several books were lying open, as though somebody had left off studying them only moments before.

He walked to the fireplace, some distance from her table, leaned his shoulders upon it and folded his arms across his chest.

'You have my full attention,' he told her. And the depth of the table between them for good measure.

Chapter Seventeen

She eyed his deliberately casual pose with narrowed eyes, as though wondering whether to confide in him. Then, clasping her hands at her waist, she took a deep breath.

'You know that in the last few days before he was murdered, Herbert had been very excited about a new lead he thought he'd stumbled across?'

He nodded. 'He told me that he'd found something new, yes, and that it might be a fresh way of discovering the head of the trail that ended up with our informant in France. That he just needed to crack a new code that the conspirators had started using.'

She pulled her mouth down at the corners. 'How like Herbert to make up a story like that.'

'You mean, he hadn't stumbled across a new code?'

'No. I mean, yes.' She shook her head. 'I will be able to explain it all much easier if you refrain from interrupting.'

He held up his hands to signify surrender. Folded his arms across his chest again.

'Where was I? Oh, yes. Well, Herbert said he'd seen

someone passing notes to someone else in a way that
made him prick up his ears, in a manner of speaking.
He couldn't believe they were lovers, but if they weren't,
then there had to be some other reason why they were
carrying on in such a furtive way.'

Yes, that was the gist of what he'd told Nick, too.

'And so,' Horatia continued, 'he stole one of the notes
he'd seen them pass each other. And, when he saw it was
in code, he brought it to me to work out what it said.'

'So all those hours he spent in the rookeries, learn-
ing how to pick pockets didn't go to waste,' he said
aloud. Herbert had lifted a coded note from a suspect.
There had been nothing on Herbert's body, nothing in
his rooms. He'd thought the trail had gone completely
cold. But Horatia had seen this note. Had deciphered it.
And it had led her here. His heart kicked into a hope-
ful canter.

'Will you stop interrupting?'

'I beg your pardon. You deciphered it...' She must
have done, or she would not have left her house, let
alone the city of London, to attend the wedding of someone she'd never met.

'Of course,' she said with a toss of her head. 'Because it was ridiculously simple.'

'What did it say?'

'What? Oh, haven't I said? I thought...' She frowned.
'I can't recall the exact words. But it definitely ordered
the person receiving it to attend the Duke's wedding,
because he wanted to speak face-to-face.'

'And a wedding might be the only time this person
could get close to the Duke without it looking suspicious,' mused Nick. 'You see? The Duke *could* be the

ringleader. He could be the traitor. He has access to all sorts of information that would be invaluable to the French. And it certainly explains why he suddenly decided to get married. And then, after inviting the cream of society, making them think he was going to choose one of their daughters, he picked a nobody. A girl with no family who might grow suspicious of his activities and no influence to stop him.'

'Well,' she said, pursing her lips. 'I can see that you would like all that to incriminate him, but I have to tell you that the note spoke of him in the third person.'

'That's irrelevant! He wouldn't say, come to *my* wedding, would he? That would give away his identity.'

'It wouldn't explain why he styles himself as The Curé, either.'

'Perhaps…' He struggled to find a theory that might hold water and suddenly found inspiration from his childhood. 'You know—well, I told you, didn't I? That he suddenly sprang out of nowhere when I was about five years old. Well, he had been sent away to live with a foster family who told him he was a bastard.'

'No!'

'Yes. Mother told me. When I was much older, of course. My father suspected his first wife of playing him false. And he was given to strange fits of temper. The way he treated Mother—' He bit off what he might have said. There were some things neither he, nor his sisters, would ever speak of outside the family. 'Well, you only have to look at the way he evicted me and my sisters from this place the moment he decided Oliver was his true heir after all. Even though he looked, and acted, like a farm boy.'

'So you think the Duke might have developed a disgust of rank and privilege because of the way your father rejected him? It didn't affect you that way though, did it?'

'No. But then as you pointed out, I had my mother and sisters with me. He was out on his own. With everyone calling him a bastard. And treating him like one.'

'Oh, the poor boy,' she said. Which made him wince. Because he suddenly saw...no, *felt*, that it must have been as bad for Oliver as it had been for him. Worse, possibly, because not only had Oliver gone through his exile alone, but he'd been much younger when it began.

'Anyway,' he said, deliberately shaking off the feeling of sympathy her words had evoked for the bewildered and betrayed little boy Oliver had once been. 'He has radical views, everyone knows that. He openly petitions Parliament for changes in favour of the underprivileged. What if he is also taking action to ensure those changes take place? In a revolutionary manner?'

'I take your point. However, we were talking about the code itself and its significance to our actions now, not who might be the guilty party.'

'Very well,' he said, holding up his hands in a gesture of surrender again. 'Pray continue.'

'Well,' she said, pushing her spectacles back up to the bridge of her nose. 'Most of the messages Herbert brought me had been in something that was not really very much more than a glorified version of the Caesar shift, for which I soon drew up a table.' She spoke to him as though what she was saying ought to make perfect sense. So he did his best to look as though he understood it all, though she might as well have been speaking in Chinese. 'But the last few, why, they were the sort of thing a child would employ, when first starting to think of ways of sending secret messages. I've done it myself.'

Yes, she would have.

'You agree on a book that you know the person you are sending the secret message to has a copy of,' she continued. 'And then to put the word into code, you tell them first the page number it is on, then the line on the page and then the position in the line,' she said, with the kind of enthusiasm that showed she found that sort of thing fun. He didn't think he'd ever seen her little face so animated. 'So that for each word there is a set of three numbers. Usually. Except in this case, each word was represented by four numbers. Which, of course, led me to deduce which book they were using as their source.'

'It did?'

'Yes. A book that every household has access to. The Bible.'

'Egad. You worked all that out from the fact that each word was represented by a set of four numbers? What a remarkable brain you must have.'

'Yes, well, there are sixty-six books in the Bible,' she carried on, as though he hadn't interrupted, the only sign that she'd heard him at all being the flush that crept to her cheeks. 'And I noticed straight away that the first number used never went above that. Then each book is divided into chapters. Then verses. Then, well, individual words. So, if you wanted to say the word *duke* you could, for example, write it as one, thirty-six, forty, twenty-three, I think. Though there must be other places where the word is used in the singular.'

'Hold on, that is…Genesis, chapter thirty-six…'

'Verse forty—yes, that's correct,' she said, smiling at him as though he was a schoolboy who'd just given her the correct answer to a complicated bit of mental arithmetic. 'Though I may have misquoted the actual chapter and verse, you have got the idea.'

Oh, yes. He'd got the idea all right. 'It's fiendish. Because every house will have a Bible. And no matter what version they have, they will be the same by chapter and verse.'

'That's it. So it is of no use trying to find a copy of a book that will look unusual. Everyone has a Bible. Why, at chapel yesterday, I dare say most of the ladies were carrying one.'

His heart did a funny little skip. 'That is why you were so suspicious of the chaplain? Because, to write such codes, he must have an excellent working knowledge of the Bible.' Nick certainly wouldn't have known there was the word *duke* in the book of Genesis.

'No, no, no. That is not the case at all!' She'd relegated him to the bottom of the class. 'You only need to have access to a concordance. Which has a list of every word in the Bible and where to find examples of it. And before you ask, yes, there is one in this library. I found it on my first night here.' She gestured to the table at which she was standing. At one of the books lying open.

He sprang away from the mantelpiece and strode over. On the open page he saw, at a random glance, the words *hair, ham, hand*, in bold print, followed by a list of places where those words could be found by chapter and verse. And the page edges were worn, as though the book had been well used.

'Anyone,' he said, his heart sinking, 'be they staff or guest, could come in here and walk over to this table, and the worst anyone would assume was that they were…pious.'

'Exactly!'

'Damnation!' He took a few paces across the room and back, running his fingers through his hair. If there was no incriminating code book to search for, it meant he was going to have to come up with a completely different plan. Think up a new way of unmasking Herbert's killer.

Which would mean being on form. And not wasting time striding about the place with his hair on end looking like a zany.

He went back to the fireplace, over which there was a mirror, smoothed down his hair and checked that his neckcloth and waistcoat were in pristine condition.

'It's a delaying tactic, isn't it,' she said.

He met her eyes in the mirror, to see a look on her face that told him she had just come up with a solution to something that had been niggling at her for some time.

'Your habit of checking yourself in every mirror you pass. You don't have any idea how to proceed from this point, now that you don't need to search for a code book, so, while you are trying to come up with a new plan, you are pretending to be preening.'

She was too clever by half. No wonder no man had ever proposed marriage to her. She must have made them all feel about two inches tall.

He, however, was not going to be intimidated, or emasculated, by a slip of a girl, no matter how acute her powers of observation were.

He turned to her with a hard smile. 'Did Herbert never tell you how we began on our present career?'

She shook her head. 'Though I don't see what relevance it can have. Or why you need to tell me about it now.'

'It was as I was *preening*, as you put it, in such a mirror, at one of the dullest functions you can possibly imagine, when I saw two people together who had no business being together.'

'Just as Herbert got on to the track of this person.' She waved her hand at the book on the table.

'Precisely. What piqued my curiosity on that first occasion, though, was that the two people in question always swore they had never met each other. Indeed, the...man in the case slipped out of the house almost at once, then denied ever having been there. And because I was bored, and because I have always had a spirit of mischief that provokes me into doing the very thing that everyone says I ought not to do, I determined to get to the bottom of their little mystery. I told Herbert what I was about and he, as always, followed me.'

A small frown flitted across her brow and was swiftly replaced by an expression of great sadness. 'I wish he hadn't been so ready to follow you into mischief,' she said. And then shook her head, a little angrily. 'No, no, that isn't true. It is of no use blaming you. The last year or so, while he was actually doing something constructive, I was glad...only...'

'Well, I blame myself,' he said, stung by the way she was trying to exonerate him. 'We never expected to unmask a criminal venture when we started attempting to unravel that first mystery. Nor did we set out with any noble motives whatsoever. We just found it amusing to thwart a pair who thought they were being really clever. And it might have been the end of it, if somebody hadn't taken note of our activities and reported it to…a group of powerful men who decided they could make use of our particular skills.'

'Yes, and that thrilled Herbert. By that point, even if you hadn't wanted to do more of that kind of work, I think he would have gone on. He was so proud of himself when he told me about how someone in government was seeking patriotic young men from good families with the brains necessary to carry out their… spying, I suppose you would call it, for them. And he thought it a great joke that even his reputation for being a bit…wild was going to be useful cover for consorting with rather low types. That he would be rewarded for behaving badly.'

'It wasn't quite like that.'

'No,' she said pensively. 'I can see that now. And although he didn't tell me how you got started by accident, I might have guessed it would have been something like that. Nowhere near as noble and important as he kept making it sound.' She bowed her head and ran a finger along the page of the open book, as though she was studying it.

'Perhaps he was trying to impress you.'

Her shoulders hunched.

'Yes,' she said in a very small voice. 'He did have a bit of a tendency to…that is, he was so pleased to be thought clever by someone, when before they'd all said that I had all the brains and he had all the beauty.'

'Whoever said that was an idiot. Herbert had brains. And you have…'

'Don't say it,' she hissed at him, glaring up at him with eyes that had narrowed to slits. 'Don't tell me any lies. Not for *any* reason.'

She looked so fierce that he quashed his first impulse, which was to persuade her that she did have a type of beauty. That if she took more care of her appearance and talked in the same, animated fashion which had so changed her features from pinched up and disapproving to open and…yes, rather charming, she could rival any Season's accredited beauties. Instead, he addressed her major concern.

'I promise,' he vowed, 'that from now on, I will never lie to you.'

'Hmmph,' she said, looking far from convinced. Which was even more irritating than her refusal to receive any sort of compliment. And yet, rather than let it slide, he found himself wanting to persuade her that he'd meant what he'd said. And win back her trust.

'Look, I can understand, only too well, what might have motivated Herbert apart from his loyalty to me. Because I was in it to prove myself, as well. To prove that I had some worth, to somebody, even if my own father…' He ground to a halt. It was one thing thinking it but quite another, he found, to say out loud that his father had as good as tossed him aside once his firstborn had come back into favour.

She came out from behind her desk, strode up to him and took his hands. Which shook him. He hadn't expected her to respond to his confession with quite so much feeling. So much feeling that he couldn't look directly into her eyes for long, as they were blazing with compassion. He bowed his head over her hands instead. And was a touch surprised to note how tiny they were, considering the strength of her grip.

'Your father,' she said indignantly, 'sounds like a complete nitwit. He should have treasured you. Well, he should have treasured both his sons, yet he did the same to you both.'

What? How had she managed to bring Oliver into it?

'You are intelligent,' she was saying, gripping his hands even harder as he attempted to remove them, 'and capable and kind...'

'Kind?' he scoffed, finally extricating himself from her rather inky fingers. 'If only you knew...'

'No. I am not going to listen to you listing your faults. You are not the rake you claim to be, or there would be a string of ruined women with a cartload of by-blows in your history. And there aren't. Yes, you have behaved badly, in many ways, but there is a streak of decency in you that has stopped you sinking into true depravity.'

'Ha! Not being depraved hardly equates to having any actual worth—'

'But the work you and Herbert were doing...'

'Do you know,' he said, deciding to be completely honest with someone for once, 'lately I've been feeling a great deal of affinity for that Greek chap, Sisyphus. Endlessly rolling a boulder uphill only to have it roll right back to where it had started the minute he thought he'd got it to the top. Because the moment I defeat one group of conspirators, another one takes its place. It's all so pointless.' He leaned across the table and flipped the cover of the concordance so that it snapped shut in a cloud of dust. He'd been fooling himself that he was doing something worthwhile. His life, his activities, they were all pointless.

'Well, this isn't just about unmasking conspirators, is it? This time, we are on the trail of whoever killed Herbert. So you cannot say this is pointless,' she said, wagging a finger at him. 'Can you?'

He sucked in a shallow breath. For once, the capture of his quarry *was* going to give him a sense of validation. Whoever had killed Herbert must not be allowed to get away scot-free. 'You are absolutely right. So, instead of standing about raking over the past,' he said in his most withering tone in an attempt to regain the upper hand, 'we should be putting our heads together and coming up with a way forward.'

He should have known that speaking to her a bit disdainfully would not have been enough to put her in her place. He should also have chosen his words more carefully. Because the way she was smiling at him told him that she'd taken his suggestion that they put their heads together as a compliment to her intelligence.

'Are you admitting you don't have a plan?' she said, her smile turning more amused than gratified. 'You?'

If it had been anyone else, he might have attempted to persuade her that, of course, he did. Only he'd just promised to never lie to her. Besides which, he had a feeling she would see straight through him.

'The problem is that we have practically nothing to go on.' He thought of all the guests already at Theakstone Court and the *dozens*, as she'd put it, due to arrive over the next few days.

'Well, no, not quite nothing. We know that the people we are looking for were both in London the day before Herbert was killed,' she said, holding up one finger as though she was about to count the number of things they did know. 'That they agreed to meet here.' Yes, dammit, she was now holding up a second finger. 'That the code name of the person in charge of this plot, whatever it is, has the code name of The Curé...'

'The what?' Never mind her fingers, this was something worth counting. 'As far as I knew, nobody in the particular network we had been investigating knew much more than the next person in the chain to whom they had to pass on what they knew. You are telling me that Herbert had discovered some information about their ringleader?'

'Well, in the new letters, the ones that used the Bible as their source, they definitely mentioned The Curé. Which means pastor, in French, doesn't it? Or a chaplain, at a stretch...'

'Hold on, hold on... I might not be the world's most religious man, but I'm pretty sure the word *curé* never appears in the Bible.'

'No, but the word cure does, and so does the indefinite article. When they occurred together, in referring to a person, I translated it as "cure a", or *"curé"*.'

'It sounds as though Herbert brought you several of these coded notes.'

'Yes, he did. And he always smuggled them back to the person he got them from before they noticed.'

'How the deuce did he manage that?'

She gave him a look of exasperation. 'I don't know. He never told me any details about his work, not re-

ally. I just copied the notes, then returned the originals
to him before anyone could notice they were missing.'

That wasn't the way they usually worked. What on
earth had possessed Herbert to copy notes and return
them? And not tell him exactly what was going on?
'How long had this been going on?'

'A week or so.'

'And during that time, you must have deciphered
several notes.'

'Yes.'

'So? Tell me what was in them. And what led you here.'

Chapter Eighteen

'Well, the first few notes, which came from this person who called himself The Curé, were actually rather threatening in tone, now I come to think of it. Though at the time, I was more interested in the work itself than the implications of them. Oh,' she said, her heart sinking. 'How I wish I'd paid more attention! I...' She found herself gazing up into his face, even though it had gone a little blurred. Because he would understand all about guilt and regret, wouldn't he? And doing things from motives that were as far from being noble as possible?

'I was being so...selfish!' She took off her glasses and rubbed at her eyes. 'I enjoyed being able to use my brain in a way that very few others can. I wasn't interested in what it meant outside the house. Outside my room. It just gave me a really good excuse for sitting there, away from Aunt Matilda and her constant fault-finding, and feeling *useful*. Even if it was only to Herbert. Even if I couldn't tell anyone else about it. Even if he did receive the wages—' which he passed on to her, since he'd said nobody would actually employ a female for such work '—and the credit...'

'You can still be useful,' he said in that tone of voice a person used when they were trying to placate a toddler who had broken a favourite toy.

'You promised you wouldn't lie to me,' she said, hooking her spectacles back over her ears, so that she could glare at him more effectively. Herbert had always said that putting them on made her look as though she had stones for eyes. Like a gorgon.

'I am not lying...'

'Just how do you think I can continue in this line of work, now that Herbert has...gone?' She tripped over the word died. It was too final. Too obscene, considering the way he'd died.

'Now that I know about your skills...'

'What, you are going to visit me, on the way home from one of your gambling hells, with a note that must have a translation by morning? Or pop round for breakfast the next morning to pick it up?'

'Yes, well,' he said, in a voice laced with bitterness, 'that would definitely ruin your reputation, wouldn't it?'

'That is not it at all! You stupid man! Nobody would believe you could possibly be visiting me for...*that*.'

She batted her hand at him as though to prevent him from interrupting.

'It's all very well convincing people here that you are amusing yourself by flirting with me simply because your brother forbade it and you want to defy him, or annoy him. But who on earth would believe that a handsome man like you, a man who could have any woman with the crooking of his finger, would keep *on* pursuing a plain, awkward bluestocking like me? They'd know there was something else going on. They would want to know what. They'd talk and ask questions, and there would go any chance of being able to work unnoticed.'

'You really don't have much idea of just how bad my reputation is,' he said bitterly. 'Far from assuming we were doing anything of import, they'd probably say I'd become so jaded with my usual fare of dashing matrons that I'd sunk to amusing myself by attempting the ruination of an innocent. That the obduracy you've shown towards me so far has made me determined to teach you a lesson, or some such thing. They'd come up with anything but the truth.'

'Really?' She peered up at the lines bracketing the corner of his mouth and saw that he totally believed what he'd just said. Her spirits plucked up, just a bit. If it was true, if society was so set on believing the worst of him that she might be able to continue with work she'd found so rewarding, then...

She sighed. She was being selfish again. Hiding behind a man who would face all the danger, all the criticism, just so she could do as she pleased. 'Once we've discovered Herbert's killer, that will be the end of it. I have to accept it.'

He frowned. 'You are going to just...give up? An occupation that means so much to you?'

'Yes.'

'But, how will you cope? Herbert told me that he passed a good deal of the money he received by way of...reward for our activities, to you.'

'I never *needed* the money,' she explained. 'My parents left adequate provision for me. It was just...very satisfying to know that I had earned it through my own abilities. That it was my very own, to spend as I saw fit. Or invest as I saw fit. Without anyone else having a say in it. It made me feel…' She shook her head. 'Well, never mind. It is of no use thinking about it. I couldn't possibly sacrifice you in that way. It wouldn't be fair.'

'Sacrifice me…' He blinked. Tilted his head to one side. 'Are you saying that you would give up your work, work that is so important not only to you, but also to the security of our country, out of some misguided notion of protecting *my* reputation?' His face changed. Grew sardonic. 'Are you sure it isn't your own reputation you are worried about? That you don't want your name to be linked to mine?'

'How like a man to suspect something like that. You, none of you, can believe that a woman is capable of acting honourably. As if I care *that*,' she said, snapping her fingers, 'for the opinions of society. After the disaster of my Season, and my behaviour since, I have no reputation to ruin. And even if I did, do you really think it would bother me to lose it? What do I care for all that vacuous gossip that passes for conversation in the salons of the idle idiots who think they are better than everyone else just because they have either lots of money or age-old titles? So what if they start saying I am a fallen woman? They already snigger at me for being an oddity, for wearing the fashions of five or six years ago and preferring to attend lectures than balls.'

He silenced her by suddenly grabbing her by the elbows and giving her a little shake. 'You don't know what you are saying, you little goose! It will be an entirely different thing and you should know it. If they once suspect you of being a *fallen woman*, as you call it, they won't just snigger at you and give you a wide berth. You will have the worst sort of scum sniffing round you like dogs after a juicy bone.'

She could feel his hands not only on her elbows, but right the way down to her toes. And she wasn't sure if it was that, or the fierce light in his eyes, that had made all her irritation vanish as suddenly as a popped soap bubble.

'No, really,' she said in a voice that would only just emerge from a throat that felt thick with...something she'd never experienced before. 'I hardly think men would...'

'Don't you ever look in the mirror?' he said, giving her another little shake. All she could do was blink up at him, rendered totally mute now by having him so close. Having his hands on her. Such strong hands, that could move her entire body with just the tiniest of effort on his part.

He frowned. 'Just how bad is your eyesight? Never mind. I'm pretty sure there is nothing wrong with your ears. So just listen. Take it from me, you are pretty. Deucedly pretty, as a matter of fact.'

Pretty? She leaned forward, just a touch, and breathed in to see if she could smell brandy on his breath. Could he have been drinking when he'd gone off to change his clothes? For he surely couldn't say any such thing if he was sober.

'And your mind is...' He shook his head. 'There must have been men who have looked beyond the dreadful clothes you wear to the woman beneath?'

Hearing him speak about the woman she was beneath her clothing made her feel incredibly aware of her skin. All over. From there, it was merely a blink of an eye to take her to a place where she could imagine she was standing before him completely naked. With his hands on her. And his eyes looking intently into hers. Her heart started pounding. It was hard to breathe. She couldn't be thinking about being naked, with his hands on her. It was…so, so wrong. She should move away.

She raised her hands and put them on his chest. Her cheeks felt as though they were on fire. What was she doing?

'I…that is, no. No man has ever wanted to…explore beneath my clothes.' She couldn't believe she'd just said that. What was the matter with her?

She cleared her throat. 'That is, I mean, most men shy away from women like me, don't they? Men don't really like women to be cleverer than they are. Especially not a woman who has a tendency to voice her opinions, whether they run contrary to their own or not.'

She would have thought he would have agreed with her. Made a joke of it. Broken the strange tension she could feel taking over her better sense. Stopped her from making a total fool of herself.

Instead, he took her face between his hands. Looked at her mouth. 'Most men,' he said gruffly, 'are idiots, though, aren't they? Cowards.'

Her heart was now beating so fast she rather thought it was making her tremble. He was going to kiss her!

Was he going to kiss her?

No, of course he wasn't. Men like him didn't kiss girls like her. Not even when they were taking part in a *pretend* pursuit. Or, perhaps they did. If they thought they needed to convince people they were really smitten, or at least, determined to make her fall for them.

But in that case, he wouldn't set about it like this. He'd have made sure there was at least one witness…

Oh, why was she thinking of a thing like that at a time like this? When he was still holding her face in his hands. And looking at her mouth. And…lowering his head!

She gasped.

And so did someone else.

And Lord Devizes turned his head from her suddenly to look in the direction from where that other gasp had come from.

And so, of course, did she, her heart plummeting. Because there stood the very witness he needed, if he'd set the scene deliberately.

Which explained it all.

Chapter Nineteen

'What,' boomed the pompous tones of his half-brother's loyal secretary, Perceval, 'do you think you are doing?'

Before he could ask himself the same question, Nick fished in his pocket for a handkerchief. 'Miss Carmichael has something in her eye.' Yes, the kind of look no red-blooded male could resist. What the hell had he been thinking, yielding to that invitation? 'I am attempting to remove it,' he said—although, actually it was Perceval who'd removed it when he'd interrupted. Nick folded his handkerchief into a neat triangle, then, rather than allowing the obstacle of her spectacles to get in the way, slid it under the lenses. He wished he could as easily remove what he'd seen blazing from that unique pair of eyes as he could a mote of dust. Albeit an imaginary one. For she shouldn't believe anything good of him. He was no good. Why couldn't she see what everyone else could?

In spite of being very short-sighted about some things, she was quick to spot her cue. Taking hold of the handkerchief, she muttered, 'Thank you, my lord. I think I can manage.'

But Perceval was no fool.

'A likely story,' he said, bustling over.

'For goodness' sake,' said Horatia with a touch of impatience. 'What do you think he was doing? Something improper, by the tone of your voice,' she said, jabbing at her eye with the corner of his handkerchief until it really did look a bit raw. 'As if that were at all likely. Men like him don't kiss girls like me,' she concluded, with a convincing touch of wistfulness.

Convincing, because she believed it.

'Men like him,' said Perceval, jutting his chin in Nick's direction, 'will kiss any female if they think they can get away with it.'

Precisely!

Though, hang on, what did he mean *any* female? How dare he imply Horatia wasn't the kind of woman a man would want to kiss?

Before he knew what he was about, he'd curled his hands into fists and was on the verge of demanding Perceval apologise for insulting her to her face. And even when he'd uncurled his fists and clamped his mouth shut tight, having reminded himself that this was no time to start a brawl, he was still of the opinion that it was past time someone stood up for her.

'You should not,' continued the pompous oaf, blithely ignorant of how close he'd just come to having his cork drawn, 'be alone in a room with him. It is most improper.'

'Fustian,' she said, tucking his handkerchief up her

sleeve, instead of hiding it away in her reticule, the way most ladies would.

'Precisely,' Nick said, following her lead this time. 'Miss Carmichael has the sense to know she is perfectly safe from unwanted advances.' The trouble was, they wouldn't have been unwanted. If Perceval had not come in just when he had, Nick would have kissed the blazes out of her. And then probably flattened her to that sofa and explored beneath her clothes, just to prove that she was as desirable as any woman her age.

And she would have loved every minute of it.

'So what,' said Perceval, 'do you expect me to believe the pair of you are doing in here? Alone?'

Miss Carmichael gave him a look that wouldn't have seemed out of place coming from a governess confronted by an exceptionally dim child. 'We are devising a treasure hunt for the children. Did His Grace not inform you? Or his betrothed, Miss Underwood?'

'No,' said Perceval, looking as though she'd slapped him. 'They did not.' He obviously didn't like not knowing everything that was going on at Theakstone Court.

He made a swift recovery, however, and was about to point out something Nick was sure he wouldn't want to hear. So Nick stepped up to him and said softly, 'Since Miss Carmichael's recent bereavement means she is unable to take part in the more frivolous pursuits in which everyone else is engaged, Miss Underwood thought this would be a way to take her mind off her grief, while also being of use. Those children,' he said, with a slight shake of his head, 'are being woefully neglected.'

'No, they aren't,' put in Horatia indignantly, proving that she'd overheard his attempt to convince Perceval he was being tactful. 'Miss Underwood just has a lot on her hands, that's all. And why anyone should take it into their heads to drag their children from their own homes and then abandon them to the care of strangers, I cannot think.'

He exchanged a glance with Perceval then, expressing a shared, masculine exasperation at the female's ability to contradict herself and the impossibility of pointing it out.

'But surely,' said Perceval, doggedly refusing to be distracted from his primary concern altogether, 'this is not a suitable place for the planning of—'

'It is not only the perfect place for the planning of,' Nick said, cutting him off before he could really get going, 'it is also one of the stages for the hunt itself.' He drew out a sheaf of paper on which he'd scribbled his ideas for a clue to lead to this very spot. *'"Though it is said the world cannot contain all the books that may be written, the room of books can hold the globe,"'* he quoted and waved his hand to a geographical globe that rested upon a stand near the window. In the lower part of the stand was a shelf with a drawer. Last night, he'd ascertained that currently it was empty. 'There is a perfect place to conceal a clue and a bag of sweets for whoever finds it first. Miss Underwood has dispatched a footman to the village to purchase them.'

'But as you can tell,' put in Horatia, with a wry grimace, 'that clue still needs a bit of work. The other ones we've written are all in rhyme.'

We've written? He raised one eyebrow in Horatia's direction at that claim, causing her to tighten her lips in disapproval.

'Well, still,' blustered Perceval, 'I must insist that a better place for you to work together would be one of the drawing rooms, where there are footmen in attendance. And other ladies would be present.'

'But Miss Carmichael needs to see the rooms where we are to place the clues.'

'Why?'

'For inspiration, of course. How is she to help me create verse that will amuse the children, while leading them to the correct spot, if she has not seen the place where I believe a clue should be left?'

'Which reminds me,' said Horatia. 'Don't we need to be moving on now? To the main hall? You did want to leave a clue in that suit of armour you were telling me about, didn't you?'

'Hush,' he said with a frown. 'I don't want you giving Perceval here any hints.'

'Oh, but surely, since he doesn't have any children of his own, he isn't going to pass any information on to anyone about where we are going to hide anything, is he?'

Perceval swelled at the implied insult. 'You cannot possibly think that I...that any of His Grace's guests would stoop to such sneaking behaviour? Just so that their child might win a bagatelle?'

Well, at least two of them were passing on information to supporters of Bonaparte in France. So, yes.

'It is not about the prize itself, but the notion of winning,' said Nick firmly. 'And we have no intention of letting anyone gain any advantage over anyone else. We want this to be a fair contest. Besides,' he added with what he hoped was a disarming grin. 'I don't want

Miss Carmichael getting distracted by the prospect of gossiping with other ladies.'

'Yes, I quite see that,' said Perceval, shooting Horatia a rather condescending look. 'The female brain is so easily distracted by such things.'

Nick had to bite his tongue to stop himself laughing at Horatia's gasp of indignation. He'd explain to her later that he'd had to say something of the sort to get rid of Perceval. Or perhaps there would be no need. Once she'd calmed down, she'd work out for herself why he'd said what he had. And would, uniquely for a member of her sex, wave aside any apology he felt compelled to make.

He was just congratulating himself on getting through the tricky situation with such ease, when there was another stir of movement in the doorway.

'Lady Tewkesbury!' Horatia looked genuinely shocked to see her friend's mother standing there. 'What are you doing out of bed?' she said, hurrying over to the woman, who did indeed look white and haggard.

Lady Tewkesbury's eyes darted round the room as though searching for someone. Her thin fingers clawed at the gauze scarf she had wound round her scraggy neck, as though she was finding it hard to breathe. Horatia clearly thought so, too, because she went to her side. 'Come and sit down while you get your breath back, Lady Tewkesbury,' she said, trying to take her arm. Lady Tewkesbury shook her off and took a step into the room.

'I don't need that kind of behaviour from a creature like you,' she spat. And then, as though noticing the men standing nearby, she said in a less abrasive tone,

'That is, I don't need mollycoddling. I just need…' She stared wildly round the room.

It was Perceval who came to her aid this time, as Nick shifted closer to Horatia in an instinctively protective manoeuvre.

'I dare say you are in need of some reading material,' Perceval said to Lady Tewkesbury. 'I understand you have been, ah, indisposed. May I hope that your venture down here is a sign that you are recovering? And are starting to wish for some occupation?'

'Yes, that's it. I am finding it very dull being cooped up in my room. I do need a book. That is why I have come to the library. Obviously.'

'As you are not sufficiently recovered to withstand the rigours of any of the more strenuous activities,' Perceval continued.

Nick exchanged a glance with Horatia. In her eyes he saw exactly the same suspicions that were forming in his own mind. Perceval was supplying Lady Tewkesbury with a valid reason for being in the library. Which clearly meant that was not why she had come here and he knew it and was covering her tracks, which put him under suspicion as well.

'Or the noise they will be making,' said Lady Tewkesbury, placing one hand to her forehead. 'I must say, when I heard that these two are encouraging children to run amok all over this great house,' she said waspishly, sending a glare in Horatia's direction, 'I could hardly believe it. A man of Theakstone's standing, permitting that sort of thing.' She shuddered. 'I thought it was going to be all elegance and sophistication here this week, not a…*romp!*'

'May I suggest,' said Perceval, extending his arm, 'that we browse the section containing the books much beloved by His Grace's stepmother. I am sure you will find something sufficiently entertaining to while away such time until you are feeling up to gracing the company with your presence once more...' Lady Tewkesbury gratefully laid her hand on that arm and allowed the secretary to lead her to a section of shelving right at the far end of the room. Where they could converse without risk of being overheard by Nick and Horatia.

And vice versa.

'Did that look as smoky to you as it did to me?' said Horatia, the moment the others had started their own muted conversation.

'Yes.'

'She never gets up before noon,' she told him in an urgent undertone. 'And always has her breakfast in bed. And never goes on her own errands, but sends Connie, her maid. If she really wanted a book...'

'Yes. I think we have established that the last thing she planned to do in this room was look for a book,' said Nick. 'The only question is, what *was* she planning to do? Or, perhaps we should be asking, who was she planning to meet?'

They both glanced at the pair who had their heads bent over an open book, as though they were studying its contents, although they were still talking in voices too low to carry far.

'It could be them,' said Horatia. 'They could be the ones who've been exchanging coded notes. I mean, the way Perceval made up a plausible excuse for her to be here, and the way she...only—' She stopped, her brows knitting. 'I mustn't jump to conclusions. What she said about the event descending into a sad romp does sound just like her. She does have some very stuffy ideas. From what Lady Elizabeth tells me, well, I shouldn't betray confidences, but…' She spread her hands wide.

He admired her for that loyalty. So he said, 'I get the point. Continue.'

'Well, it's the same with Perceval, isn't it? I mean, although what he said could be suspicious, it isn't as if it was out of character for him to talk to a female as though she has not a single thought of her own of any worth. He did it to me the entire time I was sat next to him at dinner,' she said resentfully. '*Exactly* the way he treated Lady Tewkesbury just now. So it could just be his pompous manner that made him say what he said…'

'Or it could be the perfect cloak to disguise his involvement in the…'

She nodded. 'Just what I was thinking. And he would have access to all sorts of sensitive information, wouldn't he, what with handling all the Duke's business. Only, was he in London at the…*the* time?'

'I can find out,' he said. 'In the meantime, I believe it would be worth my while to keep him under close observation. Because it looked to me as though they arranged to meet here and we foiled their attempt to be private together. That was what all the indignation was about.'

'Unless it was genuine,' she put in. 'It could have been. I mean, they do both have a point. We were behaving with impropriety.'

They had been about to, certainly.

He couldn't help grinning.

'The one thing about clandestine meetings going awry,' he drawled softly, 'is that the pair involved will be determined to arrange another. So all we have to do is keep a close watch on them both and catch them at it.'

'Catch them at what, though?' said Horatia with a pensive frown. 'It has just occurred to me—'

But she broke off before she could confide whatever it was that had just occurred to her, because Perceval was marching away to the door while Lady Tewkesbury was making straight for them.

'Perceval,' said Lady Tewkesbury to Horatia, 'has just had the gall to remind me that as you are here under my aegis, it is my responsibility to look out for your reputation.'

'What cheek,' said Nick, allowing a smile to curve his lips just the slightest bit.

'Indeed,' said Lady Tewkesbury frostily. 'However, he is right in saying that if you do ruin her reputation—' she slid a resentful glance in Horatia's direction '—I will be held responsible. Which means that I cannot allow you to stay here on your own with her.'

Horatia looked as though she was about to make an objection, but Lady Tewkesbury held up her hand. 'I shall sit on that sofa there and look at this book,' she said, holding up the slim, board-covered volume that had the distinct look of the kind of thing his mother would read. 'That should satisfy anyone's notion of propriety.'

'Oh,' said Horatia. 'But in a few moments, we may be removing to another room. We really are working on clues for the treasure hunt, you know, in spite of what that Perceval person was insinuating.'

'Then I shall have to come with you,' said Lady Tewkesbury with a martyred air. 'Drat the man.' She trailed across to the sofa and sank on to it.

Horatia turned to him with a grin. 'Amazing! Right after you saying we had to keep an eye on the pair of them, she makes my job easy for me. Just as I was thinking that I would be the first unmarried female to dog the steps of her chaperon, rather than the other way about.'

'Which reminds me. I need to keep watch on Perceval.' He frowned. Looked to the door. Looked to the sofa.

'No, we can't just abandon the treasure hunt.'

He couldn't help smiling at her. 'I can see you don't want to disappoint the children, but have you forgotten that I have the treasure hunt well in hand? That our sole purpose for going from room to room with a sheaf of clues was a ruse to enable us to hunt for a non-existent code book?'

She flushed guiltily. She clearly had got carried away with the whole charade. But instead of floundering about, she frowned, then said, 'What if I appear to take pity on Lady Tewkesbury, then, and take her back to her room? Say we are going to leave the positioning of the rest of the clues to you.'

He could have kissed her. Attention to little details such as this made all the difference between a mission failing and being a resounding success. And Herbert had always left attention to this sort of detail entirely to him. He'd been a loyal follower, but not a partner in their enterprises. Not like…

'Good thinking,' he had to be content with saying. For there was no way he was going to start kissing Horatia, or admitting that it was a rare treat to have someone apart from him doing all the thinking, not with Lady Tewkesbury watching him. Or glancing up at him every now and then from the pages of her novel, anyway.

He would have to wait until they were on their own again.

'I will get after Perceval, then. See where he is going next. We can compare notes at nuncheon.'

She nodded. 'I will look forward to it,' she said, gracing him with one of her rare smiles.

So would he. Very much.

Chapter Twenty

Horatia watched the door close softly behind Lord Devizes, then turned to Lady Tewkesbury, who was still sitting on the sofa.

Could this woman really be a traitor? Part of a group who would stop at nothing to smuggle information out of England to France? Not even murder?

She ran her eyes over the woman's face, halting at the bitter set of her mouth. She certainly had much to be bitter about. Her husband had died leaving a mountain of debt, according to Lady Elizabeth. He'd run through what should have been his wife's portion, as well as Lady Elizabeth's dowry. Which was why her mother had been urging her to marry a rich, titled man, rather than the one she truly loved. Why she had been so angry when the Duke, who had put Lady Elizabeth on a list of possibilities, had instead fallen heavily for Miss Underwood, who was nothing but a pretty little country miss. So angry that Lady Elizabeth had been surprised that she'd accepted the invitation to attend this wedding at all. Lady Tewkesbury had *said* they needed to be practical, that if they spent another week here, her daughter might meet another wealthy scion of the Duke's family and still marry well. But if that was the real reason for them coming here, why hadn't she been making more of an effort to push Lady Elizabeth at the various eligible gentlemen who were arriving daily?

It *could* be because she'd been ill ever since she'd arrived, Horatia argued with herself. She'd looked increasingly wan and then yesterday she'd finally had to retreat to her bed.

'Are you going to stand there staring at me all day, impudent miss?'

'I beg your pardon,' said Horatia. 'I was just thinking that it might be better if you went back to your room.'

'I dare say you do,' snapped Lady Tewkesbury. 'But I am not going to let you go making a fool of yourself over that…' she waved one clawlike hand at the door through which Lord Devizes had just gone '…that scoundrel. Oh, I can see why you've fallen under his spell,' she added, her mouth twisting into a sneer. 'He is an expert at sweeping silly women off their feet, then trampling over them once they have fallen.'

'I hardly think…'

'That is just the trouble. Elizabeth tells me you are intelligent, but the moment a man like that smiles at you, a woman ceases using her brain at all.'

'That is…' She'd been about to say it was unfair, but Lady Tewkesbury had pretty much hit the nail on the head. She did find it hard to use her brain when Lord Devizes smiled at her in that certain way. And, if Perceval hadn't come in just when he had, she might well have let him kiss her. If he *had* been about to kiss her. Which sort of proved Lady Tewkesbury's point. All she could think about, when he got close, was kissing.

'Yes,' sneered Lady Tewkesbury. 'I can see that hit home! You silly goose. It isn't even as if he's likely to offer marriage, since you have nothing to offer apart from a momentary diversion. You need to stay away from him, if you value your reputation.'

Well, that was just it. She didn't value it all that much. Not when weighed against the importance of tracking down Herbert's murderer. However, she did want to keep Lady Tewkesbury under observation. So she bowed her head in what she hoped looked like meek obedience.

'I can leave him to finish off preparations for the treasure hunt on his own, if you think that would be for the best,' she said.

'It most definitely is,' said Lady Tewkesbury, getting to her feet. 'So let us return to our rooms and... unless you wish to...'

'There is nothing I wish to do this morning, if I am not to help with the treasure hunt.' Apart from perhaps looking for clues in Lady Tewkesbury's room. 'Shall I come to your room and...read to you?' She waved her hand at the book. Lady Tewkesbury pulled a face and tossed it on to the sofa. 'I don't read rubbish like that,' she said haughtily. Which begged the question—why had she permitted Perceval to hand it to her, then?

Oh, yes, it would certainly be a good idea to look through Lady Tewkesbury's room for...for...well, she wasn't sure what. But she could start by having a peep into the Bible she had taken to chapel on Sunday morn-

ing. There might be marks in the margins, if not actual
coded notes for her to find. There might be all sorts of
clues she might notice, now that she was regarding her
as a possible suspect.

Lady Tewkesbury's mouth firmed into a line, as
though she was biting back some remark. Which wasn't
like her. She didn't usually spare Horatia's feelings.

'We will go to *your* rooms,' she finally said. 'The
ones you are sharing with my daughter. I shall perhaps find her there? And we may…well, I haven't seen
much of her since we got here. She has become thick
as thieves with that dreadful girl—'

There was another dreadful girl here? Apart from
Horatia? Oh, yes, Miss Underwood. The girl who'd had
the temerity to win the Duke's heart, when all anyone
had expected him to offer was his hand.

Lady Tewkesbury tossed her head and stalked to the
door. 'Come along, Miss Carmichael. I should probably
have inspected my daughter's accommodation before
now. Only I haven't felt…' She let that sentence drift
to a close rather than finishing it properly.

Bother. When was Horatia going to get a chance to
search through Lady Tewkesbury's room for incriminating evidence? Although, wasn't her reluctance to permit
her into that room at all, even when she was there, a sign
that she was hiding something? Lady Tewkesbury had
been behaving in a most inconsistent manner for some
time, Horatia reflected as she followed the lady along
the corridor and up the stairs. She'd never liked Horatia.
Not from the first moment Lady Elizabeth had taken
her home and introduced her as someone she'd met at
a lecture on the transit of Venus. And yet when Lady

Elizabeth had asked if she might come to Theakstone Court with them, saying that it might help to give her thoughts another direction, she could have sworn tears had come to Lady Tewkesbury's eyes. And she had definitely said that Horatia must not dwell too much upon her brother's death, nor the manner of his passing, but look to her own future. At the time, Horatia had put her uncharacteristic display of sympathy down to the fact that she'd been through a bereavement herself. Only Lady Elizabeth had said that she hadn't mourned her husband as much as appeared relieved to be free of him. Until the lawyers had explained that he'd left nothing to them but debt and disgrace.

Or perhaps that did explain her inconsistent behaviour. That tirade about Lord Devizes just now had sounded more as though she was talking about the men in her own life than offering Horatia advice. And the late Marquess of Tewkesbury had most certainly been a libertine and a rake. So perhaps she had experienced a flare of fellow feeling for a woman left alone in the world...

Bother again. There were two ways to look at everything, where Lady Tewkesbury was concerned. She wasn't going to be able to reach any conclusion without gathering more evidence.

Nick was having an almost equally frustrating time of it. No sooner had he reached the end of the corridor than the man he'd been attempting to pursue doubled back and made straight for him.

'If you have a moment,' said Perceval, 'His Grace would very much like to have a word with you.'

'Is that so? Why did you not say so in the library?'

'I was…on other business,' he said, looking deuced defensive. Other business, such as making contact with his fellow conspirator?

'More important than a message from His Grace?'

'Absolutely not! It slipped my mind, that is all.'

A likely story. Perceval had the reputation for being the most efficient and knowledgeable man in England.

'That is…' A muscle in Perceval's jaw twitched. 'I have…there is a lot of extra work at present. What with one thing and another. And…well, anyway, you are clearly free at the moment, so you may as well come with me to see His Grace now,' he finished with a touch of belligerence.

'May as well,' he drawled, waving his arm to indicate Perceval should precede him. He would at least know where Perceval was, and what he was doing, which had been the plan.

And what, he wondered as they set off in the direction of the downstairs offices, had the man meant by *one thing and another*? 'Are the preparations for the impending nuptials not going smoothly?'

'Perfectly smoothly,' snapped Perceval.

'Oh? It doesn't look like it to me. Not with Miss Underwood practically begging me to help out with the nursery party.'

'That is merely a sign that she is taking up the reins of governance with great skill and diplomacy,' said Perceval staunchly. 'Nobody expected so many children to arrive. No plans had been made for their management.'

Skill and diplomacy, eh? Horatia's suggestion that Miss Underwood was attempting to heal rifts in their family by getting him involved and obliging her fiancé to be grateful wasn't sounding so far off the mark now.

However, something had definitely got Perceval flustered enough to forget a message from his employer. Could it possibly be because he'd somehow found out that Nick and Horatia had joined ranks to hunt down Herbert's killer? Though, how could this man even know they were on the hunt? It sounded as if the group of traitors Herbert had discovered knew a damn sight too much. Somehow, they'd first found out that Herbert was on to them, and killed him to stop him from getting his hands on any more coded notes. But did they know that Herbert planned to pass on any information he'd gleaned from them specifically to Nick? Did they know that Horatia had been the one deciphering them?

Or, if Perceval was one of them, was he just putting two and two together and panicking?

'You will wait here a moment,' said Perceval, knocking on the door to the Duke's study and slipping inside.

Rather than missing an opportunity to hear what the pompous fellow might be saying about him, Nick set his hand to the door and, when the footman stationed there would have intervened, pushed him aside. Because the footman had expected his size and bulk to deter anyone from doing anything so outrageous, Nick's shove caught him by surprise. With the result that Nick walked into the study in time to hear Perceval saying, '...as you suspected...'

Nick shut the door behind him, walked to the window and leaned on the sill, crossing his legs at the ankle and his arms over his chest.

'Suspected?' He looked from one scowling face to the other with a bland smile. Even though his heart was beating fast and he had a sick feeling in his stomach. Because the moment he'd walked through the door he remembered the last time he'd been in here. When it had been his father sitting behind the desk and the present Duke standing, hat in hand, beside it.

'Dear me,' he said flippantly. 'This sounds serious.'

The footman then burst into the room. 'Beg pardon, Your Grace,' he said. 'Lord Devizes slipped past me. Should have—'

His Grace held up one hand to silence him. 'No harm done, Braggins. As a member of the family, I dare say Lord Devizes didn't feel the need to follow strict protocol before coming in.' He then turned to Perceval. 'You may leave us now. Both of you,' he added, eyeing the agitated footman.

Damn. Once Perceval had left, who knew where he might go and who he might contact?

'No need to leave on my account, Perceval,' he therefore said. 'I am sure that you know all about whatever it is my half-brother wishes to discuss with me and will be getting a report on it later. Why not save time by staying and getting it all at first hand?'

While Perceval hesitated, looking to his master for guidance, the footman, looking even more agitated, darted out and shut the door behind him.

The Duke flicked one hand at Perceval, summarily dismissing him.

'I am surprised,' said the Duke, the moment Perceval had gone, 'that you really think I could have a discussion of this nature in front of a member of staff.'

'Well, since I don't know what you've brought me here to discuss…' Nick spread his hands wide and gave a shrug for good measure. His half-brother's brows drew down into a deep V on his forehead that put him forcibly in mind of their father, when he'd been about to fly into one of his rages.

'In spite of my warning, I have heard reports,' said the Duke calmly, 'from several sources that you have been toying with Miss Carmichael.'

'Have you indeed?' Several sources?

'And since I saw you, with my own eyes, with her in the alcove on the corridor outside my apartments yesterday…'

'Hiding,' Nick supplied helpfully.

'You were not hiding. You were…' His face contorted with disgust. 'I won't have it, do you hear? I won't allow you to ruin some poor innocent female under my roof. I won't have you create a scandal at my wedding.'

'And that is it in a nutshell,' he sneered. 'You don't want a scandal at *your wedding*. You don't give a rap for poor Miss Carmichael's reputation.'

'No more do you, or you wouldn't be luring her into secluded spots and filling her head with nonsense.'

'Nonsense? What do you mean by that?' Had one of his sources overheard them talking about Herbert? Was that what was really at the root of his half-brother's disquiet? The fear that Nick and Horatia were about to uncover a conspiracy of which he was a part?

'The kind of nonsense you always tell women, I should think,' the Duke growled. 'The kind that gets them to lift their skirts for you, to put it bluntly.'

'Are you saying you think Horatia is the kind of

woman who would…?' He pulled himself up short. Both because he had spoken of Horatia by her given name and also because of the way he'd leapt to defend her honour.

'She is the kind of woman who stands no chance against a practised seducer like you, that is what I am saying. You have some kind of…power over women that makes them…but that is not what I wished to say. I know you hate me and would do anything to cause me embarrassment. But for God's sake, don't drag anyone else into our quarrel. Especially not a poor helpless creature like Miss Carmichael.'

Poor helpless creature? If only the Duke knew.

'I am warning you,' he continued in that same calm, cold voice, 'that if you ruin that poor creature while she is under my roof, then I shall personally make you pay for it.'

His voice might be calm, but his half-brother's face was thunderous.

He was very, very angry.

Which made Nick smile. It would have been worth flirting with Horatia just to get this result, even if it wasn't so necessary for their plans. What was more, if he now dogged Horatia's steps day and night, the Duke here would think he was doing it, and would persuade everyone else he was doing it, just to annoy *him*.

He was, in short, providing Nick with the perfect excuse to carry on spending as much time with her as he needed.

'I shall bear that in mind,' Nick said, as he made for the door. 'As I redouble my efforts. Because, do you know, if you were so set on not having any scandals at your wedding, you shouldn't have confided as much in me. Besides the fact,' he added as he opened it, 'that whenever anyone has ever warned me not to do a certain thing, or it will have dire consequences, I simply can't resist rising to the challenge.'

Chapter Twenty-One

Lady Tewkesbury turned her nose up at the rooms she discovered her daughter was having to share with—though she wasn't ill-mannered enough to say so out loud—a common person like Horatia.

And in spite of saying how worried she was about her mother's health, Lady Elizabeth did not show it. On the contrary, Horatia had the distinct feeling that if she hadn't been there, mother and daughter wouldn't have made any effort to make even stilted conversation. The atmosphere between them made her think they would much rather have stripped off their metaphorical gloves and gone at it hammer and tongs. In the end, she suggested going to the yellow salon for refreshments. They both greeted her suggestion with relief, and, the moment they got there, all three went their separate ways.

Though Horatia was not on her own for long. Lord Devizes, wearing yet another waistcoat, this one white with black embroidery, joined her at the tea urn. He was sporting his usual cynical smile, but his eyes were dancing.

'What has happened?' Horatia asked, under cover of the rattle of teacups and general buzz of conversation going on around them.

'My esteemed brother,' he said, strolling away from the nearest group of people in the direction of the fireplace. Even though he was clearly dying to tell her something, he placed his teacup carefully on the mantelpiece and started fussing with his appearance in the mirror before saying a word. And then, because she'd so often wanted to put a mantel shelf to the same use, she set her own cup next to his.

'It's working,' he said, flicking away an imaginary speck of dust from his shoulder. 'My esteemed brother is so enraged by rumours about my dastardly intentions with regard to you that he made all sorts of dire threats. It tempted me,' he said, tidying his hair, 'for a moment or two, to dislike him less, hearing how he planned to avenge you should any harm befall you while staying under his roof.'

'Yes, well, what did you expect? He is a man with solid principles.'

He shot her reflection an exasperated look as he tugged at his neckcloth.

'Only look at the way he treats his child, even though she isn't legitimate. Going to the lengths of flouting convention for her sake. Never a thought of farming her out to be raised in secret...'

She floundered to a halt when she caught a look of hurt flash briefly across his face.

'Unlike our own father,' he continued for her, 'who tossed both his legitimate sons aside when the mood took him.'

'I am so sorry,' she said, reaching out a hand to lay apologetically on his sleeve. 'I shouldn't have said that.'

'You did not. You stopped before becoming offensive.' He smiled at her then, in a not very pleasant way. 'And one advantage of your slip is that the way you are looking at me now will convince anyone who had not made up their mind about us before that you have fallen utterly under my spell.'

'What?'

He looked down, pointedly, at where her hand still lay on his sleeve.

'Oh,' she said, snatching it back. She glanced round the room. So many people rapidly looked away, with expressions of either amusement or disapproval, that she could tell Lord Devizes was correct. They all believed she'd fallen for him.

Oh, goodness. She took a sip of tea so that she could hide her face, even though only briefly, from all the people who'd been staring at her. But after taking only one sip, her eyes began to fill with tears. How she wished people could see the good in him. And there was good, plenty of it. Or he would be using his maltreatment as a child as an excuse for betraying his country and trying to bring it down round his ears, instead of actively trying to stop such a thing happening.

And he wouldn't be willing to sacrifice his own reputation while shielding hers by encouraging her to keep rebuffing him at every turn, so that he would be the one to look foolish. So that she could carry on working with him to track down Herbert's murderer.

She sighed. No man had ever encouraged her in any

of her ambitions before. Well, come to think of it, no woman had, either, apart from Lady Elizabeth.

'It is grossly unfair,' she said, setting her cup into its saucer with a snap, 'that people believe you would really pursue and ruin an innocent female simply to annoy your brother. Oh, Nick.' She placed her hand on his sleeve again and this time not caring who was watching or what they thought. 'It must be horrid to have people believe the worst of you all the time. Especially as you aren't a bad sort.'

'Am I not?'

'Not really. Oh, I know you have behaved in a rather wild fashion, but then so did Herbert. And he wasn't truly bad either. Only a bit rebellious. And I could hardly blame him, what with Aunt Matilda being so strict and disapproving of everything we did on principle, I sometimes thought. It was hardly surprising that Herbert sometimes did things to deliberately shock her. Said he might as well be hung for a sheep as a lamb.'

'So hot in your defence of him,' murmured Lord Devizes. 'And of me, but H—Miss Carmichael, I am not your brother.'

'No, but...'

'And you are not my sister. In fact,' he said, leaning in a bit closer, so close that she could feel the heat of his breath on her cheek, 'the way old Dr Grimes is looking at you, as though you are a seasoned seductress...'

She took a step back. Not only because she'd felt herself start to lean towards him and they were in a public place, but also because just one mention of that horrid old cleric made her feel as if a slug had just crawled down her back.

'I wouldn't be a bit surprised to learn that it's him.'

Lord Devizes turned and raised his quizzing glass at the chaplain, studying the way he was still looking at Horatia as though she was something that was giving him indigestion.

'What makes you think so?'

'Well, what was he doing in the main block, near the Duke's private apartments, do you suppose? Shouldn't he have been in his own rooms? Surely his quarters are in the south wing, with all the other male staff?'

'Yes, they are, but...'

'But nothing. He was behaving suspiciously. And the name of the leader of the conspirators, you know, sort of describes a clerical person.'

'You *have* taken him in dislike, haven't you?'

'No more than you have taken against Theakstone,' she countered. 'And with more reason. He was wandering about where he had no business being—'

'That we know of,' he countered.

'And he acted oddly. And what's more...'

They both looked across the room at the man in question, who was eyeing them back with disfavour.

'Yes? What's more?'

'Well, he...' She grabbed her teacup. 'He knew,' she said, mouthing the words over its rim, in the hopes that covering her mouth would prevent anyone else from understanding what she was saying, 'what you were referring to when I was kneeling in his way to stop him approaching the Duke's rooms.'

'And just when,' he said with what looked like a touch of surprise, 'did you find out what I was accusing him of?'

'Lady Elizabeth told me,' she said, taking a gulp of tea as though to wash away a nasty taste.

'I wonder how she knew?'

'I cannot bear to even begin to imagine,' she replied with a shudder. 'But that is beside the point.'

'True,' he said. 'Also, I think we have loitered in this spot long enough. Let us make our way to the buffet, get something to eat, then find a table a bit out of the way where we can discuss…the treasure hunt,' he said with a meaningful look.

Once they were settled at a table with their plates of food, Lord Devizes pulled out his plans of the house. 'Who else,' he said as he spread them out with a lot of unnecessary rustling, 'do you suspect?'

'Well,' she said, leaning in. 'What about Dr Cochrane? How do you suppose he got to the portrait gallery so quickly?'

'Quickly? What do you mean?'

'Oh, I beg pardon, you did not know. Well, Lady Elizabeth said he was attending to her mother. In her room. And yet five minutes later, up he pops miles and miles away from there.'

'Lady Tewkesbury's behaviour was downright odd, as well, wasn't it?' he mused.

'And Perceval turned up just at the most inopportune moment.'

Her face heated a little as she recalled exactly which moment the Duke's secretary had interrupted. The moment when she'd thought Lord Devizes might have been about to kiss her. She couldn't help looking at his mouth and wondering what it would have felt like to be kissed by an expert…

No, not by an expert anything. It was Lord Devizes she wanted to kiss, not some…random rake!

Oh, dear. She had to do something to take her mind off kissing him, or she'd be grabbing him by the neck-cloth and dragging him across the table and shocking everyone. Especially him.

To start with, she removed her spectacles, which had the effect of reducing him to a blur. And then, to make it look as if she'd removed them for some good reason, she started polishing them on the handkerchief she had tucked up her sleeve. Which smelled of him. Or at least, whatever soap he used to wash his linen.

She tried not to breathe in. But she couldn't help it. Well, everyone had to breathe, didn't they? Or they would faint. And how would that look?

As though she was so besotted with him that merely taking lunch with him was enough to make her swoon at his feet. Oh, dear. If she didn't watch out, she would be falling in love with him. And where would that get her? With egg, she reflected, looking at the slice of a hard-boiled one on her plate, on her face, that was where.

With a little huff of irritation, she hooked her spectacles back over her ears.

Nick couldn't tell what, or more likely who, had put that expression on her face, but he felt heartily sorry for whoever it was. She was something to behold when she was roused.

He shifted in his chair.

'So, we have a list of suspects. The Duke, his secretary, his doctor and, yes, his chaplain.'

'And Lady Tewkesbury.'

'Hmm...' He'd assumed that a man was behind it. But it could be a woman, he supposed. If that woman was as clever and as driven as Miss Carmichael.

'In the light of all we've learned so far, and, yes...' he held up his hand in a gesture of surrender '...you have uncovered most of it...'

He had to pause as she treated him to a smile of such radiance it hit him somewhere in the solar plexus. Not many people, he would warrant, had ever seen her smile like that. Or known they'd been the cause of transforming her serious face into something that resembled... well, if she used it more often, men would be falling at her feet. 'I, er...' He took in a breath, scrambling for something that would follow on from what he'd been saying before she distracted him. Something about the chaplain. And uncovering something. But thinking about the man brought back a vision of Horatia kneeling at the man's feet and the salacious conversation that followed.

Which conjured up images of that mouth doing the most wicked things to his body.

Which was wrong. Totally wrong. This was Herbert's *sister*. *Herbert's* sister. A man who was no longer around to guard her from men like him. He cleared his throat as that last reflection cleared his mind.

'Change of plans... Yes, that was what I was going to say. We need to change our plans.'

She tipped her head to one side, as though awarding him her full attention.

'We were going to use the treasure hunt as cover to search rooms for a code book. But now that we no longer need to, we should take a new tack.'

'Which is?'

'Ah.' Would she stop looking at him that way if he admitted he hadn't a clue? 'I am not completely sure.'

No. Her eyes hadn't changed. She was still looking at him as though he could accomplish anything. 'I need to mull it over,' he admitted.

'But you will find a way to flush out the guilty party,' she said with conviction.

Lord, he hoped so.

'Thank you for being so frank with me,' she said.

'Well, I've learned my lesson. There is no use pretending to know it all around you, is there? You soon saw through me last time I attempted that. Besides, now that I know you better, I...' He pulled himself up short. He was about to say he trusted her. And he did, when it came to hunting down Herbert's killer.

But that was all. All he would allow it to be.

'Anyway, until I come up with a plan, we may as well get the treasure hunt out of the way. Ah, Miss Underwood,' he said, noting that she was looking their way. 'May we have a word?'

Once he'd established that the footmen had successfully raided the local sweet shop and found a carpenter who made ingenious toys from offcuts, he explained that they'd completed the clues and saw no reason not to run the treasure hunt that very afternoon. Which put a smile on Miss Underwood's face, too.

'I do need to just assemble the relevant footmen and give them their clues and instructions,' he said, getting to his feet. 'I will see you again at three,' he said to Horatia, 'or thereabouts, in the schoolroom.'

Horatia supposed she shouldn't have been surprised when Lady Tewkesbury said she ought to act as chaperon while she and Lord Devizes were gallivanting all over the house with the children, after what Perceval had said that morning. When it was time to set out, Lady Tewkesbury grumbled all the way up the many flights of stairs and the moment they reached the schoolroom sat down in the first chair she saw, fanning her face and breathing heavily.

Miss Underwood was already there, as was the Duke himself. He was sitting on the window seat that his daughter had perched on before, gazing down to where she knelt at his feet, petting the little white dog that was never far from Miss Underwood's side, his features, for once, not looking the slightest bit stern.

Horatia instinctively dropped into a deferential curtsy, but the Duke barely acknowledged her, so intent was he on his daughter. He did stiffen, however, when Lord Devizes came in some moments later. Miss Underwood went to the Duke's side and gave him a speaking look. The Duke rose to his feet and stalked across the room.

'I believe that thanks are in order,' he said to Lord Devizes. 'You have clearly gone to a lot of effort to help entertain these children.'

Miss Underwood beamed at him, though the Duke could not see her, since she was still standing by his daughter.

'You should know that I didn't do it to gain your

approval,' drawled Lord Devizes. He inched closer to Horatia. 'It simply gave me a perfect excuse to be alone with this adorable creature.'

Horatia's face grew hot. The Duke's grew stormy. Miss Underwood's smile vanished. And Lady Tewkesbury gave a disapproving sniff.

'Lord Devizes, do you have the first clue,' said Miss Underwood, breaking through the tension that was mounting between the adults. 'The children are all so excited and are longing for the treasure hunt to begin.'

'Of course,' he said, bestowing one of his knee-melting smiles in her direction, which caused the Duke to make a low, menacing noise in his throat that, coming from a lesser man, would have been described as a growl.

With a flourish, Lord Devizes withdrew two sheets of paper from one of his pockets.

'First of all, you children need to form into two teams.'

'Boys against girls,' cried the two little boys who'd been torturing the smaller girls the last time Horatia had been up here. The girls looked as though that suited them fine.

'And which of you two ladies,' he said to the governesses, 'will be supervising which team?'

They looked at each other. 'We ought really to look after our own charges,' said the taller, thinner of the two. 'Only we each have children of each sex.'

'I can look after the girls,' said the nursemaid, hoisting the baby on to her hip. 'If you like.'

'Then that's settled,' said Lord Devizes before anyone could raise any objections. 'Here is your first clue,' he said, handing one sheet of paper to her. 'Which of you wishes to take the clue for the boys' team?' he then added, holding out the other sheet in the space between the two governesses.

The shorter one grabbed it and, beckoning the boys of the nursery party, went over to the desk, the taller governess hot on her heels.

The Duke's daughter, who'd been reading the clue over the shoulder of the nursemaid, suddenly said, 'Oh!' And then, checking the end of the room where the boys were still watching the two governesses quarrelling over who should be in charge, beckoned the other girls to her side.

'I know where that is,' Horatia heard her inform the girls, although she had kept her voice low so that the boys wouldn't overhear. 'Come on,' she said and dashed to the door.

'And that is our cue, I think,' said Lord Devizes, 'to leave also.' He held out his arm to Horatia. 'Lady Tewkesbury,' he said, holding out his other arm.

'I can't,' whimpered Lady Tewkesbury, raising her hand to her forehead. 'I simply cannot go charging all over the house after a pack of—' She broke off as the boys, with an assortment of hunting cries, went charging past the adults who were standing by the door. 'No,' she said again with more determination. 'I will not be a party to...*that.*'

'Don't you worry, Lady Tewkesbury,' said Miss Underwood. 'I can act as chaperon to Miss Carmichael, if you really think it is necessary for her to have one.'

'As if you have not enough to do,' growled the Duke.

'No, truly, I should love to see Livvy trouncing those

horrid boys…' She bit her lip and cast an appalled look at Lord Devizes. 'I didn't mean…that is, I'm sure your nephews are…'

To Horatia's surprise, Lord Devizes laughed with what sounded like genuine amusement. 'No need to apologise,' he said. 'They are horrid at that age. Perfect monsters, in fact. And Livvy, if that is her name?' Miss Underwood nodded. 'Is going to thoroughly enjoy… er…*trouncing* them. And will become, if I am not very much mistaken, a heroine in the eyes of the other girls.'

The Duke's frown eased by about a hundredth of an inch. And Horatia knew exactly why. Because it was the approval of society's females Livvy needed to acquire. And no matter what had passed between them all this far, or what motives had driven their parents to position them close to her, after today, they were likely to start forming genuine friendships.

'Shall we?' Lord Devizes held out his arm again and this time Horatia lay her hand on it without hesitation.

The Duke nodded at his wife, then extended his arm to Lady Tewkesbury. 'Allow me to escort you to the terrace. I am sure I can find you a shaded spot where you may sit and sip a cooling drink, and watch the game in progress on the lawn. It should prove very soothing.'

'Oh, that does sound pleasant,' said Lady Tewkesbury, taking his arm.

And all five of them left the nursery.

Chapter Twenty-Two

'Um...where should we head for first?' Miss Underwood had waited until the Duke and Lady Tewkesbury had descended the first set of stairs leading in the direction of the main bulk of the house, before tentatively asking the question.

'The yellow salon,' said Lord Devizes.

Ah, yes, Horatia remembered the clue he'd written, about finding a second clue under something blue.

'It really is good of you,' Miss Underwood said, 'to favour Livvy this way...'

'No,' he said. 'Do not fall into the error of thinking I am being good.'

'Then, why...?'

'Anyone who knows me well could tell you that I cannot help getting up to mischief whenever I can. But bullying is something I cannot abide. And those boys of my sisters are, as you pointed out, well on the way to becoming little monsters. It is about time that they learned that they cannot always win by dint of using their muscles.' A tightening of his jaw betrayed the fact that he felt very strongly about the subject.

For a moment, Horatia saw him in the guise of a knight errant, going about slaying…well, not dragons, but perhaps bullies, to save damsels from…only that wasn't right either. He was giving the girls a chance to prove they were just as good as the boys, not rescuing them, precisely.

And from the look on her face, Miss Underwood was thinking pretty much the same.

'It is such a pity,' she said, 'that you are at odds with Oliver. That is, my fiancé. I know that what your father did created a huge amount of…that is, I suppose it isn't my place to say anything. Only I am sure he would prefer it if you could get on…'

'Do you, indeed?'

Horatia had never seen Lord Devizes looking so cold. If she'd been Miss Underwood, and he'd turned that glacial look upon her, she would have shivered.

But Miss Underwood only smiled and shook her head. 'You are so alike,' she said, giving him a look that was almost affectionate.

'We are nothing alike!'

'That's exactly what Oliver said,' said Miss Underwood with amusement. 'One day…'

But Horatia wasn't paying attention any longer. Because she could hear a most peculiar noise. As though a horde of invisible children were running, giggling, down the staircase behind them. And from the look on his face, Lord Devizes had heard it, as well. Only there were no children in sight.

'It's the children,' said Miss Underwood, noting the way Horatia and Nick were looking all round in confusion. Even the dog had pricked up its ears and was looking about in a bewildered way. 'Well, to be more specific, the girls, I should think. Using the servants' staircase which is on the other side of that wall there,' she said, waving one arm in the direction of the wall from which, now Horatia was thinking more clearly, the sound of footsteps had really come, 'to reach wherever they think the next clue will be, so that the boys can't follow.'

'The...servants' staircase?' Horatia felt Nick's arm tense beneath her hand.

'Yes. Livvy claims to know all of what she calls the secret staircases and corridors. And all the best hiding places, too. She used to run away from her governess and hide whenever she could. Apparently, Theakstone Court is riddled with them.'

'So.' Nick's eyes narrowed as though he was trying to work something out. 'You think she has managed to reach the yellow salon and find the clue, and is on the way to discovering the next one already?'

Miss Underwood cocked her head. 'From the direction those footsteps are heading, I would say yes. If the next clue happens to be in the portrait gallery.'

Lord Devizes made no comment, but started striding off in the direction of the portrait gallery. They arrived in time to see the footman stationed at the foot of the portrait of King Charles in all his ermined glory, handing over a bag of sweets and a sheet of paper to an exultant Livvy.

'Oh, dear, at this rate the treasure hunt will be over in less than an hour,' said Horatia.

'Yes, and then we shall have to find something else to occupy the children.'

'The main prize is a selection of toys,' said Nick. 'I should think they will keep them occupied for some time.'

'Oh, yes, yes, of course,' said Miss Underwood. 'I should have—' She broke off, her face falling. 'Now what?' she muttered as Mrs Manderville, the housekeeper, came scurrying in their direction.

'It is His Grace,' said the woman, without preamble, twisting her hands together.

'Oliver? What has happened? Has he met with an accident?'

'No, no, not His Grace. *His Grace.* The Archbishop. He has just arrived.'

'But he isn't due until tomorrow!'

'Exactly,' said the housekeeper. 'And although I have his room prepared...'

'Of course you have. You are always so efficient. Nevertheless, I suppose I should come and greet him. Is that what Oliver says?'

'Bullimore has gone to inform His Grace. I came straight to fetch you.'

'Yes. He may well wish to speak to us both together... oh,' said Miss Underwood, turning to Horatia in a way that suggested she'd almost forgotten about her and Nick and the treasure hunt. 'I ought to go and meet the Archbishop. He has agreed to marry us, at very short notice, and since he's arrived a day early, it might mean—' She broke off and sighed. 'Well, I don't know what it might mean. And though I did promise to chaperon you...'

'I am sure I have no need of chaperonage,' said Horatia. 'Lord Devizes is hardly going to attempt to ravish me in broad daylight, is he?'

The housekeeper gave Horatia a very frosty stare. Miss Underwood looked a bit shocked. 'No, no, the very idea! And I would never suggest...' She glanced up at Lord Devizes a touch apologetically. 'It is just a question of observing the proprieties. You understand.'

'Perfectly,' said Lord Devizes with a completely expressionless face. 'You may go and meet your archbishop with a completely easy conscience. And for my part, I solemnly swear not to attempt the ravishment of Miss Carmichael or anyone else during the course of the treasure hunt.'

'I...' Miss Underwood blushed. 'You have a very odd sense of humour.'

Lord Devizes gave her what Horatia could only consider a rather ironic bow. But it served its purpose, for Miss Underwood and the housekeeper and the dog went trotting off together without a backward glance.

'Well,' said Horatia, once they were out of earshot. 'That leaves us free to get on with our own hunt.'

'Our hunt? Ah,' said Lord Devizes, with a nod of comprehension. 'So, where do you plan to start?'

Horatia blinked up at him. He was asking her what she wished to do? He wasn't going to dictate terms?

'Lady Tewkesbury's room.'

'And might I enquire as to why? It is only,' he said diffidently, 'that you persuaded me we had no need to search for a code book, but would do better to observe the behaviour of anyone who might be considered to be behaving suspiciously.'

'Yes. But then I saw the flaw in that plan. Which is the difficulty of working out what constitutes suspicious behaviour. When they are all such good actors.'

'Actors?'

'Yes. You know very well what I mean,' she said, with exasperation at his pretending not to understand. 'Just about all the ladies here can say smiling things to your face, then say cutting things behind your back. Which I would never have guessed they were saying, had I not only overheard them...'

'This happened during your come-out?'

'Yes.'

'I am sorry for that...'

'Yes, well, thank you, but it taught me a valuable lesson. Which I remembered just in time. That all of them are two-faced enough to carry off this kind of deception. And so, I thought—' she said, then broke off. 'Look!'

She pointed along the gallery, to where the girls had all suddenly gone surging away from the footman and then, one by one, appeared to vanish through the wall.

'Well, that saves us wasting time searching for the door to this *secret* passage,' said Lord Devizes. 'All we need to do is follow the children. And, since we can be said to have a special interest in the outcome of the treasure hunt, nobody is going to be at all surprised at us doing so. Shall we?'

She didn't bother answering. Just hitched up her skirts and dashed off after the children, before the secret door could close. It turned out to be in the form of a slight alcove, rather similar to the one into which she'd dragged Lord Devizes, when she'd been trying to hide from the Duke.

She peered into the corridor on the other side. It was narrow, with a woven rush mat running down the middle of the stone floor, presumably to muffle the sounds of servants going about their business. And it was lit by a succession of small squares of glass, high up on the facing wall. She'd probably be able to see them from outside, if she stood in the courtyard and searched for them. But they were so tiny she'd just think they were part of the elaborate decorations that smothered every inch of the outside walls.

Lord Devizes followed her into the narrow passage and allowed the door to shut behind them. 'Well, this certainly explains how Dr Cochrane managed to get from Lady Tewkesbury's room to the portrait gallery so quickly.'

'Indeed it does. This way,' said Horatia, darting off in the opposite direction from that in which the girls, and the hapless nursery maid, were running. 'It should bring us out somewhere in the ladies' wing.'

'Where we are going to search Lady Tewkesbury's room for something that is *not* a code book.'

She glanced over her shoulder at him and almost caught him smothering a smile.

'You find this funny?'

'I find you vastly amusing,' he said with a grin.

'Look, I have good reason to want to search Lady Tewkesbury's room.'

'I am sure you do,' he said. Patronisingly.

'Yes. She grew very agitated when I suggested going to her room with her. I'm pretty sure she's hiding something. Not a code book. But…*some*thing.'

'And will you know what it is when you find it?'

'I hope so. I mean…it is as I was saying before. About everyone being good at hiding their feelings.

The only one who is agitated, as far as I've been able to see, is Lady Tewkesbury. Only, I can't see why she would betray her country. Or get mixed up with the sort of people who would murder Herbert just because he was on to them. She is far too high in the instep, surely?'

'Ah, well, that is no indication of loyalty to the Crown, so I have discovered,' said Lord Devizes, for the first time sounding anything but amused. 'Being high in the instep, as you put it, can be a motive in itself. The way the present monarch and his son have been carrying on is enough to turn the most High Church Tory into a screaming radical. Especially those from families who are old enough to consider the pair of them German upstarts.'

'Oh!' Horatia had never considered that before. 'But…to pass on state secrets to agents of the French government…what would they hope to gain from that? I mean, even if they could get rid of the Hanoverians, the French model of government wouldn't be much of an improvement, would it? Especially when you consider that most of the French nobility either got killed or had to run away, and lost pretty much everything.'

'As to what they hope to gain, in this particular instance, it is the hope of restoring the French emperor, I believe, since the agents we have in France have been informing us that there are many of his ardent followers attempting to get him released from his exile because they don't want the monarchy restored there. Bonaparte did, after all, bring order out of the chaos that their revolution created.'

'But…' She paused and turned to him. 'Surely, if he

did leave Elba, not all the French would support him. Wouldn't it mean…war?'

'Yes,' he said grimly. 'Which is why people like myself have been working so hard to discover who, in England, is sending those…agitators so much information.'

'And why you are even prepared to listen to *my* suspicions about who might be involved.'

'Well, that, and the fact that we have to find some way of passing the time, since I have promised faithfully not to attempt to ravish you. On the name of an archbishop.'

'You did no such thing! Not…the name of the Archbishop bit, anyway, because they never said his name. Oh…you…' She just, but only just, resisted a strong urge to slap him. Then shook her head at allowing him to provoke her into reacting exactly the way his sister had done. A way which she'd despised as being childish.

And he had deliberately provoked her, she rather thought. Because he'd been getting too serious. Letting her see too much of what he really felt, deep down. And making a joke of everything was his way, or at least one of his ways, of keeping people at a distance.

Keeping *her* at a distance.

'Stop teasing me,' she said firmly.

'Must I?'

'Yes.' There was no need for it. And it wasted so much time. Time they didn't have. 'Now,' she said, scanning the corridor. 'I wonder which of the doors along here will take us into Lady Tewkesbury's room.'

'How about,' he said, peering at a slate in the wall next to the nearest door, 'the one which has her name on it?' He then turned and grinned at her over his shoulder.

Drat the man for being so clever. Of course, the servants would have the names of their guests chalked up. Servants in a ducal household, that was, with a housekeeper as efficient as Mrs Manderville. No risk of any of the visiting staff stumbling into the wrong bedrooms, or using the excuse of getting lost when their mistress or master rang for them.

'Should we knock, do you think,' he said, 'or simply barge in and hope there is nobody there making up the beds, or hanging up freshly laundered clothing?'

'We will knock. At least,' she said, '*I* will knock and, if there is a maid there hanging up the clothes, I can make some excuse about...' Well, she was sure something would come to her. 'And you can stay right here, next to the door, where nobody inside will be able to see you.'

He nodded and gave her a mock salute.

She shook her head at his levity. Gave a brief rap on the door, squared her shoulders and pressed down the latch.

Chapter Twenty-Three

The door opened into a bedchamber. An unoccupied bedchamber.

'There's nobody here,' she said and stepped inside. She stood perfectly still, looking about the room. Rather than being divided into a separate sitting room with two small bedchambers off it, like the apartment she shared with Lady Elizabeth, this was one enormous space. There was a screen near the bed behind which she supposed there was a washstand and so forth, and a dressing table at one end. Chairs and a sofa grouped round the fireplace. A writing desk standing beneath one of the floor-to-ceiling windows. 'What do you think I should be searching for?' she said, whirling round to ask Lord Devizes, who was lounging in the open door-way, his arms folded over his chest.

'This was your idea,' he pointed out. Annoyingly.

'Yes, well… I might have been wrong.'

'What!' He feigned astonishment. 'You?'

She ignored the jibe. 'I know she was behaving oddly. For her. But perhaps she just didn't want me in here because she dislikes me and values her privacy.'

'That is,' he said gravely, 'a distinct possibility.'

'You aren't helping!'

'What would you like me to do? Argue with you?'

'No. Yes. I don't know. Come up with some ideas.'

'You already have plenty.'

'Why are you being so calm? There are only a few days before the Duke's wedding, after which we will all have to leave, then we'll never find out who is behind Herbert's murder. And I'm standing here, arguing about the wisdom of searching Lady Tewkesbury's room, when for all we know the real culprit hasn't even arrived yet.'

'Or has just arrived,' said Lord Devizes, inspecting his finely manicured nails. 'Has it not occurred to you that the term "The Curé" might be a jocular reference to a religious man who might be more than a mere parish priest?'

'You are surely not suggesting that an archbishop might be involved?'

He glanced up from the inspection of his nails, an unholy grin on his face.

'Oh, you are impossible! You are deliberately trying to annoy me. Why must you always goad people into losing their tempers with you? No, never mind, I know exactly why,' she said, stalking back to the doorway and putting her hands on her hips. 'It is a kind of armour, to repel people, in case they get too close and...'

'Well, you should know,' he said, the smile vanishing as he straightened up. 'You do the same with those dreadful clothes of yours.' He indicated her rather shabby, dyed gown. 'I know Herbert could have made you fashionable, if you'd taken his advice. But, no. You would rather retreat into your shell like a myopic snail.

I wouldn't even be surprised if there was nothing but glass in those ugly spectacles of yours,' he said, snatching them off her face.

He was wrong. About the spectacles, if not the rest. The part about her hiding from society behind a shield of awkwardness and unfashionable clothing—that was all too true. It had been her inability to cope with the cut and thrust of so-called polite society that had made her dig in her heels and emphasise all the things people had criticised her for, insisting that she could never fit in, so why should she bother?

'I need my spectacles,' she said, shaken. 'I can hardly see my hand in front of my face without them. Please.' She held out her hand. 'I need… I need…'

'Here,' he said gruffly, placing them back in her outstretched hand. And sighed. 'We are two peas in a pod, you and I,' he said, running his fingers through his hair. 'Hiding our true selves from the world behind masks of rudeness and clothing. Flashy clothing in my case. Ugly clothing in yours.'

'Opposite sides of the same coin, you mean, then,' she said pedantically, hooking the wires over her ears and taking a step back. 'Not two peas in a pod.'

'Horatia, I…'

'I am going to…' They both spoke at once. He gave her an ironic bow and extended his hand in a gesture that told her she should go first. 'I have decided to have a quick look in Lady Tewkesbury's Bible, now I am here,' she said defiantly, turning and heading for the dressing table where she'd noticed one lying out in the open. 'Just in case she has made any notes in the margins, or underlined any words for no apparent reason.'

'And if that bears no fruit?'

'I don't know,' she said grumpily.

'You could, perchance, listen to what I think we should do next?'

What, he'd had a plan all along? And had let her come blundering up here anyway? Ooh, if she wasn't already halfway across the room, she would have been sorely tempted to slap him. Though, since any attempt to do so would have resulted in him grabbing her wrist well before her palm got anywhere near his smug face and making her feel even more inadequate while he had a good laugh at her, it was just as well she was halfway across the room.

She took a deep, calming breath. Picked up the Bible that was laying, so conspicuously, on the dressing table next to her ladyship's hairbrushes.

'You have a plan,' she said, as nonchalantly as she could, while flicking through the pages.

'Of course I have a plan,' he said, shaking his head in mock reproof. 'I...' He froze. Held his finger to his lips. 'I think...' He darted back into the servants' corridor, swiftly pulling the secret door to just as the door to the main corridor opened and Lady Tewkesbury came in.

'You!' Lady Tewkesbury also froze, for a moment. 'You impudent...' she took a step forward '...meddling...' another step '...infuriating creature!' She looked at the Bible Horatia held in her hand and her face turned a ghastly shade. 'He was right,' she said, as though to herself. 'I should have stopped you long before this. In London. But I couldn't believe it was true. You couldn't have known...' She shook her head. Gazed desperately round the room. 'Make it look like an accident, he said,' she muttered to herself. 'No more loose ends...'

From the disjointed way she was talking, Lady Tewkesbury must either be touched in the upper works, or in the conspiracy up to her neck.

Part of Horatia wanted to shout huzzah! She was almost certain that she'd tracked down one of the people behind Herbert's death. Another part was shocked that it could be a lady with whom she was on, well, perhaps not exactly friendly terms, but she'd been in her house a few times and certainly considered her daughter her friend.

But the most part of her wanted to make sense of those cryptic comments, if there was any sense to make of them. Could the *he* of whom she spoke be The Curé? The man behind it all? And had they really suspected Horatia was involved in Herbert's work? Before she'd left London? And what did she mean about loose ends?

Well, the obvious way to find out was to ask.

'Who is making you do this? Who is The Curé?'

Lady Tewkesbury went a shade paler. 'How do you know his name...? He warned me you were dangerous. I wouldn't listen. He told me I had to stop you, but I didn't think it was necessary. You are just a...' She waved a hand at Horatia in a gesture of disdain. And then her face twisted with hatred as she started stalking across the room. But not towards Horatia. Instead she was heading for the writing desk, from which she snatched up a long-bladed letter opener.

Horatia only realised what Lady Tewkesbury intended a split second before she came running at her, slashing wildly with the letter opener. She just had time to raise the hands that were holding the Bible, using it

like a shield, as the blade came slashing down with ter-
rific force. Horatia was pushed back into the dressing
table as the knife glanced off the thick leather cover of
the Bible, then scored a line of fire across the back of
her left hand. One of her elbows struck the mirror as
she reeled back from the blow. And something went
wrong with her fingers of her left hand. She found she
couldn't hold on to the Bible any longer. As she tried to
right herself, clutching at the Bible which had saved her
before, Lady Tewkesbury raised her arm to strike again.

But the second blow never came. For Lord Devizes
was there and he'd seized Lady Tewkesbury's up-
raised hand, holding it firmly in both of his own. Lady
Tewkesbury screamed and for a moment or two went
wild, kicking and clawing at him. In the struggle, Horatia got knocked to the floor. Where she sat, stunned and
panting, and feeling slightly sick.

'That's enough of that,' said Lord Devizes, pushing
Lady Tewkesbury in the general direction of the bed,
while somehow also wresting the weapon from her hand.

'What,' came a new voice from the main doorway,
'is going on in here?'

Horatia tore her eyes from Lord Devizes, who was
standing over the bed with the bloodied letter-opener
in his hand, to see Lady Elizabeth, staring at him as
though he was a murderer. Horatia knew she was going
to have to speak up before her friend could jump to the
wrong conclusion.

'Your mother tried to stab me,' Horatia said. Then
frowned, for her voice sounded funny. Come to think of
it, the whole room looked funny. As if it was rippling.
And going misty.

'Mother, really,' said Lady Elizabeth, striding over to the bed. 'I know you have never liked Horatia, but surely attempting to injure her is out of line. One cannot give way to one's urges to stab people we don't like, no matter how strong the compulsion, else every ballroom would soon be littered with corpses.'

'You don't understand,' moaned Lady Tewkesbury. 'She means to ruin us. She knows…'

'Knows what?'

'Never mind standing there talking,' said Lord Devizes, suddenly looming over Horatia. 'You need to call for help.'

Grim-faced, he started clawing at his neckcloth, while behind him, Horatia saw Lady Elizabeth run across the room and tug on a bell-pull.

'Don't,' Horatia whispered as he started winding the strip of muslin round her hand. 'You will ruin it.'

'As if that matters,' he growled, pulling it tight. Making her wince. 'I have to stop the bleeding.'

'Bleeding?' Horatia tore her gaze from his face and looked down at her hand, which was now wrapped in a makeshift bandage, which was going red. There was a small red puddle on the floor beneath her hand, too. And, come to think of it, her hand hurt. Rather a lot.

'It will take for ever for someone to answer the bell,' said Lady Elizabeth, from somewhere out of sight. Horatia heard her run across the room again and saw the door fly open, then heard her friend scream for help. At the top of her lungs.

But then everything went dim.

And then faded away altogether.

Chapter Twenty-Four

She'd fainted away. From loss of blood. Or was it just the shock? How would he know? It was a doctor she needed, not a man who had never taken care of anyone else in his life.

Nick looked impatiently at the empty doorway, then at Lady Elizabeth, who was fussing over her mother who was now lying face down on the bed, moaning. And then at Horatia, lying so still and pale in his arms. He fought the urge to crush her to his chest and weep into her hair. It wouldn't do her any good. Like as not it would only make matters worse.

Dammit, why didn't anyone come? What would he do if Horatia died? He would be alone again. Horribly alone, after knowing what it felt like to have someone at his side these past few days. Someone *on* his side, come to that. At that point his own stomach rose up and almost choked him.

But then, thank heaven, Horatia's eyes flickered open. 'What…?' she murmured.

'You fainted,' he said.

'Nonsense. I never faint.'

'No, you are far too sensible,' he said, stroking an errant strand of hair from her lovely face. She was back! His darling, prosaic, sensible girl...

'Yes, and nobody has ever tried to stab me before,' she pointed out. Although she was not making any protest about being held in his arms, or about him stroking her face. Even though they were not alone.

'A glass of water might help,' suggested Lady Elizabeth, from the bed. 'Or sal volatile.'

Since he had not the faintest idea where to procure sal volatile, he looked about the room for a jug of water and a glass, and spotted them on a table next to Lady Tewkesbury's bed.

He let go of Horatia, reluctantly, to go and fetch the glass that Lady Elizabeth had swiftly poured and was now holding out to him. At which moment, Dr Cochrane finally arrived. His eyes flicked from the tableau round the bed, to where Horatia was lying propped up against the dressing table, her bloodied hand limp at her side.

'What has happened?'

Lady Elizabeth darted Nick a glance that was half-despair, half-pleading, over the rim of the glass.

'There has been the most stupid accident,' said Nick, taking his cue from Lady Elizabeth. 'Miss Carmichael cut her hand and Lady Tewkesbury apparently dislikes the sight of blood so much she is near to swooning. And then Miss Carmichael really did swoon. Only for a moment or two,' he added, at the sound of a faint protest from Horatia.

Dr Cochrane, far from going over to attend to her, stalked over to the bed. 'Is that true?' he enquired of Lady Tewkesbury, coldly.

'No!' Lady Tewkesbury sat up and threw out one hand in a beseeching manner. 'I did my best. But he—' she indicated Nick '—was hiding nearby, somewhere, and got the knife from me.'

'Oh, Mother,' groaned Lady Elizabeth. 'Please, don't listen to her, Doctor. She doesn't know what she is saying. She hasn't been in her right mind since Father's demise...'

'That,' said the doctor with a strange smile, 'is a story we could put about to explain this, yes.'

'What?' Lady Elizabeth stared at him as though he'd just sprouted horns and a tail.

And Nick suddenly saw why the man hadn't gone to bind up Horatia's wound right away. Why he was always attending to Lady Tewkesbury for her headaches and why she never seemed to get any better. Why she'd burst in on him and Horatia in the library, looking as though she'd flung her clothes on haphazardly, shortly after the doctor had confronted them in the portrait gallery after they'd been discussing how they planned to hunt down Herbert's killer. He'd heard it all. He must have been skulking in the servants' corridor. Because, now Nick came to think of it, he'd appeared right about at the spot where the children had just shown him the location of the hidden door.

'It is you,' snarled Nick. 'You are The Curé. You are the one leading the group of traitors who are passing secrets to the French and who had my friend murdered.'

'What?' Lady Elizabeth was now looking at Nick as though *he'd* sprouted horns and a tail.

But Dr Cochrane was smiling at him, in a way that sent a shiver down Nick's spine.

And then he saw the pistol in the doctor's hand, which he was pointing at Horatia.

'No,' cried Lady Elizabeth, clinging to the bedpost as though her legs were no longer strong enough to hold her up. 'You cannot mean to shoot Horatia!'

'Not only shall I do so, but you,' sneered the doctor, 'will tell everyone that it was an accident.'

'Don't be ridiculous,' said Lady Elizabeth tartly. 'Why should I say any such thing?'

'Because if you don't,' said the doctor with a soft laugh, 'your mother will pay the price. And so will you. You might have been able to hold up your head after your father gambled away his fortune, but you won't survive the scandal of having a mother who is a traitor to her country. And a murderess besides.'

'I didn't kill anyone,' protested Lady Tewkesbury feebly.

'I will tell everyone that you killed her brother,' said the doctor. 'And that I have been shielding you from the consequences of that act ever since.'

'But it was you,' she protested. And then, when Horatia gasped, turned to her daughter and added, 'He wanted to kill your friend then. But I said there was no need, that she couldn't possibly be any threat to us.'

'This cannot be true,' said Lady Elizabeth faintly, clinging even more tightly to the bedpost.

Nick had heard enough. 'Don't worry, my lady,' he said, taking up a position directly in front of the doctor. 'I won't let him hurt Horatia. He will have to kill me first.'

'What a splendid idea,' said the doctor, turning the pistol on Nick. 'And then we can say she shot you...oh, perhaps because she caught you making advances to Lady Elizabeth. And she will hang for it.' He grinned. 'Two birds with one stone.'

'No,' cried Lady Elizabeth and flung the glass of water in the doctor's face. As he flinched, and blinked his eyes, Nick seized the opening she'd given him to lunge at the doctor's gun hand, hoping to wrest it from him the way he'd parted Lady Tewkesbury from her knife. As he leapt, the gun went off. He felt no pain, only heard some glass shattering somewhere behind him and a piercing scream. By God, if the villain had hurt Horatia, Nick would kill him with his bare hands. The force with which he then fastened them round the older man's neck sent them both tumbling to the floor.

Nick had never been much of a one for this sort of dirty, rolling-on-the-floor fighting. Boxing in Jackson's saloon was much more his style. And he soon discovered that in spite of his advancing years, the doctor had plenty of the meaner sort of fighting moves.

But then, all of a sudden, the room seemed to be full of boots and fists, and he was being pulled away from the doctor and held round his chest with his arms pinned to his sides.

'Enough,' came the voice of his half-brother. 'Stop fighting my man, Nick. It's over now. It's over.'

Sure enough, the Duke's secretary was kneeling beside the doctor, who seized the moment by affecting a most piteous groan. The Duke himself was standing in the doorway.

'Would you care to explain how you came to be mixed up in...' the Duke waved his hand at the trio of terrified women, the groaning doctor '...this?'

'You wouldn't believe me if I told you,' said Nick, attempting, and failing, to throw off the hold of one of his half-brother's footmen.

'Try me. And, Peter, do let go of my brother, there's a good fellow,' he added. 'He won't be going anywhere until we have got to the bottom of this.'

'I won't be going anywhere,' Nick corrected him, 'until Miss Carmichael has been properly attended to. She has lost a lot of blood, I think,' he said, going over and dropping to his knees at her side.

She reached out for him and flung her arms round his neck. 'He was going to shoot me,' she said. 'You saved me.'

'Well, I couldn't let anything happen to you, could I?' he said, sliding his own arms round her waist. 'You are far too important.'

'I'm not,' she protested. 'I'm nobody.'

'No.' He lowered his head and whispered into her ear, 'You are a valuable asset to the Crown. Or you could be.'

She seemed to slump against him, then removed her arms from about his neck. 'I do beg your pardon,' she said stiffly. 'I seem to have got blood upon your coat.'

'Peter,' said the Duke meanwhile to the footman who'd been holding Nick in arms that had felt like a vice, 'run and fetch Miss Underwood. She will know what to do. Now, Devizes,' he said as the footman hurried from the room. 'The truth, if you please.'

'He was trying to ravish that poor young woman...' Dr Cochrane began to bleat. But before he could get any further, Perceval balled his hand into a fist and struck him so hard that his skull bounced off the floor.

'Begging your pardon, Your Grace,' said the portly young man, shaking his hand as though it hurt him a great deal. 'But I've been wanting to do something of the sort for some considerable time.'

'Naturally,' said the Duke. 'And he was clearly about to tell us a pack of lies, anyway. But you, Devizes,' he said, turning to Nick again, 'I should very much like to hear your statement.'

Nick glanced up at Lady Elizabeth. 'Go ahead,' she said wearily. 'I've had enough of trying to keep up appearances. Let's all admit to the truth, for once. No matter the cost.'

Nick looked at Perceval, then at his brother. He really didn't want to admit to the role he'd taken up with Herbert. Nor mention the men who had been employing them. Nor expose Horatia's part in it. As it stood, she could well be England's secret weapon against spies, with her remarkable ability to decode even the trickiest of ciphers. But only if her ability remained a secret.

'We heard most of it from the doorway,' said the Duke. 'I am only curious as to how you came to be on the trail of the same...' his nostrils flared with distaste '...criminal as myself.'

'If you were listening at the doorway,' said Nick, rapidly reviewing exactly what had been said during the past few minutes, 'then you must have heard him confess to having murdered Miss Carmichael's brother. My good friend, Herbert.'

'Ah. You and Miss Carmichael were trying to see if you could discover who was behind it, were you? Was her brother by any chance working for...the government?'

'Yes,' said Nick, relieved that the man had given him a slant to it that he could work upon, without giving too much away. 'And Miss Carmichael came into possession of a note which led her to believe the…traitors were going to meet here…'

'Ah. Now it makes sense. Nothing less than the hunt for a murderer could have induced you to put aside the enmity you have nursed against me for so many years and attend my wedding.'

Nick hung his head. It had been nothing so noble. He'd been at a loose end without Herbert and, consumed with thwarted rage, had decided he might as well turn it on this man.

Who had never deliberately done him any harm.

'No wonder you spent so much time with each other,' observed the Duke. 'While pretending to organise that treasure hunt, were you in fact searching all over the property for evidence of some kind? Which led you to sneak into Lady Tewkesbury's room while you thought she was safely outside on the terrace with me?'

'No,' said Lady Tewkesbury, suddenly sitting up. 'Doctor Cochrane was telling the truth. Lord Devizes was attempting to ravish my daughter…'

'Oh, spare me that tale,' said the Duke impatiently. 'Aside from the fact I was standing there listening to you and your accomplice concocting that catalogue of lies, do you seriously think I would ever…' he strode to the bed where he stood glowering down at her '…believe that he would attempt rapine upon a damsel of good birth, not even to cause me maximum embarrassment. He is many things, but an out-and-out villain is not one of them.'

It wasn't exactly a glowing encomium, but even so, the faint praise reached a place deep inside Nick that Horatia had already started to thaw.

'Besides,' put in Perceval, still rubbing his knuckles ruefully, 'we have been watching Dr Cochrane's movements for some time.'

'You knew he was a traitor?' All his animosity for his brother flared up again. 'You knew about him and did nothing? He almost killed Horatia!'

'We did not know,' said the Duke testily. 'Not for certain, until just now, that it was him. We only knew that *someone* from Theakstone Court had such strong sympathy for the French that they have been stirring up trouble. They arranged for saboteurs to wreck a fireworks display put on to celebrate the Peace with France, among other things. Although, to start with we suspected Mrs Stuyvesant. The governess,' he explained to the room at large, 'since the incidents tailed off after we dismissed her from her post.'

'But the woman was recommended for that post by Dr Cochrane,' put in Perceval indignantly. 'A woman who we later discovered had no experience with children at all. A woman who spent so much time whipping up local people with her revolutionary notions that His Grace's little girl ended up running wild round the estate, with nobody knowing where she was. And *anything* might have befallen her.'

Ah, well, that explained why the secretary had been so distracted he'd forgotten a message from his employer. He was on the hunt for whoever had infiltrated the Duke's household, right under what he'd thought was his efficient nose. And, now he'd discovered it was the doctor, a man he'd trusted, it explained why the normally placid young man had been driven to punch him in the face.

'Revolutionaries?' Lady Elizabeth was looking from one to the other of them in astonishment. 'Saboteurs? Murderers? Good grief, and I was told this was going to be an elegant, sophisticated gathering, not a...' She looked down at Nick and Horatia. 'But I still don't understand why on earth anyone would want to kill Miss Carmichael.'

'Because her brother was investigating the ring of traitors,' said Nick, 'of which Dr Cochrane seems to have been the ringleader from the London end. And when he got too close to them and they killed him, Horatia vowed to track them down.'

'Yes, but...how was Mother mixed up in it?'

Lady Tewkesbury burst into noisy sobs. 'Your father left us in such a mess! N-no m-money, n-no h-home, n-no p-provision at all! And there were papers...l-lying ab-bout his d-desk. And then h-he said I c-could get good money for them.'

'He? The doctor?' the Duke barked at Lady Tewkesbury, causing her to put her hands over her face.

'Yes! He said my husband had already sold him valuable information. And that he would only keep quiet about him being a traitor as well as a bankrupt if I handed over some outstanding papers he'd already bought. And it was only a handful of documents, which he'd left out on his desk. Not even in a drawer!' She lifted her head then and waved her arms wide, as if in appeal to the whole room. 'But then, once I'd done that, he contacted me again and said he would expose me, for what I'd done was treason. And then I had to k-keep w-working for them…'

This time when she broke down the tears looked more genuine than before. Even Lady Elizabeth seemed moved by them, for she went to sit on the bed next to her mother and tentatively patted her knee.

This was the moment the footman returned, with a rather flustered-looking Miss Underwood in tow.

To her credit, she neither screamed nor began asking foolish questions. She just came straight over to where Nick was kneeling, gently took hold of Horatia's hand and began examining the blood-soaked make-shift bandage.

'Shut the door now, Peter,' said the Duke. 'And make sure nobody comes in. We have,' he said grimly to those remaining in the room, 'some decisions to make.'

Chapter Twenty-Five

'Can you deal with Miss Carmichael's injury?' the Duke asked Miss Underwood. 'If possible, I would rather not bring anyone else in until we have decided how to account for this...episode.'

Miss Underwood nodded. 'I will do what I can. It doesn't look all that deep.'

'She lost so much blood she fainted,' said Nick angrily. At which point, realising she was still lying slumped in Nick's arms, she made a half-hearted attempt to sit up. His arms tightened round her. And she gave up even attempting to look as if she wasn't exactly where she wanted to be. Even though she would rather he valued her as a woman and not an *asset to the Crown.*

'We did it, Horatia,' he said, hugging her a bit harder. 'Together we found the traitor. The murderer.'

'I'm not a traitor,' wailed Lady Tewkesbury, drawing attention back to herself as though her concerns far outweighed anyone else's. 'Nor did I kill anyone. I couldn't!'

Horatia was tempted to remind everyone that wasn't

strictly true. That Lady Tewkesbury had just flown at her with a surprisingly sharp letter-opener and, but for her quick reflexes and the sturdiness of that Bible, would have plunged it into her throat.

'He *made* me come here,' she declared, pointing at the prone figure of Dr Cochrane. 'He wanted me to take the place of that Mrs Stuyvesant person, passing messages and information on to his minions as though I am some kind of errand boy,' she said indignantly.

'Would you be prepared to testify to this?' said Nick.

'I can't go to court. I cannot face the shame,' wailed Lady Tewkesbury. 'I would never be able to show my face in society again!'

'No, it would be a private hearing. Just a few men who are involved in…' Nick darted a look at the Duke, who was frowning down at them both.

'I take it,' said the Duke, his expression changing into something bordering on respect, 'it wasn't just your friend who has been working for the Crown.' Nick's mouth firmed, as though debating what line to take. But the Duke spared him the bother of admitting it, by swiftly moving on.

'What do you suggest we do about the pair of them?' he said, indicating the sobbing Lady Tewkesbury and the unconscious Dr Cochrane.

'You are willing to let me concoct the cover story?'

'Let us say I am willing to listen to your suggestion.'

Nick's mouth quirked up on one side. 'I suggest we pack them off to London in the care of a few of your burly footmen. To those men I, ah, happen to know. Through Herbert. They will be very interested in hearing Lady Tewkesbury's account of things.'

'And what do you suggest we tell my guests? They will have heard the gunshot, even if they do not know exactly how many people were present when the weapon was fired. And they will be agog when both Lady Tewkesbury and my own physician depart without witnessing the wedding,' said the Duke, folding his arms across his chest and propping himself against one of the bedposts, reminding Horatia so much of Nick that it was uncanny.

'Well, we could say that the doctor attacked Lady Tewkesbury. That Horatia leapt to her defence and that he shot her. That the shot attracted our notice and we all came rushing in and subdued him.'

'He didn't shoot me,' Horatia pointed out. 'He missed. The bullet went through the window.'

'Yes, but we don't need to let anybody see your hand without the bandage. So nobody will ever know that you were stabbed, rather than shot. And as for Lady Tewkesbury,' said Nick without taking a breath, 'she is so overcome by the horror of the attack that she will have to retire to some quiet spot, where her nerves may recover.'

'Whereas she will actually be in London testifying.'

'Yes, but I shouldn't think it will take long. Most of what she says is only corroborating what we already knew. Or guessed. And then…'

'I think I know the very place where she might go,' said the Duke, 'to recover from all aspects of her ordeal. I have it on good authority,' he said, turning to Lady Elizabeth, 'that Leipzig is a most salubrious spot. Not only will she be removed from all the gossiping tongues, but I hear that one can live very economically there.'

'Leipzig,' cried Lady Elizabeth. 'You are really sending us to Leipzig?'

The Duke nodded.

'Then, since Mama cannot show her face in society again, and we will all be poor as church mice, there will be nothing to stop me marrying Mr Brown!'

He nodded again. 'I always did think you should marry nobody *but* him.'

'And you have made it possible,' she said, beaming at him. 'I take back every ungenerous thing I ever said about you.'

'And,' said the Duke, turning back to Nick as though Lady Elizabeth's faint praise was making him uncomfortable, 'how do you propose we explain Dr Cochrane's journey to London?'

'Surely you cannot continue to employ a man who is a danger to females. I dare say you know of some asylum where he may be confined?'

'I can soon find one,' said Perceval.

'And you,' said the Duke softly. 'You will, of course, marry Miss Carmichael.'

What?

'Naturally,' said Nick stiffly.

'No,' said Horatia. 'There is no of course about it. You know now that Nick was only pretending an interest in me so we could work together to find Herbert's killer. That it was just a ruse.'

'Yes,' said the Duke. 'But a lot of people will talk about…the way you two have been behaving. Culminating in this…'

'Let them talk,' she said. 'I don't go about in society, so I shan't hear it.'

'You will, in effect, go into seclusion and allow my brother to face public censure alone?' He looked at her as though he was extremely disappointed in her.

But Nick remained silent.

'You could always come to Leipzig with us,' said Lady Elizabeth, causing her mother to throw up her hands in horror. 'It was just an idea,' said Lady Elizabeth, backing down at once.

'If you truly don't wish to marry my brother,' said the Duke, ignoring Lady Elizabeth's suggestion, 'then, of course, we will come up with some other way to bring you through this without any stain attaching to your character.'

Not want to marry Nick? Oh, it would be the best thing that could possibly happen to her, if he truly wanted it. But he didn't. He was just dealing with her in the way he was dealing with all the other loose ends. And she had no intention of being tidied away, then spending the rest of her life shrouded in a falsehood.

'And what if,' said Nick, 'somebody—' he glanced up at Lady Tewkesbury '—should spread the tale of how I held you in my arms and you put up no protest.'

'Why, obviously it is because I am too weak from loss of blood, and too shocked by the whole experience, to properly know what I am doing,' she said waspishly.

'I see,' he said and shifted away from her, then stood up, walked over to the window and began examining the shattered pane.

It felt very cold and lonely once he was no longer holding her in his strong embrace. But she was going to have to get used to the feeling. Of being cold and lonely, that was. Because he wasn't going to *beg* her to marry him, was he? Because he didn't truly wish to be married. To anyone. He'd just gone along with the Duke's suggestion, as a way of tidying up the whole affair in such a way that gossip would quickly die down.

Suddenly, she felt very ill again.

'Do you think,' she asked Miss Underwood, who was, she discovered, holding her hand, 'I could go back to my own room now? I need, I need…' Her lower lip began to tremble. Oh, no, she wasn't going to burst into tears, was she?

She was. And nothing, not even the way Miss Underwood put both arms round her and started making shushing noises, was able to make her stop.

Chapter Twenty-Six

She was an idiot. A prize idiot. She could have been looking forward to her own wedding, instead of lying here, all woozy from whatever it was that Mrs Manderville had given her to drink, wishing she'd agreed to marry Nick when she had the chance, even if it would mean betrayals and humiliation and heartbreak for the rest of her life. Wouldn't it have been better than sinking into a sort of grey sludge of a life, with Aunt Matilda in that gloomy little house? At least if she was fighting with Nick she'd feel alive.

But it wouldn't have been fair on him. He'd only gone along with what the Duke said out of some sort of notion of tying up loose ends, or protecting her reputation, or possibly even cementing the fragile bond she could see beginning to form between him and his half-brother, or some warped sense of duty, or...

Oh, who knew what had motivated him to agree to the Duke's absurd plan? And she'd never know. Because she wasn't likely to see him again. He'd be too busy now, escorting Dr Cochrane to London and the men who wanted to question him. And probably making sure Lady Tewkesbury didn't get away without making a full confession, either. *That* was his duty. His real duty.

And no doubt he'd make it sound as if his sudden absence right before the wedding was in keeping with his long-standing enmity for his half-brother. People would say he couldn't stomach attending the ceremony. Or that he was allergic to weddings altogether.

People would say...

People.

She hated people!

She rolled on to her side and reached for a fresh handkerchief. She didn't know what had come over her. She'd never been much of a one for tears. Not even after Herbert had died. Back then, she'd just been fired up with a furious determination to avenge him. Well, she'd done that now. Perhaps that was why she could finally cry. Why she was doing so much of it.

Or perhaps it was the medicine that Mrs Manderville had given her to try to calm her down and deal with the throbbing pain in her hand. Perhaps that was what was making her feel as though her limbs were made of lead and her future look so depressing. Why she was wishing she'd never come to Theakstone Court.

No, no, she mustn't wish she hadn't come. She'd discovered the ringleader of the people responsible for Herbert's death. And now they'd pay. Dr Cochrane would pay.

But Herbert was still dead. And her life could never go back to the way it had been, with him bringing her all those coded messages to decipher. Though it wouldn't be just the work she'd miss. She'd miss him.

Herbert. Without him in her life, she'd have nothing to look forward to.

And without Nick, she'd dwindle into an old maid, because she wouldn't dream of marrying anyone else. Not that anyone else would ever ask her. She was doomed to become an irritable old maid, who would take out her frustrations on the servants and any hapless relatives who had the misfortune to darken her doorstep. She'd end up as bad as Aunt Matilda. Probably worse, because at least Aunt Matilda had a coterie of friends. Friends who'd invited her to go to Bath with them while Horatia was at this wedding. And the only person who could tolerate Horatia was Elizabeth. Who was going to swan off to Leipzig to marry her impecunious scientist.

Yes, she was going to dwindle into a lonely old age and die unmourned. And then...

A furtive sound from the other side of her room had her turning her head in alarm. Miss Underwood had said nobody would disturb her. That they were going to let her sleep it off. So who was...?

'Nick!' She sat up, clutching the sheet to her breast as she saw him sidle into the room through one of those doors that led into the servants' corridor. 'What are you doing?'

She looked a mess.
She looked adorable.
But what made his heart lurch was the fact that she was neither shrieking in alarm, as if she suspected him of having evil intentions, nor giving him come-hither looks. She knew that if he had come in here, in a

stealthy manner, then it was because he had something both important and confidential to tell her. Because, in short, she trusted him.

And as to her question, what he was doing, well, it was something he'd never done before. Because nothing had mattered to him as much. So naturally, instead of saying so, he turned and shut the door behind him with a decisive snap, before he could dart out through it and run.

He turned to face her, his heart pounding. Wondering where to start.

She was looking at him with her head cocked to one side, waiting to hear him out. Still not shrieking or casting out lures. Just waiting for him to explain himself.

'This is something I've never done in my life before,' he said.

Immediately she pursed her lips in a cynical way.

'Oh, I don't mean creeping into a lady's bedchamber by a back door,' he said, interpreting that pout as easily as he could read just about every expression that flitted across her face. 'Yes, I have done that plenty of times. But what I have never done is stand up and fight for what I truly want.'

Now she simply looked puzzled. Lord, but she really couldn't see how much he wanted her! Encouraged to think he might have cause to win through, he took a couple of steps away from the door, clasped his hands behind his back and squared his shoulders.

She ran her eyes greedily over his frame. And then sighed, as though with regret. Yes, he knew he looked good, adopting this particular pose. It was why he'd adopted it. He wasn't above using every weapon available in his arsenal, not if it meant conquering her.

Although, he hoped that his most potent weapon would be the truth.

'Look, I cannot blame you for not wanting to marry me,' he said.

'What?' Her eyes flew wide. So she hadn't been expecting him to renew his proposal. Was that a good thing, or not?

Giving a mental shrug, he kept on going with the speech he'd prepared while he'd been pacing the floor of his room, after he'd had that horrible vision of what life would be like without her at his side. How he'd go back to the aimless frittering away of his days. Without even Herbert, or the work they'd begun to do, to give him some sense of…well, that he wasn't totally worthless.

Which brought him neatly to his first point.

'To start with, I thought you were right to turn me down…'

'Turn you down?' All traces of confusion vanished. She looked downright cross. 'That statement,' she said in her most nannyish tone, 'implies that you made me an offer. And you didn't. The Duke said that you ought to marry me and you just went along with the suggestion. With obvious reluctance.'

'Well,' he said, 'you would be much better off without me. I thought so from the start. I didn't want to let you into my world, a world of spies and violence and lies. Because I don't want to see you hurt. Not on my account. And, God, Horatia, when he fired that pistol and I heard you scream…'

'I did *not* scream,' she said indignantly. 'I may,' she conceded, 'have shouted in surprise...'

'When you shouted in surprise,' he said, since this wasn't the time to start arguing about things that really didn't matter. Besides which, she looked so adorable, with her hair all over the place like that, scolding him as though he was a naughty schoolboy. 'Well,' he forced himself to continue, rather than pointing out that her nightgown was slipping off one shoulder. Revealing a delicately rounded shoulder...

He cleared his throat. 'It felt as if the world had gone dark. Completely dark. If he had killed you, it would have... I would have felt as if...' He ran his fingers through his hair. 'The thing is, Horatia, I realised then, in that moment, that if I never saw you again, never held you, never kissed you, I would have lost something infinitely valuable.'

'But you just shrugged and walked away when the Duke said he'd think of some other way of explaining my involvement.'

'Yes. But then, surely you know me well enough to understand that it's what I always do? Pretend I don't care when people hurt me. So that was what I did.'

'Yes, that is what you do,' she mused. And settled back into the pillows. The pose was so inviting, that if it wasn't so important to convince her to accept his proposal, he'd have been at the edge of her bed and going into his tried-and-tested seduction routine. He did take a step nearer the bed. But only so that he could grab hold of one of the bedposts, hoping that if he hung on to that, it would help him resist the urge to reach out and take her into his arms before they'd got everything properly settled.

'It was only later,' he explained, 'when I considered just how very much I want to marry you, that I realised that for once in my life I needed to…to bare my soul to another person. And fight for what I want, rather than pretending I don't care. So, then, Horatia,' he said, gripping on to the bedpost for all he was worth, 'would you do me the very great honour of becoming my wife?'

There was a long pause. She looked him up and down. Put her thumb to her mouth and started chewing on the nail.

And then, with an expression of utter bewilderment, simply said, 'Why?'

He hadn't known he'd been holding his breath until it all went rushing from his lungs.

It wasn't a refusal, at least. She just needed convincing.

He pushed aside the temptation to kiss her into surrender. Because in years to come, she might say he'd taken advantage of her at a weak moment. Besides, it wasn't her body he wanted to conquer…although, yes, of course he did want that. But more importantly, he needed to convince her mind that he was in earnest. And know he'd won her heart.

So what could he offer her? He scrabbled for an answer. 'If you are asking what I have to offer, I must admit most people would say not very much. I am not considered a prize catch—' He broke off as she shook her head, with a touch of impatience.

'No, no, no! The question is, why on earth do you claim to want to marry *me*? I mean, apart from anything else,' she protested, applying her handkerchief to her nose, which was clearly still running after what looked, from the redness of her eyes, like a hearty bout of weeping, 'we've only known each other a matter of days.'

Well that was an objection he could easily dismiss. 'Yes, but during these days, we have spent as much time with one another as many couples do during an entire Season. And what is more, since most of it has been unchaperoned, we have been more open and honest with each other than is the norm. Besides which, we did know each other, through Herbert, for many years.'

'You are splitting hairs.'

'Possibly. But only consider the easy intimacy into which we fell from the moment we agreed to work together. As though we'd been a team for a considerable time.'

She snorted. In a most unladylike fashion.

'What does that snort denote? You surely cannot deny that we worked well together.'

'Once I'd forced you to abandon your prejudice against working with a female.'

'There was no prejudice of that nature. I told you, I didn't want you getting dragged down into the murky business of lying and spying on people. Nor expose you to the very people who killed your brother. It was only when I saw that if I didn't help you you'd go after them alone that I decided I would be better keeping an eye on you and making sure you came to no harm.'

'Exactly,' she cried, jabbing a finger at him. 'You didn't trust me!'

'Whereas you trusted me from the start. Even now, though I startled you by coming in here, I did not alarm you. You believe in my integrity in a way that nobody else ever has.'

'Well, of course I do. You would not have bothered sneaking in here without a jolly good reason.'

'You see? You make me feel...as though I could be worthy of...' He gave a half-shrug. 'You know, I fell into the work with Herbert by accident and let him believe we were carrying on with it for a lark. But it wasn't just that. For the first time in my life, there were people, besides my hen-witted mother, who believed I had value. And when you told me how solving ciphers made you feel, well, it was like finding...'

'A soul mate?'

Was that a wistful note in her voice? Lord, he hoped so.

At any rate, she hadn't yet told him that she had no intention of marrying him. The objections she was raising were all about superficial things.

'I would prefer to say that it felt as if we...recognised each other,' he told her, since that was more how it had felt to him. And he'd promised always to tell her the truth. 'It was also the total loyalty you displayed, time and time again. The way you defended me, instead of letting me take the blame...'

'Well, it was my fault you got into any of the situations we found ourselves in, wasn't it? If I hadn't kept on pestering you until you grew sick of me, you would not have been searching for Herbert's killer among the Duke's wedding guests, would you?'

'I could never grow sick of you,' he said, unfurling his grip from the bedpost, and leaning against it instead.

'Don't you know,' he said, a smile touching his lips as he folded his arms across his chest, 'how unique you are?'

'I am nothing out of the ordinary.'

'But you are. I have never once heard a woman shoulder the blame for a catastrophe, if there was a man standing by...but never mind other women. You are the one I want to marry. And if you don't I am going to die a lonely, bitter old bachelor.'

'*Pfft!* Not lonely. Not you. You will always have some willing woman warming your bed.'

'But none of them will ever be able to make me gasp with admiration at their cleverness. Nor will I be able to trust any of them the way I trust you. Nor will they make me feel that I have someone on my side, taking my part, no matter what. I tell you, Horatia, after you turned me...after I *thought* you'd turned me down,' he amended hastily, when she took a breath as though to object to the slight inaccuracy of that statement, 'I went back to my room and looked into my future. And I didn't like what I saw. Because it didn't have you in it. Oh, yes, I would have plenty of...' He scrambled for a description that would not offend her. 'Bedroom activity. And I would go out and about in society, and drink and gamble, and all the rest. But it would all be hollow. Inside I would be missing...well, you,' he concluded.

To his consternation, instead of looking pleased by the way he'd just bared his heart to her, she looked as if she was going to start weeping again.

'But I'm so plain,' she wailed. 'And you are so...' She waved her hands in his direction when her voice choked up in a despairing sob.

Was now the time to scoop her up in his arms and soothe all her insecurities with kisses? He pushed himself off the bedpost and began to reach for her.

Then thought better of it. Because her insecurities about her own appearance needed dealing with first.

'Now, Horatia,' he said sternly. 'I cannot believe you are letting a little thing like my appearance put you off. Not when so far you have always looked right through the mask that usually fools everyone else to the man I am beneath. And treated me with the respect you think that man deserves. Don't, I beg of you, turn me down because I wear the clothes of a dandy and preen every ten minutes like some fop. You know that is not who I am.'

'No, but... I am so—'

Yes. That was what he'd thought she was thinking.

'Enchanting,' he interrupted before she could say anything derogatory about herself. 'With a mind like a steel trap. I have never met anyone as clever as you, male or female. That is what I love about you most. Your mind. Your intellect is like...to me it is like...a bright, shining jewel. Now that I have glimpsed it, I covet it for my own.'

'You love me?' Her mouth gaped. Her eyes widened. But instead of beaming with joy, a frown pleated her forehead. 'Am I dreaming this? Did all this come out of that little brown bottle of Mrs Manderville's?' She pinched herself. 'Ow!'

So she did want him. He was the stuff of her dreams. Resisting the urge to throw back his head and crow with triumph, Nick finally abandoned the safety of the bedpost and went to sit on the edge of her mattress.

And took her hand, her poor little bandaged hand.

She looked at him with what, finally, looked like yearning blazing from her eyes. But only for a moment, before it dimmed as something else occurred to her.

'But when a man who looks like you, with a reputation like yours, marries a plain, awkward woman like me...' she said.

He lifted her injured hand to his lips and pressed a kiss to a patch of bare skin above the bandage. Giving her, into the bargain, the benefit of one of his most smouldering looks. She shivered, as though all the heat he put into it had percolated right down to her toes. Visiting all the relevant places in between.

'To start with,' he said, 'I have never considered you plain.' Which was the complete truth. 'And anyway, the kind of beauty that is only skin-deep fades with age. Skin that was once likened to a rose petal always wrinkles, in the end. Firm figures swell and sag. But your mind, your heart, the things that make you *you*, they will never change. Those things will continue to dazzle me, for years and years.'

'Oh...' She sighed, the anxiety fading from her eyes, and that yearning look taking its place.

'Besides, you haven't fallen for my face, have you, but the man I am inside.'

She looked worried again. 'I...I cannot deny,' she said, guiltily, 'that part of your attraction *is* the way you look.'

Now, how was he to counteract that objection?

'You always turned your little nose up at me,' he recalled, 'when you thought that *all* I had to recommend me was my looks.'

'That's true,' she said, brightening up at once. 'I am not shallow enough to simply fall for a handsome face and elegant tailoring, am I? It wasn't until I got to know you, the man you keep hidden from everyone else, that I started feeling as if you were my every dream come true.'

Her every dream come true? His heart quailed, just a bit. Being her every dream was going to take some living up to.

But hadn't he vowed it was going to be better to fight for what he truly wanted, than to slink away like a coward, pretending he didn't care? If he hedged off now, because he couldn't believe in himself, he would live to regret it.

He sat up straighter. 'So, is it a yes, then?' He gripped her hand tightly. Willing her to take a gamble on him and help him become the man she thought he could be.

Yet also willing her to come to her senses and turn him down, for her own good.

'Oh, how I want to say yes,' she said, rather than giving him either answer. 'But...'

Now was the time to kiss her. Before she could think of something he couldn't argue away. So he did. And she stopped arguing. With her whole body. Instead she looped her arms round his neck and kissed him back with all the inexpert enthusiasm he'd hoped for.

It felt like his first kiss. And it was the first time he'd kissed her, though he'd been longing to do it since... well, he couldn't recall a time when he hadn't wanted to kiss her, to be frank. But more than that, it was the first time he'd kissed a woman and meant it. Heart and soul.

But he had to stop. Because if he didn't, he'd be

giving in to other, baser urges. And that wouldn't be fair to her.

So he drew back. Gazed down into her face. Her sweet, trusting, innocent, lovely little face. Although, he couldn't help noticing that her nightgown had slid a bit further down her shoulder. Revealing the beginning of a curve...

'Can I ask you something?'

He yanked his gaze from the upper slope of her bosom and assured her that she could ask him anything.

'It's just... I was wondering...how it will work. Being married, I mean.' Her eyes clouded. 'Will you want to carry on with the work you did with Herbert? Will I be helping you track down criminals and traitors, or will you want to keep me out of it all, like you said? Oh, but I could still work behind the scenes, couldn't I? If anyone is sending messages in code. But I suppose,' she went on before he could think of a reply, 'that means you will have to keep on going to those horrid gaming hells and cock fights and low taverns. And you will expect me to go to balls with you.' She pulled a face. 'Everyone will pity you for having a drab little wife like me. The women will redouble their efforts to console you. And I will become a veritable shrew...'

There was only one way he could think of to stop her downhill slide into an imaginary future that looked so unappealing. He kissed her again. Until she melted and squirmed, and would, he rather thought, have hooked one leg over his hip if it hadn't been for the bedding getting in the way.

'Enough of that,' he panted, dragging his mouth from hers. 'If we don't stop, I won't be able to stop.'

'Does it matter?' She was panting, too. And her eyes were shining.

'Yes. Because you are...well, I don't know what Mrs Manderville gave you, but not so long ago you were pinching yourself because you weren't totally sure you hadn't imagined me.'

'That's very true,' she said, looking rather impressed.

'So, here's what I think would be best.' Best? Best for whom, a certain part of his anatomy protested. 'You will snuggle down and get some sleep. And then in the morning, you will tell me again that you want to marry me. In the cold light of day. Because I am not going to do anything that will make people say I *had* to marry you because I ruined you.'

It said a great deal about the state of her mind that she took that statement at face value and smiled at him as though he'd said something really noble. Then did as he'd suggested, by snuggling into his chest.

'I will tell you something, though,' he said, settling into a more comfortable position.

'Mmm...?'

'Our marriage will be whatever we choose to make of it. But one thing I promise is that I will never try to shield you from the uglier truths of what is going on in our country, simply because you are a woman. So, if I do get given a case I want to investigate, you will be the first to know. And I will trust you to work with me, in whatever way you think best. If you wish to. Because you are likely to have more insight into it than any person I know.'

'That's the best—' she broke off to yawn '—compliment anyone could pay me. To say my mind is as good as anyone else's.'

'It isn't at its best right now, though, is it,' he said ruefully, looking down into her trusting face.

'You mean, because I haven't pointed out that I will be every bit as ruined in the morning as if you really did do what you say you want to do?'

He looked at her more sharply. She was peeking up at him from under her eyelashes. Her lips were twitching with mirth.

'Do you know what I think? I think,' she continued, before he could say a thing, 'that we should start as we mean to go on.' She reached for the tie at the neck of her nightgown. 'And to hell with what everyone else thinks.'

For a second or two, his heart was pounding so hard that he wasn't sure how he was going to resist. But at the last second, his hand shot out and covered hers before she could undo her gown.

'Exactly. And I care what you will think of me in the morning, when your head is clear. I don't want you thinking I have taken advantage of you.'

'How about if I took advantage of you?'

'You couldn't. Because I want you too much.'

'How about...considering how angry your brother will be at the scandal it will cause, if everyone were to know what we got up to?'

'That...that does add an extra piquancy... I...no, damn it, it doesn't. I don't care what he thinks. I don't care what anyone else thinks. And nor do you, not really. This is our life, Horatia. Yours and mine. And I'm going to start out our life together doing the right thing.'

She looked up at him with an expression of fake innocence. 'You mean, spending the night in my room? So that in the morning everyone will think we did what we both want to do?'

'I… Damn it, are you always going to outwit me?'

She smiled and snuggled back into the pillows.

'Absolutely,' she said. And promptly fell asleep.

* * * * *

If you enjoyed this story,
be sure to check out
the Brides for Bachelors miniseries

The Major Meets His Match
The Marquess Tames His Bride
The Captain Claims His Lady

And check out this other great read
by Annie Burrows

A Duke in Need of a Wife